PENGUIN METRO READS
SOMEONE LIKE YOU

NIKITA SINGH was born in Patna and grew up in Indore, Madhya Pradesh. After pursuing a degree in Pharmacy she decided to try her hand at writing. She is the author of the best-selling books *Love@Facebook* and *Accidentally in Love* and co-author (with Durjoy Datta) of *If It's Not Forever...It's Not Love*.

DURJOY DATTA was born and brought up in Delhi. He has an engineering degree from Delhi College of Engineering and a management degree from MDI, Gurgaon. He is the author of several best-selling books including *Of Course I Love You!, You Were My Crush!, She Broke Up, I Didn't* and *If It's Not Forever...It's Not Love* (with Nikita Singh). Durjoy was recognized as a young achiever by the Teacher's Achievement Awards and in 2011 he was chosen as one of two young achievers in the field of Media and Communications by Whistling Woods International.

NIKITA SINGH DURJOY DATTA

SOMEONE LIKE YOU

Penguin
metro reads

PENGUIN METRO READS

Published by the Penguin Group

Penguin Books India Pvt. Ltd, 11 Community Centre, Panchsheel Park, New Delhi 110 017, India

Penguin Group (USA) Inc., 375 Hudson Street, New York, New York 10014, USA

Penguin Group (Canada), 90 Eglinton Avenue East, Suite 700, Toronto, Ontario, M4P 2Y3, Canada (a division of Pearson Penguin Canada Inc.)

Penguin Books Ltd, 80 Strand, London WC2R 0RL, England

Penguin Ireland, 25 St Stephen's Green, Dublin 2, Ireland (a division of Penguin Books Ltd)

Penguin Group (Australia), 707 Collins Street, Melbourne, Victoria 3008, Australia (a division of Pearson Australia Group Pty Ltd)

Penguin Group (NZ), 67 Apollo Drive, Rosedale, Auckland 0632, New Zealand (a division of Pearson New Zealand Ltd)

Penguin Group (South Africa) (Pty) Ltd, 24 Sturdee Avenue, Rosebank, Johannesburg 2196, South Africa

Penguin Books Ltd, Registered Offices: 80 Strand, London WC2R 0RL, England

First published in Penguin Metro Reads by Penguin Books India 2012

ISBN 9780143417699

Typeset in Bembo by InoSoft Systems, Noida
Printed at Manipal Technologies Ltd, Manipal

ALWAYS LEARNING   **PEARSON**

For Mini, the best sister any girl can ever have. You will always be missed.
(Neha Singh—4 July 1992 to 23 April 2011)

Chapter One

Panic

' All right. It isn't going to be *that* bad. You're just getting paranoid,' I tell myself for the zillionth time and take a deep breath in and slowly let it out. I have always been a closet drama queen, that's what my sister says. After all, it is just a matter of one week. That's just seven days. How likely is it that in a mere seven days' time, someone will find out that I am the most socially ill-equipped and maybe, just maybe, the most boring person ever?

I have never managed to keep myself interested in myself, forget about anybody else. Over the years, the growing disinterest that people show towards me has turned me vengeful and I, in turn, have no interest in anybody at all. And that disinterest is etched all over my face, accompanied by the big *Fuck Off* sign pasted on my forehead.

Seven days also means one hundred and sixty-eight hours or four thousand and sixty-two minutes. Every second of which, I'm supposed to spend surrounded by girls. Girls who take pains to dress up and look pretty. Girls who actually *know* how to dress up and look pretty. Girls who have boys fawning all over them, following them around, hoping for a glimpse.

Point is, for the next one week, I am supposed to be surrounded by girls who are . . . well, *girls*. That is not to say that *I* am *not* a girl. Of course I am. I mean, if we go by the physical attributes that I am blessed with. I could have been a little more *endowed* at certain parts of my body, though that's off the topic. But just because I happen to have physical evidence, it does not make me a girl. *A guy with boobs*, a guy had called me once. It was very embarrassing, as he didn't say it playfully; it was meant as a snide remark on my wretched looks. I would've happily done the honours of knocking his teeth off, but I stopped myself in time. For two reasons. First, honestly—that guy, Navroz, is the only guy who talks to me (the only *person*).

And secondly, his accusation was not completely untrue. I don't have mannerisms that essentially say that I'm a girl. I've never got myself a pedicure or even a manicure—even when Simran, my elder sister, literally bit my head off to get one done for that wedding last year. I get hair-cuts only twice a year, even though the hairstylist pleads with me to come back every two months for a trim. In fact, if I were to list the number of articles I use that fall under the vanity department, it would contain only—

Body wash
Face wash
Shampoo
Conditioner
Moisturizer (Strictly during winters)
Lip balm (Vaseline, actually)

I know most of what is on my list does not fall under **vanity**, but under *hygiene*. But hygiene is the closest I have come to vanity till now. It's not that I don't want to be pretty or look like the girls on television. It's just that I haven't had the time or the drive to do something about it. And more than anything else, I think I am too late. When

I was young and no one was dolling up, I guess I was pretty too. But slowly, we grew up and people started to dress up and I got uglier by comparison. I study myself in the mirror and I am disappointed. In my dreams, where I am a grown up and take my own decisions, I live in a house with no mirrors. Mirrors remind me of things I am not, things I see other people are and things I would like to be. And also—sadly—things that I can never be.

Look at my wardrobe for instance. No chiffon. No satin. No silk. No skirts either. You won't find anything that has frills or embroidery on it. I don't own a single article of clothing that can be worn to a party, let alone a date. I don't have a single pair of footwear that has heels higher than one inch. I still end up wearing my sneakers everywhere. I don't have a boyfriend. The only guy I have ever dated was Piyush Mehra. Bastard of the highest order.

I've always been pretty good at academics and I, somehow, always felt at home being surrounded by books. It was the tenth standard and I was engrossed in my dreams of scoring the maximum in the board examinations. Then Piyush happened. Piyush, the wide-eyed rich boy in school noticed me. He was charming, had a way with words, and was the most coveted company in school. The way he held my hand on the last bench of the class, and told me how I had the prettiest eyes in the whole world melted my teenage heart. I was too naïve and loved him to bits. I have to admit, he made me feel like a girl!

Three months later, I realized my responsibilities as a girlfriend, which ranged from completing all *his* assignments to forging *his* attendance in classes. No ice creams, no small bits of love notes exchanged during the class, no loving glances shot across the school campus, and surely no dates.

A month later, he was holding someone else's hand and saying the same things to her.

I was crushed. I thought I would never forgive him, but he had made me feel like I had never felt before, so now I think I have. He was my first experience with love, and though it ended on a bad note, I don't hold it very much against him. After we broke up, I spent days locked up in my room, crying and watching sad movies and cursing everyone. Eventually, I did badly in the board exams. My parents had been expecting a lot from me and I hated letting them down.

My father was a government employee for the first fifteen years of his career. My grandfather, a lawyer with the local government, had died a premature death—a heart attack—when he was forty-three. Dad was only eighteen then and the eldest in a family of three sisters and two brothers. By government rules, he was offered a clerical job at the office and he took it up. He spent the next fifteen years working three jobs—the clerical job, tuitions, and as a part-time accountant for small businesses—and bringing up his siblings.

Just before I was born, he joined a local university as a professor, having done the rest of his studies through correspondence and evening college. Things have been better since and he wants a better future for both Simran, my older sister, and me. Simran is already on her way. She was always interested in English literature and went off to Delhi to study. We have no doubts that she will be doing her Master's from Oxford on a full scholarship next year.

Meanwhile, my future was in shambles when Piyush left me. The tenth standard board results were more disappointing for my father than they were for me, not that he ever let it show. I remember him coming into room, holding my hand and saying, 'I know this is not your best but I have full faith in you, Niharika. You're meant for bigger things.'

'I have let you down, Dad. I don't know what to do. I will never be as good as Simran Di. I am sorry. I am. . .'

'Come here,' he said and hugged me.

I don't know how much he meant it, but I was moved to tears. When the other kids were beaten up and disparaged for their less than satisfactory performance in their board exams, I—the expected topper—was just greeted with a warm hug. And an ice cream thereafter.

The very next day, I found myself neck-deep in my books again. I cracked the Bansal's admission test and left for Kota to prepare for IIT-JEE and to complete my +2 from a dummy school there. Once there, I immersed myself in complex numbers, differential calculus and organic chemistry.

My mother never wanted me to go, unlike my father—who harboured a simmering ambition to see me succeed. She was more like the quintessential mother from the movies. She just wanted her daughters to grow up as the prettiest, most cultured girls in the neighbourhood. I don't remember her ever raising her voice at either of us. She is such a sweet soul. To think that she has to handle such messed up daughters like Simran-Di and me seems unfair.

Eventually, after a lot of pleading and cajoling, she let me go to Kota. There, I was too busy with my coaching classes and late-night studies to have time for *love*. So after Piyush, there was no one. I sometimes do wish that someone had been there for me. Like when I watch a romantic movie where everything is perfect in the end. Or listen to a Bryan Adams song. That's when I think I need someone to wrap me in his arms, say the sweetest things, and make me feel like a girl again. But otherwise, I don't think I *need* a guy to *complete* me.

But then, who would want to take *me* out? I am that skinny girl from school, who sat on the first bench, wearing her thick glasses, always immersed in her books, religiously noting down everything taught in the class. The kind that you never hear speak, unless it is to answer a teacher's question, or when she is on stage, presenting a debate or an extempore speech.

That's *me*. Niharika Singh—the girl that doesn't exist.

It's strange that I am what I am because my sister Simran—from the same gene pool—turned out *perfect*. And now, she wants me to stay with her for a week.

I am still out of ideas of how to turn her down because going to her college—Miranda House, Delhi—is the last thing I want to do right now. Even as my mind starts coming up with all possible excuses I can make for not going, I get a sinking feeling in my heart. I know she won't listen to anything I say. I am all set to join college—the Indian College of Engineering, Nagpur—in a few days and Simran wants to see me before I lose myself in the engineering books again. She will not take no for an answer and will give me an earful about how I never listen to her and how I never . . .

Is that my phone ringing?

Simran, I say in my mind and sure enough, *Simran* is what the display says, with her picture on the screen, smiling sweetly at me. She's pretty. I look like a frog in front of her. More like a toad, actually, because frogs are less ugly and there is a chance that they might change into beautiful people from royal families after a mythical kiss. Nothing of that sort will ever happen to me.

I contemplate whether to take the call or not. And if yes, what should I say? I let the phone ring. But as expected, the phone starts ringing again almost as soon as *Simran Missed Call* flashes on the screen. I know I can't dodge her forever. Her next call will be on Mom's phone, who will come bursting into my room, saying, 'Simran wants to talk to you. Why aren't you taking her calls?'

I take the call as I bury my head in the pillow, sadly aware of the impending argument that I am set to lose. I think I have already accepted defeat, but I will still try to put up a feeble fight.

'Hello?' I sigh into the phone.

'Where the hell *were* you? Would it really kill you to pick up your phone a tiny bit earlier?' her voice shouts at me.

'I'm good, Simran. I hope you are doing well too.'

'Shut up. Keep the sarcasm to yourself.'

'Okay. Sorry,' I say. I don't know what it is about my sister, but I'm perpetually intimidated by her. No matter how hard I try, I just can't stand up to her. Maybe because I love her. Maybe because she matters to me more than winning these stupid arguments. Maybe because I cherish our relationship. *Naah.*

It's because she is . . . her. The girl every other girl wants to be. She is tall, with flawless, glowing skin, facial features that are delicately carved, long, lustrous, waist-length, midnight-black hair and jet-black eyes which command attention. Whenever she enters a room with her confident stride, a trademark smirk on her face, and a charming *I-am-a-friend-but-don't-you-mess-with-me* attitude, everything else ceases to exist. Whenever I am in the same room with her, I become the furniture—dull and lifeless.

'So, are you done with the packing?' Simran asks.

'Hmm . . . almost,' I say and look at the suitcase, lying open on my bed. Empty.

'Good. Hurry up. At what time does your train leave? Make sure you're not late.'

I say nothing, trying to frame the right excuse.

'Niharika? Hello?' Simran says. 'When is your train?'

'In three hours . . .' I reply.

'Okay. Cool. I'll see you tomorrow morning then.'

'Umm . . . Di . . .?'

'Yeah?'

'Actually . . . can we meet later some time wh . . .?'

'I *knew* you would say something like this. But I'm not listening.'

'I really do think this is a bad idea,' I say, deciding to be honest. I cannot find another feasible excuse. And she is way too smart for excuses anyway.

'What?' she asks. 'I want to see my sister before she goes to some nondescript college in some corner of the country for four long years, and I can't do that? Is it too much to ask for?'

I can tell that she is getting impatient. But this isn't about me. This is about her.

'Please.'

'*What?*' she shouts at me.

I say nothing. I don't know what to say. She is and has always been very persuasive. Her persuasiveness was one of the major reasons why she was the champion debater in school who had never tasted defeat. Very early in life, I was pushed into debates by her but I was never as good as her. I felt like a star kid, trying desperately to live up to the predecessor's fame and talent. I was always the ugly duckling—the lesser known sister—while she was the dazzling swan, the star.

'What is it, Niharika? Why don't you want to come?'

'Honestly, if I come to stay with you . . . for a week, I would only ruin your reputation,' I say. 'I still remember my first debate at the Presidency Convent. Everyone thought I was your sister and expected me to be like *you*. But you know what happened . . .'

I had choked. It was a crowd of over five hundred students from twenty different schools and we—sisters, and supposedly the best debaters our town had seen—represented our school. I froze on stage in the third minute of my passionate yet restrained speech and our team finished seventeenth. She won the best individual debater and best interjector awards and I came back home with a crippling inferiority complex that would last a lifetime.

'*Come again?* That was eight years ago and you were a little kid. And don't let me count the number of times you have stood on your own now.'

'Simran, please. I know you're very famous there. And I'm not someone people should associate you with.' I say, and add with a pause, 'I am ugly. I don't know how to dress. Or walk. Or talk. I don't know the difference between kohl and eyeliner and mascara. I can't walk in high heels. I don't own a dress. I don't carry a handbag . . . I'm your complete opposite.'

'So? How does that . . .?' she starts to ask but I cut her off.

'Oh, come on. When people look at you, they're dazzled. If I come there, they would expect me to be a two-year-younger version of you. They always have. I can't handle that.'

'Are you kidding me? You don't have to be *me*.'

'I can't be *me* either,' I reply, disappointed. 'When you tell your friends that I'm coming, they would probably picture me as . . .' I try to explain.

'I've already told my friends that you're coming. And I've told them all about you too. And they like you already.'

'What did you tell them?' I suck my breath in.

'That you are very intelligent and have made us all proud. And that you are the sweetest person on the planet who does not need pretty shoes and shiny lip gloss to look good. That you don't give a damn what the world thinks of you. I respect you for that.'

I stay silent for a brief moment before asking meekly, 'Did you really say all that to them?'

'Yes. Of course I did. And I did so because I truly believe in it. I don't know what's wrong with you. Why are you suddenly so insecure about yourself?'

'I'm just . . . you know, in front of your friends . . .' I trail off.

'The people here don't even come close to how nice *you* are as a person. Just come. They will love you.'

'What if I embarrass you?'

'Shut up. You can never embarrass me. You're my sister and I love you the most. You're my best friend. And you know what—even if you were not my sister, you would still be my best friend. That's how much I love you,' Simran says.

I smile. I love my sister. She understands my silence.

'So go now. Pack and come to me,' she says.

'I'm coming,' I say, almost happy.

'Good. Ask Mom to send those pickles with you. My friends love it.'

'Sure,' I say and we hang up.

I return to packing my clothes in a solitary bag that I am taking to Delhi. Only this time I actually pack, instead of just looking around aimlessly and torturing myself with depressing thoughts. What Simran said made me feel good about myself. She's proud of me. And she thinks that I don't try to look pretty not because I *can't*, but because I don't *need* to. It feels nice to know that Simran actually thinks that way about me. It's nice that anyone thinks that way about me. I stuff all my things into my bag and make my way to the washroom to get my toothbrush. As I turn to leave, my gaze falls on my reflection in the mirror. I stop to study my face.

Simran got all the good genes from my mother, though I do pride myself on my hair—thick, dark, rich, and long. I have never been noticed otherwise, but whenever I decide to cut my hair short, some people, without fail, come up to me and tell me how they liked my long hair better. Other than that, I have a face which gets lost in the crowd. No one would come forward to gather my things if I dropped my bag and spilled my things on a crowded road. I've been given eyes so I can see. Nose so I can breathe. Lips so I can . . . well, not kiss, for sure. Who would want to kiss me?

But then, there are a few things that I can thank God for. Like, I don't have a pimples issue. My teeth are straight.

And my breath doesn't stink. Neither does my body. I'm not like one of those really hairy girls. I do get a wax done on a regular basis, but I am not really a pain for whoever decides to wax me.

I have put on some weight recently, but that is a good thing, as people used to say that I was too thin before. I have never had the propensity to gain weight. It's a part of God's plan for me. No matter how much I eat, I never gain enough weight. Just like it's God's plan to make me go unnoticed on this planet.

All in all, at five feet five, a decent body type and not-so-good but not-so-bad either facial features, teamed with lustrous, long hair, I think I look okay. My mother says she can see the world in my big brown eyes. But she is my mother and she thinks that I'm a princess without a tiara and treats me so. All said, I believe that not every girl has to be good-looking, anyway. I will do fine, I tell myself.

I just hope I don't embarrass my sister in Delhi.

Chapter Two

Gosh, I Need a Boyfriend

Delhi is a big city and it can leave you befuddled if you don't know anyone here. I remember the first few days Simran had spent here. She had been excited to come to Delhi because she always thought, and we did too, that she was a little too big for a small town like ours. Plus, Delhi was always a few hours away and the lure of a city was too hard to resist for someone like Simran.

But things changed when she landed in Delhi. Her phone calls used to last for hours and she used to feel so homesick that Mom had almost booked a taxi to Delhi to stay with her for a few days. My father and I knew better. Within the next few days, she had made herself at home in Delhi and started to fall in love with the city and its culture. Or the lack of it. Now, she loves the place and says she will settle down here if possible.

My first impression of the city isn't that bad either. Big, wide roads and tall buildings greet me, even though the summer heat and the leering men on the streets throw me off balance slightly. I have never been stared at, so it feels a little strange.

As soon as I reach Simran's hostel, I'm greeted by a hurricane of words. At least five different fragrances waft their way into my nose.

Hey, Niharika.
It's so nice to finally see you.
Simran talks about you all the time.
You look . . . uh, nice . . .
Simran's sister? Umm . . . . okay.
You've got such nice hair.

I smile at them. The reactions are more positive than negative. I let out a sigh of relief, as I look at the bunch of girls surrounding me. There are seven of them, all looking at me very curiously. Or maybe it is just my active imagination. Simran introduces me to all of them, and I instantly forget who is who. They all sound like Delhiites and look like Delhiites. I can hardly tell them apart. Pink pyjamas, floppy slippers, straight hair and long eyelashes—they look exactly the same.

I decide to take the trouble of remembering only two of the girls, Prerna and Chaaru. I've heard a lot about them from Simran before, and they seem really nice too. They were the ones who had said—*It's so nice to finally see you.* And—*Simran talks about you all the time.* Unlike the other girls, their eyes look kind behind the eyeliners and mascaras.

After the first five minutes of smiling at everyone and making small talk, Simran notices my discomfort and ushers me to her room from the common room.

'So? You like it here? It's not that bad, right?' Simran asks, looking visibly excited. And exceptionally pretty. Like always.

'Hmm . . . I don't hate it,' I shrug.

'What is there to bloody hate?' she almost screams.

I choose to stay silent. Simran has always been a sort of a rebel. Swearing in every sentence seems to be her most recent way to being so. And unlike other people, it doesn't sound out of place either.

'Wait till you get the hang of things here, Niharika. I bet you, you'll beg· me to let you stay for longer. I think you will never want to leave.'

I just look at her in utter disbelief. Doesn't she see the look on my face? Doesn't it just shout 'I wanna run'? Simran's overconfidence has seldom let her down, but for once, she's wrong. I'll never want to stay in this place any longer than absolutely necessary.

~

It takes me about half an hour to find an empty cubicle in the washroom. And it isn't like I've been lazy or sleeping too long. I went to bed early last night, while my sister stayed up and watched repeats of 'How I Met Your Mother'. That's what everyone seemed to be doing in the hostel. Movies. English sitcoms. A few girls were drinking. I wonder if this is what my college life will be all about too.

I woke up early, as Simran had asked me to, gathered my clothes and ran here. Still, I have not been able to find an empty cubicle in an hour. So now, when I see this girl in the green robe come out of a cubicle, I run to it.

After the shower, I go back to Simran's room to find out that she has already left for her class. I have no idea what I'm supposed to do all day. There's no one around. Not that I mind. I pick up Simran's laptop and I am almost shocked at her movie collection. It has every movie I have ever seen or heard of. And more. I jam my earphones deep inside my ears and start watching a movie. I wonder where Simran is, and what she is doing. I somehow doubt that she is attending her class.

Suddenly, I find my phone buzzing again. It is getting kind of creepy now, almost telepathic. Every time I think of Simran, I get a call from her.

'Hello?'

'What the hell do you think you are doing? Why can't you pick up your phone when I call you?' her shout greets me.

'What? I was watching a movie!' I defend myself.

'I asked you to meet me outside the campus in fifteen minutes. Where the hell are you?'

'You did not. When did you?'

'I left a note on the bed and I texted you too,' she says. And sure enough, there is a piece of paper—a large, A4 size sheet—lying in the middle of the bed. God only knows how I could have possibly missed it. You have to be blind to do so.

'Oh. Yeah,' I say.

'Now do you need me to send you a jet? Come quick. We are all waiting for you.'

'Okay.'

When I get there, I see that she has company. It is just the kind of a day when I don't want to meet anyone. But it's not like I have a choice. There are three people who flank her, two of those faces I am already familiar with. Prerna, Chaaru and a guy. I have never seen the guy before, but the way Simran's arm is wrapped around his gives me some idea about the kind of relationship they share. I feel a little strange in my stomach because she hasn't told me about a possible . . . boyfriend.

'There she is,' Simran says, looks my way and smiles weirdly. It looks like she is going to tell me something.

'Uh, hi,' I say, looking around, awkward as always.

'Niharika,' Simran holds my hand and pulls me into the group, 'this is Viraat. My boyfriend.'

Then she turns to the guy and her eyes twinkle for a bit as she says, 'Viraat, this is Niharika, my sister.' I notice that she is blushing all the while. I have never seen her like this before.

'Hi, Niharika,' Viraat says, and thrusts his hand out. He smiles at me and there is a lot of warmth in that smile.

'Hey,' I say.

'How are you?'

'I'm good.'

'I heard you're leaving in just three days? You should have stayed here at least for a week. We had so many plans for you,' he says and smiles at me disarmingly.

'Really?'

'Obviously. We have been waiting to see you. Simran talks about you all time and quite frankly, I feel like I already know you.'

'Oh shut up, Viraat,' Simran says. 'You don't have to try so hard to impress my sister. I love you anyway.'

We share a laugh, after which we all fall silent. Everyone looks around at everyone else, but no one says anything. I am not to blame for the silence, though. I just got to know that my sister has a boyfriend. I have never heard any mention of him, so it is justified for me to be shocked. I don't even know for how long they have been dating.

'Viraat—' I start meekly, but am cut off by a louder voice.

'We should probably leave now. We are already getting late,' Prerna says.

'Shit, yeah,' Simran says, 'we should get going.' She looks at Viraat.

'Right,' he says. 'It was nice to see you, Niharika. See you tonight.'

'Tonight?' I ask.

'Sure,' Simran says and ushers me away.

'Where are we going tonight?' I ask her.

'You'll see.'

Chapter Three

The Transformation

'Where are we going now?' I ask Simran as the auto zips through the afternoon traffic. Simran turns a deaf ear to my questions and instead complains about how we should have taken the metro instead. Beads of sweat dampen our brows and streak down our cheeks.

'We are going shopping,' she finally answers me, when I repeat the question the fifth time.

'But I have clothes,' I mutter in protest.

'I don't think so, Niharika. What you have is junk. You're going to college this year. And I want my sister to be the hottest girl on campus. All the guys will love you.'

'I can live without that happening,' I say, but she ignores me and continues, deep in her own thoughts.

'Though . . . I don't want you to fall for the wrong guy. You're too naïve.'

'At least I will let you know if I fall for someone there,' I say and hope she gets the snide remark.

'I was about to tell you, but you are such a drama queen. I thought you might tell Mom,' she says. 'And you know how Mom reacts.'

Yes, I know how Mom reacts but that can't be her reason. I would never rat her out to our Mom and she knows that.

'I would have told Mom?' I ask.

'Actually . . . I wasn't sure myself.'

I can understand. Viraat, in the few minutes I spent with him, seemed like a really warm and a nice guy. But standing next to my near-perfect sister and her friends, he stuck out like a sore thumb. He was barely five nine, had terrible skin and was not the fittest of guys I have seen. He was far from perfect. The first time I saw both of them together, his hands holding hers, I was shocked and disappointed. Not because my sister had hidden it from me, but because I had always thought she would date someone much better-looking.

'Did you like Viraat?' she asks softly.

'He is sweet, Simran.'

She pauses a little and says, 'I know what you're thinking. You think that he is not good-looking or physically attractive. I know that. But he loves me, Niharika.' The look on her face confuses me. Her lips quiver like a little child and she is blushing like a school girl who is in love for the first time.

'I think he is okay,' I say, not knowing what to say.

'He is more than okay; he is amazing. He makes me feel so special and wanted. Niharika, finally I feel like I am into something real, something that is beyond just holding hands and spending time together. I love him for everything he says and the way he treats me. He is such a nice person that it's almost unreal. When I first heard about his feelings for me, I was almost disturbed that he even thought that he had a chance to date me. But he was persistently so sweet to me, that I couldn't help it. My friends still don't understand it, but I am so freaking obsessed with him.' I am embarrassed by how much I love him and I am surprised by how much he loves me. I don't care what people think, I just love him truly and completely,' she says with tears in her eyes.

I hold her hand and she comes forward and hugs me. It seems like she had been waiting to say what she just did but she didn't find anyone to pour her heart out to.

'I am so happy for you,' I say and find tears in my eyes too.

'You know what—I hope every day that you find someone like Viraat too. Someone who treats you the way you should be treated. And that's why we need some new clothes for you,' she says and asks the auto driver to pull up.

Finally, after an hour and half of sweating profusely in the back of the autorickshaw and cursing the weather and the driver in equal measure, we have reached Saket—the southern part of Delhi—where a few new malls have come up. We walk in and are relieved as the conditioned air hits our faces.

'Gosh, it's so hot out there. I need something to drink,' I declare and look around.

'Come, let's sit here,' Simran says and points to a Barista inside the mall. It's a Saturday and the mall is crowded to the brim with people of all ages and sizes flocking to every outlet inside it. The waiter tells us that there is a fifteen-minute waiting time, but Simran charms him into giving us a table before anyone else. She then finds some magazines and asks me to go through them.

'Are you serious? You want me to read this?' I protest.

'Of course! You have a problem?' Simran asks.

'This is . . . uh . . . I don't . . . I don't read all this,' I say, pointing to the cover page of one of the magazines, which has a picture of a semi-nude, super-thin, glossy-looking actress and says *The No. 1 Sex Move He Craves—Dare To Do It. You Won't Regret It!*'

'Grow up!' Simran laughs at the look on my face and says, 'Here—read these. Just skip the relationships segment and concentrate on fashion. Observe and learn.'

She pushes some magazines—ranging from *Cosmopolitan*, *Verve*, *Marie Claire* and *Bazaar* to some whose names I cannot even pronounce—towards me. She points out hairstyles, colour

combinations, and options for shoes, and I stare at them all,
mouth agape. The girls in the magazines are pretty and their
clothes are even prettier. The kind of clothes Simran wears.
Even today, she is in a yellow summer dress that ends at
her knees and she looks beautiful in it. But these are also
the kind of clothes I do *not* wear. I want to, but I'm afraid
I would end up looking stupid in them.

'But Simran, I can't wear all this,' I say and dig into the
chocolate pastry we had ordered. If there is one thing that
I have come to love in Delhi, it's the food. It's amazing and
no matter where you go, something awfully delicious will
find its way to your mouth.

'Yes, you can wear all this,' Simran insists. 'See, most of the
clothes here are for models and really skinny people. You are
skinny and you can look prettier than these models here. For
now, we will buy you something toned down and once you're
used to it, we will buy the more outrageous and outlandish
clothes. But yes, we do have to get you a dress.'

'I am not sure.'

'You're never sure. Screw the pastry, let's go to a salon
now,' she says and pays the bill. The charmed waiter
makes sure the card is swiped and the slip is signed swiftly.
We leave Barista and my heart aches for the unfinished
pastry—a little piece of heaven—that I had been forced to
leave behind.

As she drags me out from the coffee shop and onto the
escalator, I ask, 'Why a salon?'

'When you look into the mirror in a beautiful dress, more
often than not, you're looking at your face and not the dress.
Yes, the dress matters, but the face matters more. We need
to get you tidied up. And trust me—cleaning eighteen years
of dirt takes time.'

My protests that it will not help my cause are turned
down. Simran is absolutely confident and very persuasive, as

usual. On the third floor of the mall, there is an upmarket
salon where we are going to spend the next three hours. I
don't get what she says to the person—equipped with a belt
that has twenty different types of clips and scissors hanging
from it—but I can make out a few words.

*Desperately needs a wash . . . cut it in layers . . . make the
eyes pop out . . . blow dry . . . re-do eyebrows . . . hideous . . .
nails . . . clean up . . . beautiful . . . ugly . . .*

The details of what happened inside the salon are painful
to recall now. My face is sore and warm and it pains near
the eyebrows and the nose. I don't know as yet whether it's
worth it, but every time I pass a mirror it's like a different
person stares back at me. My eyebrows look like they have
been hand-sketched, my complexion looks at least three shades
fairer and my hair is now tangled into a beautiful mess with
keratin and hair wax. I can smell how good I smell.

I look *beautiful*! This is the first time I am using that word
for myself.

'See? You love yourself, now, don't you?' Simran asks,
catching me lingering around a mirror for a little too
long.

'But didn't you say I didn't need to do all this?' I ask
her. 'That I was comfortable in my own skin and I didn't
need make-up.'

'Yes, I said that, but don't you like yourself better now?'
she asks with a smirk, and puts her arms around me from
behind. I look at our reflections in the mirror and I have
tiny tears at the corners of my eyes.

'Simran,' I say, 'we look like sisters.' I smile and look up
at her, like a child needing assurance. 'I look nice?'

'Yes, you do. But to look like sisters, we need to get you
out of your rotten jeans and show off a little bit of your legs.'

'I have never worn anything like that. Or like what you're
wearing,' I say, as I turn red in the face thinking of what it

would feel like to slip into a dress. Though, I have to admit I am also a little excited thinking of it.

'Do you hate me for taking you to the salon?'

'No, not at all,' I say and look into the mirror again. My heart starts to beat faster again; it feels like my first real moment of loving myself. My hair looks fabulous and I can't take my eyes off it.

'Then, trust me. It will be good,' she says and drags me behind her.

She takes me to shop after shop, brand after brand, not asking me to try on anything. I am thankful for that but I am sure she will start doing that soon. Meanwhile, I start to bombard her with questions about whether my complex hairstyle will stay as it is when I wake up tomorrow. About how frequently I will have to visit the salon. And what I will have to say when I go to one. Slowly and steadily, I start spending more time in front of every mirror that we pass by. As we flit from shop to shop, I notice more than a few eyes on me . . . on us. It feels nice. Simran, occasionally, bends over and whispers, '*He was looking at you.*'

And I begin to think to myself, 'Yes, he should.'

Finally, we reach a *Forever 21* showroom that Simran has been talking about all morning. The clothes are inexpensive and very trendy, just like what I am *not* used to wearing. Simran frantically starts picking up tops, skirts and everything she can get hold of and dumps them on my shoulder. Occasionally, she shrieks, 'We *HAVE* to get this!' and everyone starts staring at us. I pick up a few things too, but Simran doesn't approve of them.

A little later, with a pile of clothes on my arms and shoulders, we head to the changing room and I ask Simran to stand right in front of my door. I don't want to scamper across the entire floor of the shop to look for her in a silly dress.

I try on a pink and blue floral dress that ends just above my knees. I wear it and stare at myself in the mirror. My cheeks flush and I start to blush as I look at myself. I feel . . . I can't describe how I feel. It's like I am born again as a different person, in a matter of four painful hours. It's an amazing feeling. I leave the changing room, my head in a whirl and look at Simran, 'How's it?'

'You know what, Niharika? I am almost jealous. My sister is the only girl in the whole of Delhi, who is prettier than me,' she comes and hugs me.

I don't know why but I have tears in my eyes. I don't remember the last time I was as happy as I am now. As we hug, I see other girls look at us. They don't look pleased, and Simran whispers in my ears, 'I'm proud of you. You're going to make *so* many girls jealous of you.'

I can already see that happening. I know now what blind people feel like when they first open their eyes to a new world, or a crippled person when he or she walks for the first time. I spend hours changing into every dress, every skirt, and every top Simran has chosen for me and keep staring at myself in the mirrors from every angle. I feel a little silly, but today is the first day when I don't hate the physical form I have been given. For the first time in my life, I can say that—I feel *blessed*.

We leave the shop and try out some other clothes and buy what we like. Simran even shoots a few appreciative glances at the clothes I choose. The last stop is the shoe store where she makes me try everything. The clothes were easier to pick and I was getting a hang of it but choosing shoes is tough. Simran almost shouts at me when I picked up a *supposedly* hideous pair of red shoes.

Also, trying out clothes is easy, while shoes are actually painful. Especially since Simran doesn't let me put on anything that has heels less than three inches high. She makes me wear stilettoes with outrageously tall and thin heels and makes me walk around in them all around the store. On one occasion, I almost fall and end up making a fool of myself. But when I look at her, she doesn't seem embarrassed by the way some people turn to stare at us. She just helps me regain my balance and flings the stupid pumps away. And that's why I love my sister.

'I think we are done,' Simran says an hour later and pays the bill. It's already eight in the evening and every part of my body is hurting. I can go on for another seven lives shopping, but I am sure we are out of cash by now. We have already spent all our savings from our pocket money, and Simran hasn't got a single article of anything for herself. I have the biggest smile on my face and she notices it. It's not just about how she made me feel about myself, it is also about how she made me feel about *us*. I finally feel like I can stand next to her and not wallow in self-pity. I owe it all to her and she knows that. I don't think we have hugged or laughed or smiled as much as we did today.

Truly, sisters are your best friends ever. And also—shopping, of course.

Just as we cross a shop that has t-shirts with little slogans on them, I stop Simran and ask her if I can get another t-shirt. She disapproves of the colour but still lets me buy it.

The t-shirt says in big, white, bold letters, '*I LOVE ME*'.

~

It has been a long day, but I have no complaints. I look at the mirror and I am amazed at myself. I am getting more and more self-obsessed and now I think I can spend quite a few days with myself. I feel like the girls I had always hated because they were good-looking and desirable and spent time grooming themselves instead of doing complex math problems.

I am still sifting through all the clothes that we bought today and I keep on trying them repeatedly. I love my new clothes! They love me back and it's an exhilarating feeling. I never realized before that new clothes could make one feel so good.

'We are late. So damn late,' Simran shouts but I turn a deaf ear to her. She tells me that Viraat is already waiting outside the hostel and that we need to hurry up, though I don't hear Simran's phone ring even once. It surprises me how patient Viraat is.

We get into our dresses and I have to say I am a little uncomfortable in what Simran has made me wear. It's a blazing red dress that ends mid-thigh and clings to my body and if Simran is to be believed, it looks titillating and seductive on me. I am not sure I want to be what she says I am. I try to pull it down as I stand in front of the mirror and she pushes me away.

'Will you stop doing that? For heaven's sake. You will destroy it,' Simran says. 'And for the millionth freaking time—it's *not* short.'

'But it is,' I protest.

'I am not even listening to you any more.'

After Simran's demonstration of 'how to apply make-up in ten minutes,' we leave and find Viraat waiting for us outside the hostel. He drives an old, beaten-down, red Alto and I am somewhat disappointed again. I know Simran loves him, but it's still hard for me to accept that she would settle for such an average guy. I hate the way I think, but I can't help it. Simran has always been the girl with a perfect life, and Viraat, at least in his material and tangible characteristics, is far from perfect.

'Oh, hi, both of you,' he stares at us for a while. 'You look amazing.'

'Thank you,' we echo.

He tells us that he talked to a few of his friends and we are going to a new club that has opened very recently. Throughout the drive, his phone buzzes incessantly and he keeps mentioning names of his friends who will be there too. I feel a little odd now. I am in a dress, considerably shorter than anything I have ever worn, and am going to be amongst strangers. It's not the best feeling ever.

On the way, Viraat tells me how Simran and he started dating, despite protests from a blushing Simran. He tells me that Simran had always intimidated him by her presence and how he had an instant crush on her when he first saw her. It was six months back and he still remembers everything Simran has ever said or worn every time they have met. It was not until two months back that Simran asked Viraat out.

'*You* asked *him* out?' I ask Simran, shocked.

'Yes, I did. I had no option. We used to go everywhere, but we always used to have friends around us. He has a *lot* of friends, as you'll see this evening. He just used to stare and say nice things about me to my friends. I had started liking him. Oh, and we used to text all the time, but the moment we were together, he used to shut up and turn very shy. It freaked me out.'

'What did you do?' I ask, now deep into their story.

'I kissed him,' Simran says and they both laugh.

'*What?* Really? Where?'

'We were waiting for a few friends to see a movie and just like every time, he sat there and looked everywhere except at me. I tried talking to him but he would not say a thing. Then I just asked him to at least look at me. And when he did, I bent over and kissed him for what seemed like an eternity.'

'You did that?' I ask, picturing the scene in my head.

'Oh, yeah! Your sister is crazier than you think,' Viraat says. 'And really, I was shocked at first. And then, it hit me.

Simran had kissed me. The thought gives me goose-bumps even now.'

'Aww,' Simran and I echo, as Simran puts her arm around his shoulder.

It's already eleven in the night and the roads are more or less free of traffic. We reach the club soon, though I don't want the drive to end. Simran's seemingly perfect love story with the imperfect guy, Viraat, has me at the edge of my seat. I never realized before that I am such a romantic at heart.

We enter the club—lit dimly with red and blue lights which hang from the ceiling—and music blasts into our ears almost immediately. I don't mind it. I love music and I have wasted days and days locked up in my room dancing to every crass, filthy song or item number that caught my fancy. I am not a very party person, as I have never felt the need to, but to see heads turn towards the two of us makes me regret all the times I have turned such plans down before.

As we go inside and hide behind Viraat, who goes on a hugging spree, embracing everyone from bouncers to managers to a million different friends, I look at him intently for the first time. It's almost strange how drastically he has changed in my mind since this morning. He looks good to me now. In fact, he looks handsome. He looks like someone I would proudly make my friends meet. And that's just because he is so sweet to my sister. I think I really like him. And in a certain corner of my heart, I see Viraat and Simran together for a very long time. They are *meant* to be together.

I am falling progressively more in love with the kind of person Viraat is, when I notice something else about him and smile. He doesn't let any of his guy friends around me and doesn't allow any conversation to last beyond the first few sentences. He firmly turns down anyone who offers me a drink; I think he has sensed that I am not comfortable.

'So, Niharika,' he says. 'Do you like Delhi?'

'Yes, I do. Very much so. I didn't think I would, but I do,' I beam at him.

'That's great. And—I am sorry for all my friends who are hitting on you. It's not really their fault.'

'Are they hitting on me? Why?'

'As if you don't know! You look very nice, Niharika,' he says and shows me about ten texts from different guys on his cell phone, all asking him about me.

'Whoa! I think I like this place. And frankly speaking, I have never really got any attention from anyone. Ever,' I confess. 'This is all very new to me.'

'You're joking, right? You're Simran's sister, after all. You were bound to look like you do,' he says and looks at Simran.

'Flirt,' Simran says and punches his arm.

'You mind?' he asks.

'Yes. It's my sister, you pervert. You're flirting with her right in front of me.'

'What? I thought I was flirting with *you*,' he says, making a funny face.

'Such a smooth talker, you are,' Simran smiles and shakes her head.

He comes forward and pecks her on the lips. 'Now if you'll excuse me, I need a refill and the waiters here are busy ignoring me. You want anything?'

'You want me drunk?' Simran asks.

'Well, let's just say—I like you drunk,' Viraat says with a wink.

As Viraat moves off, I see Simran's eyes following him. She's looking at him with an expression of pure adoration on her face. I say what I'm thinking. 'When I met him in the morning, for a moment, I had thought you were one of those girls who change in front of guys. But you're just the same. You swear a lot and you really give him a hard time.'

'I don't need to change. He likes me the way I am. And that's the best part about him. You like him?'

'I like him? I love him! He is so nice. It's almost unreal.'

'I know,' she says, looking at my face intently. 'I wanted you to like him. I was nervous that you wouldn't. I really wanted you to meet him.'

A lot has changed since the morning. I see no reason why Simran should be nervous. What is there *not* to like? The guy is perfect. If I make a list with bullet points for qualities I'd look for in a guy, every point would be a tick for him. Plus, just as a bonus, Simran told me this morning that he is very passionate and is an amazing kisser.

Simran looks away from and in the direction of Viraat; she is lost again. Her smile is dazzling. Wow. Sometimes I forget how beautiful she is. It is times like these when the fact hits me straight in the face and leaves me reeling with the impact.

'You really love him, don't you?' I ask stupidly. If you could see the look on her face, you would realize the futility of the question I just asked.

'Yes,' she smiles sweetly. Her face has that *at peace* look. Like she's happy to the core of her heart. Blissful. She goes on, 'It's not about how great he is. It's about how great we are together. It's the fact that I love him. I don't think I am ever going to get enough of him. He just makes me go *wow* every single day that I have been with him.'

We stop talking as Viraat walks back towards us. Suddenly, from a short, average-looking guy he turns into a legitimate superstar walking towards two star-struck fans. She is looking at him as he comes back, with nothing but love in her eyes. Fairytale-ish love. The kind of pure, unconditional love that does not actually exist. Except, sometimes, it does. I can see it in the dreamy expression on her face.

I want this, I decide. It's not really something you can decide, actually. It's not like you have an option. If you witness such a thing, you're *bound* to want it. I want my very own Viraat, someone who will sweep me off my feet, wait for me for an hour while I get ready, drive me across the city in his small, broken car and be nice to my sister. I want it. And I want it quick.

I envy her. It's not like I resent her awesomeness or happiness. I love her, yes, more than I love anybody else in the world, probably, including myself. But I hate her almost equally for being so perfect. It's something siblings always have. At least we both do. Pure and unadulterated envy. Now that I look at her, she is the happiest I have ever seen her. I like this. And since she has it, I want it too. It's simple, right? I send a mental prayer to heaven—*give me this. Please, give me this too.*

'What are you guys talking about?' Viraat asks as he takes his seat.

'You,' I say.

'Really? Did she tell you that I'm a good kisser? Or did she just tell you that I am too average-looking to be her guy?' he asks me.

'Doesn't matter what she said. I think you're hot,' I laugh.

'I think I like your sister better, Simran,' he says and looks at her.

'How mean!' Simran punches him playfully.

Viraat whispers something in her ear and makes her giggle. I have never seen her do that before, and I am a little surprised. I start to blush a little and look away. I decide to concentrate on my drink, and as I turn to it, I notice that mine is a different colour from theirs. Were they serious about getting drunk? I don't want to seem prudish, but I can't help asking either. 'Simran, is that . . . alcohol?'

'What?' she looks up at me, pushing Viraat away and turning towards me.

'Are you guys drinking?' I repeat. I have always hated drinking and people who drink. It has never appealed to me or made sense to me.

'Yes, it's Long Island Iced Tea. You should try it some time, too. It's really nice.'

'Are you serious? When did you start drinking?'

'What do you mean? What is wrong with drinking?' Simran asks.

'What is not? I can't believe this . . .'

'Relax, okay? I drink because I like to drink. And it's perfectly okay. Grow up already.'

'Growing up doesn't mean I need to—' I begin, but Viraat cuts me off.

'Hey, hey, hey. Girls! Chill a little bit. Niharika, it's okay to drink sometimes . . .'

'What do you mean? Are you taking her side?' I ask, looking pointedly at the drink in his hand.

He puts his glass down and puts his hands up in the air in surrender. 'Fine. Not drinking any more. Alright?'

I turn to look at Simran's glass.

'You're not scaring me, Niharika. I'm not going to put it down,' Simran challenges.

'What is wrong with you? Drinking is bad!' I blurt out. 'Tell her, Viraat. Tell her not to drink.'

'Niharika, even if I do tell her that, you know that she's not going to listen, right? You know your sister,' Viraat says and Simran smirks.

'But—' I begin to protest.

'Hold on. I was saying that I can't make her stop it, but I can promise you one thing. That if she drinks too much, I will take care of her. You can trust me on that. So, quit worrying, okay?'

I nod meekly, completely convinced by what he says.

And from then on, the evening starts to change for the better. There's awesome food, awesome music and awesome company. Well, awesome drinks too, but since I don't drink, I hardly care. I also notice that despite the protests she made, Simran eventually did discard her drink. It makes me happy. Other people join us after a while, friends of Simran and Viraat. And again, Viraat ensures that no guy tries anything on me. But for once in my life, I don't feel out of place. Even though everyone here is worlds apart from what I am, they make me feel like I'm one of them. Even the short, red dress feels okay.

As the night draws to a close, and I sit sprawled awkwardly on the couch because my feet hurt, I look in the direction of Viraat and Simran. They are in the middle of the dance floor, Simran's arms around his neck and his arms on her waist and they are swaying together slowly and totally out of tune with the music. It's like the world has just the two of them in it and the music that is playing in their heads is all that matters to them.

I see Simran close her eyes and rest her head on Viraat. I wonder what she is dreaming about.

I wonder if I will ever feel the same.

Chapter Four

All It Takes Is Three Short Minutes

I can't have that. It's sad, I know. But that's how it's going to be. There's just no other way to it. As I pack my bags, which are bursting at the seams because of all the new clothes I have bought, my thoughts are still on Simran and Viraat, and more importantly—the loving bond that they share. It's like I have a crush on their relationship and I badly want it for myself.

'Are you done?' Simran asks.

'Almost,' I say and stuff the last of my clothes into the bag and zip it. 'Done.'

'Alright. We should leave for the station now. Else you'll—'

'Simran,' I interrupt her. I just *have* to ask her this. 'Do you think I will find ever someone like Viraat?'

'Why Viraat? You will find someone even better,' she says. *Yeah, right.*

'Hmm. I wish I could stay a little longer,' I say softly.

'So that you could find a Viraat for yourself?' she smirks playfully.

'Whatever,' I say and pick up my bag. Simran really bugs me sometimes. I'm all sad and serious here, and she's mocking me.

As I make my way to the door, Simran holds my elbow to stop me. She hugs me and tells me that it was the best three days she has spent in the longest time and she wishes I would never leave. She sees me still distracted and asks me what's wrong.

'I just see you and Viraat together . . . and I feel sad for myself. I'm happy for you. I am just thinking—what if it never happens to me? Am I being very needy? This is so pathetic. I feel sorry for myself,' I say as soon as I hear myself.

'It'll happen when it's meant to happen, Niharika. You can't do anything to *make* it happen.'

'But . . . what if it *doesn't*?' I ask in a low voice, again cursing myself for what I am doing to myself.

'It will. There's someone for everyone, trust me,' she says this with such conviction, that I have no option other than to believe her.

'What if he passes me by and I don't recognize him?'

'You will. Just know that you really will find him one day. Wait for him.'

'So I just . . . look for him in everyone I see from now?' I joke, trying to feel better about my needy, pathetic self.

'Not a bad idea, actually,' she laughs. 'It's not too much of an effort, anyway.'

'What do you mean?' I ask.

'I mean, it's not like it takes a lot of time to decide if the guy is dateable. Maximum, what? Three minutes?'

'Three minutes?' I ask, really taken aback. I had been expecting a more three-months type of an answer, because that's what it took Viraat and her. After all, how is a girl supposed to know a guy in a mere three minutes' time?

'Yeah,' she answers simply. 'Oh, try it. You'll see. Within three minutes, you'll definitely get to know if you can go out with the guy or not. If the answer is yes, latch on to the guy and never leave him.'

'Really?' I ask.
'Really.'

~

Though it seemed unbelievable at first, now I totally understand what Simran meant. Three minutes is all it takes. If the first three minutes make you feel something about the guy whom you meet for the first time, you should hang on to that feeling. The first minute is usually devoted to how the person looks, the second one is how the person behaves with other people (you!) and the third one is what the person makes you feel about yourself. So, while Viraat had lost out a little on the first one minute, he had definitely made up in the last two and quite substantially so.

~

It's been a week since I've been back at home—Jaipur. On my way back, I had been thinking about what Simran had said. And I believed her. I mean, of course, I would find my guy one day, it's just that if I wanted that *one day* to be soon, I would have to keep my eyes open. And as Simran said—it's not too much of an effort.

I don't think it's intentional, but I have started looking for my Viraat and it's almost like a boy hunt. The first day I spent in Jaipur, I found myself texting every guy in my friends' list, wondering if I had missed my Viraat in one of them. By the end of the day, I was sure they were all creeps and I hadn't missed out on anything that would make my life blissful.

I'm really not reaching for the stars here. But it's been a week, and I am nowhere. It seems he is just one of a kind and he is taken. I have never looked for a guy to date or to even talk to, but I realize now how difficult it is to find a decent guy to date these days. When I got back home, I had high expectations. I started to look at every guy in a different way. With a question in my mind—*can I date him?*

And you would be amazed at the number of guys I mentally rejected. After the makeover Simran and her friends had given me back in Delhi, I came back to Jaipur looking somewhat hot. I had been transformed in a week. So even though I can't go ahead and win a beauty pageant or anything, I like to believe that I will not be thrown off in the very first round either.

'It's not really about what you are blessed with. It's about how you present what you are blessed with,' Chaaru had said. 'It's about accentuating your best features and downplaying your worst. It helps that you have more good than bad.' (That last sentence had boosted my self-esteem a lot.)

Three minutes is all it takes! I can't get over this. That is all the time you need to find out if the guy is the one you're looking for. Mostly because he is bound to make at least one horrible, unforgivable mistake in three minutes. Especially if you've set yourself some really, *really* high standards, but I have not. I'm looking for *regular*. I know I'm average and I'm looking for an average guy. I'm not expecting him to be better than me, but he should at least be as good as I am.

Other than this, I'm looking for the basic things. No bad breath. No body odour. Non-smoker. Someone who can say all the right things, do things that make me happy, understand my silences, get what I don't say and understand when I am lying. Someone whom I can talk to and who makes me feel tomorrow will be even better than yesterday.

I am looking for a guy who knows what true love really is and is capable of it. I just want someone I can love, and someone who will love me back selflessly. And I swear, if I find a guy like this, I promise you, I'll love him. And I'll love him with all my heart. If I find a guy like this, I'll devote every fibre of my being to his love. I'll combust spontaneously and lose myself in him. All in three minutes.

Chapter Five

Yes, No and Maybe . . .

'Really? I wonder how you look,' Navroz says over the phone.

'I look . . . I don't know. I'm still the same,' I reply, checking my reflection in the mirror and thinking what a blatant lie it was.

'But I'm sure you must look better without the glasses.'

'Hmm. Simran says losing the specs was a good idea. She says I have nice eyes.'

'I won't know about it. I never noticed!' Navroz laughs.

'I think you're gay. For two years, you saw me every day, for hours on end. And you didn't notice my eyes?'

Navroz really amazes me sometimes. I know him so well, that I can describe each and every feature of his face in perfect detail and he can't even tell how my eyes look? I don't blame him though, as he never really looked at me like a guy should. We first met when we accidentally sat next to each other in the first physics class at Bansal's and we ended up sharing an auto back to our paying-guest accommodations.

He liked physics and I liked organic chemistry; both of us hated maths with a vengeance but managed to score all right. The healthy competition, the problem-solving sessions and the late night chats about how it would be at IIT made us the best of friends. If I had to choose between the two of us, I would have wished him to go to IIT. His father, who owned a small business in Burla, Orissa, had spent all his savings to send Navroz to Bansal's. I still remember the look of immense happiness and pride on his dad's face, when he told him that he was going to IIT Delhi to study textile engineering.

'Your glasses were too thick for me to notice,' he says.

'You're mean . . .'

'I just never lie.'

'You should probably learn to. Else you won't ever find a girl,' I say.

'Oh, never mind. I don't *want* a girl. I'll just go to Delhi and fool around. What makes you think I even *want* a relationship?'

'Right.'

Navroz has just broken up with his girlfriend, after a seven-year-long relationship. Even though I had always thought that long-distance relationships were difficult to maintain, Navroz had led me to believe otherwise. Navroz and Priya used to talk through the night, send each other letters and talk lovingly about their near-perfect relationship. But things changed. Studies, the hectic schedule and the pressure to get through IIT took its toll. The spark vanished into thin air.

Ultimately, after seven long years, there was nothing romantic left in the relationship that could have saved it. They knew each other too well. The break-up was mutual and no tears were shed, at least in public.

'Anyway,' Navroz says, 'what are your plans? Excited for ICE, Nagpur?'

'Look who's talking. You're the one going to IIT, Delhi. Your life is going to change.'

'It's going to suck. I will be stuck with all these brilliant people with nothing else to do but study. It's going to be four long years. I wish you were there too.'

'Don't make me feel bad now. Anyway, I still have some shopping to do. I will get that done today, I guess,' I say, more to myself.

'Oh, yeah. Just a week, right?'

'Yes.'

'Carry on then. Call me if you need help lingerie-shopping,' Navroz says.

'Sure,' I roll my eyes and hang up.

~

I have spent the last three hours shopping and I am glad that I didn't get anyone to come with me. Over the last three hours, I have constantly been talking to Simran and telling her about every piece of clothing that catches my fancy. Before I left home, my mother had given me her debit card and had asked me not to worry about how much I spent. What she doesn't know yet is that I have changed over the last week. Now, I know how to shop and about the joys of splurging.

'You found no one else in the whole of Jaipur to take you around shopping?' Simran asks, sounding almost tired after the three-hour-long phone call.

'There is no one I can trust with my clothes now; you have spoilt me. Plus, I really don't have friends here,' I say, almost dejected.

'Never mind, you will have a new life when you get to college. Pick your friends wisely,' she says.

I have about twenty shopping bags in my hands and I find it tough juggling them and the phone, which has remained glued to my ear all this while. Occasionally, I shift the bags from one hand to another to make it easier. It's a Sunday and the roads are jammed with traffic. Just as I try to cross the road with the phone still glued to my ears, a loud honk blasts my ears and I freeze. I look around to see a Tata Safari screeching to a sudden stop inches away from me. *Inches*, really. Like four inches. I had been so lost in my phone call that I hadn't noticed the big black beast of a car coming towards me. The phone drops from my hand and the battery falls out. I stand there and my mind is blank. The traffic piles up behind the car, and I can hear people shouting all around me.

I quickly gather up my shopping bags, pick up the remaining parts of the phone and cross the road without looking anywhere. As I reach the pavement, I see people come out of the SUV, I see their angry faces and I see their mouths move, but I don't register what they are saying. I am numb. My senses have stopped working. I look around to see a crowd gather around the car to see what happened. I slowly force my legs to move and get away from the bunch of onlookers. I cross the road and see a door right in front of me. I look up at the board and see that it's a Barista.

Suddenly, my throat feels parched. I need to drink something. I go in and ask the waiter to get me a glass of water. As I gulp down the water, I feel my breathing become more regular. I sit there, dazed, thinking about what had happened. What if I had died? I put the battery back in and call Simran to let her know that everything is fine. Just imagining what would have happened if the car had not stopped in time brings tears to my eyes. I quickly brush the thought away and try to concentrate on the menu card the waiter has placed on my table instead.

'Excuse me?' a voice calls from behind. I tear my eyes off the menu. I don't know for how long I have been staring at it.

'Yes?' I say and look at the owner of the voice.

'Are you alright?' he asks.

'I guess.'

'I am really sorry. You came out of nowhere so suddenly. I apologize for that. Is your phone okay? You dropped it, right?'

'Huh? Do I know you . . .?' I ask, now confused.

'Oh. You don't recognize me? I was driving the car you decided to get run over by. The car you just jumped in front of?'

'Oh,' I say, not knowing how to react. He had almost killed me, so I should be angry at him. But it wasn't really his fault. I finally add, 'It wasn't your fault.'

'I know, but I scared the shit out of you. I am sorry for that.'

'That you did,' I say and smile shyly, embarrassed by what had happened.

'Let me get you something and we will call it even?' he says.

Is he flirting with me or is he just being nice? I nod my head in affirmation. As he picks up the menu card, I look at him properly for the first time. He's good-looking in a *very-nice-guy* sort of a way. Everything is in place and he looks exactly like he behaves—very polite and measured. His hair is cut short—yet is incredibly shiny and makes me want to run my fingers through it—and is neatly combed, shirt smartly tucked into his neither-too-formal-nor-too-casual trousers, and a pair of nice brown shoes. Pretty neat, I think to myself. Just the kind of guy you would feel safe with.

'Coffee?' he asks, as the waiter comes to take our order.

'Oh, no. I don't drink coffee,' I say.

'Tea?'

'Tea neither.'

'Really?' he asks.

'Really. All my caffeine is only from Coke.'

'Coke, then, for her and a cappuccino for me, with garlic bread,' he says to the waiter.

When the waiter leaves, we turn to look at each other. Suddenly, we have nothing to talk about. He looks at me with a glint in his eye and I start regretting my decision to let him apologize. I should have shouted and stormed off.

Not knowing what to do, I take out my cell phone and start pressing random buttons on it, to look busy.

'Is everything okay?' he asks. I look up to see him looking at me with concern in his eyes.

'Other than the fact that you almost killed me moments ago, I think I am just fine,' I say, contriving to be funny.

'Oh, yes, it was my fault. I am sure you had better things to think of, than looking at the stupid road while crossing,' he laughs.

'I was just completing my shopping. I have to leave for my college in a few days' time,' I respond flatly.

'Oh, great. Which year are you in?'

'First year. Just joining college this year,' I say, as the waiter returns with our order.

'Which college?'

'Indian College of Engineering, Nagpur. Heard of it?'

'Come on. You've got to be kidding me!' he says, disbelief etched across his face.

'No. Why? Do I have a reason to lie?'

'No, it's just that I go there a lot.'

'You are a student there too?' I ask, wondering if he is playing with me.

'No, I don't study there. I just know a lot of people there. A few of my very close friends study there. In fact, my best friend is doing his PhD from there. I meet him every second month. And my business takes me there often too, so instead of staying in a hotel, I stay at his quarters. It's great fun. Such a coincidence. Great,' he says, still shaking his head in disbelief.

'Seriously?' I ask, still not believing him.

'Seriously,' he says.

We start talking about him and what he does. He tells me that his father has a textile factory up-north and they make clothes and fabrics for all major brands in India. He points to my bags of clothes and says that he may have supplied fabrics for those too. I probe him about his education and he tells me about his time in London—where he did his undergraduate studies in economics and got himself a degree in business.

Slowly, I realize that he is stinking rich. He doesn't mention anything, but I ask him a lot of questions about his education and business and it becomes quite obvious that he was born into money. I mentally calculate his age and guess that he must be around twenty-four. Though he doesn't look his age. He could have passed off as a sensible, sophisticated—maybe a little too much so—twenty-year-old too. That's not too bad, I tell myself. He is just a few years older than me.

Just as I start to really enjoy myself in his company, my phone starts ringing. *Mom calling*. It's well past seven and that's past my allowed time. I have to get home. I answer her call and assure her that I'll get back in fifteen minutes.

'I have to go,' I say to him.

'Oh, sure,' he says and asks for the bill. When the waiter gets it, he settles it with his fancy American Express card. 'It was nice meeting you,' he says and gets up. 'Do you want me drop you back home?'

'No, I think I can manage,' I say, unconvincingly. 'It's hardly ten minutes from here.'

He doesn't put me in a spot by insisting. Just as he holds open the door of Barista for me, he asks, 'Er . . . can we, uh, meet some time? For a movie or something?'

I look at him. In the after-shock of what had happened, I'd totally forgotten to put him through the Three-Minute Test. I remember the first three minutes. He's a definite *yes*. He is good-looking, charming, considerate—since he took the trouble of inquiring how I was despite my fault—and seemed very agreeable.

'Sure,' I say.

'Superb,' he smiles with boyish charm. He asks for my number and I give it to him. 'It would be kind of weird if I save it as the-pretty-girl-with-the-big-brown-eyes, won't it?'

'I'm Niharika,' I hold out my hand.

'Akshat Verma, the guy who almost killed you today,' he smiles warmly at me and shakes my hand.

As I climb into an auto to get home, I see him get into his car. I am pretty sure it's different from the one that I almost got under an hour back. As the car whizzes past me, I notice it's an Audi.

This guy is perfect, I tell myself.

Chapter Six

Way Too Perfect

Over the last three days, I have often found myself staring at inane things and wondering if Akshat is the one. What if he is just like Viraat, only better-looking? After all, the unfortunate way that we met—when he almost killed me, then cared enough to come to apologize and we got talking—seemed right out of a silly, romantic movie with a happy ending.

After that first encounter, we had met again the next day. Akshat had called two hours after I had left Barista to ask me out. I had agreed, blushing all the while. When he called, I was still in a daze. It's not every day that guys shower me with attention.

But then, it was quite weird in the beginning. We both did not know whether it was a date, or if we were both just being friendly. All we knew was that we both wanted to spend time with each other. Our first encounter had sparked enough interest in us to make us want to get to know each other better. So, not knowing where to go, we decided to meet at the same mall where our little accident almost happened, and take it from there. Once there, we stared at each other awkwardly after exchanging pleasantries.

Before it got too uncomfortable, he suggested we go for a drive and decide the venue on our way. Once in the car, we got talking and forgot about deciding on a place. After over an hour, we found ourselves on the outskirts of Jaipur, where there was nothing but miles and miles of road ahead of us. There was very thin traffic and we were practically alone. When we realized that, Akshat pulled over. We turned to look at each other—he, with an unreadable expression on his face, and I, slightly nervous—and eventually burst out laughing when we met each other's eyes.

After that, we spent hours lying on the bonnet of his car, talking about anything and everything under the sun, literally. It was almost unbelievable how quickly and easily we bonded. He put me completely at ease and I opened up to him with surprising effortlessness. It felt like I had known him for ages and I am sure that the feeling was mutual. I never realized that something as simple as looking at the setting sun together, and watching the birds fly back to their homes could be such an amazing experience. What we had there was what is really referred to as—*quality time*. And I crave more of it.

Luckily, I do not have to wait for very long to get it. We are meeting again in half an hour. I have been ready since the last hour, though. I spent the whole of last night thinking about what I would wear today, amongst the zillion new clothes I have bought for myself. And even after that, I ended up trying everything twice before finally coming to a decision.

I still have not told anyone—and by *anyone* I mean *Navroz* and *Simran*—because I am not sure what to make of it. Everything has happened way too quickly and I think I need a little time to actually make sense of it. Till then, I have decided to keep it my little secret and see how it goes. By the look of things, it's going really well.

I check the time and decide that it's time I should leave, to avoid being late. Akshat had offered to pick me up, but

I was scared that my neighbours, or worse still, my mother would spot us. And I have seen him in three very conspicuous cars—one big and the other two terribly expensive—and I didn't want to be seen in any one of them. I grab my handbag and rush out of the house, hail an auto and get to the theatre in record time. I'm two minutes late. I look around and see Akshat standing next to the door, waiting for me, leaning against his car. Again, I don't know which one it is, but it's never-endingly long and extraordinarily expensive. Also, it's none of the three I have seen him drive before. I smile at him.

'You look beautiful,' he says.

I smile wider.

'Maybe, it's because I don't see you killing me now,' I say and he smiles.

'You're late, but I can see what took you so long. I love what you're wearing,' he says.

He always says the right things, I think to myself. I blush and look away. He starts to walk towards the movie hall and holds his hand out, and instinctively, I grab it. He wraps his long, bony fingers around mine, looks at me and smiles.

Like every Shah Rukh Khan movie, this one is impeccable too, and I think I love the man on the screen, more for the person that he is, than his acting abilities. He is a great human being, a responsible husband and a loving father, despite being the superstar that he is. Much like what I can see Akshat grow up to be. I shake myself. *Why is everything I see making me think of Akshat in one way or the other?* I feel that I am thinking too much and start to concentrate on the movie, though I find it tough to do as Akshat caresses my fingers endlessly. I blush throughout the movie and try not to look at him, but I know his admiring eyes are constantly on me.

The date is turning out to be amazing. We leave the movie hall, hand in hand and he takes me to a restaurant in a heritage hotel. I remember the hotel clearly, not because it's huge and has won many tourism awards, but because Navroz had asked me to treat him in the same place if I got through to IIT—and Akshat sits right opposite to me. Everything is just perfect. It's not about the way he is, it's about the way he is making me feel. Simran's words ring in my head, *'He makes me feel special.'*

As he excuses himself to use the washroom, I watch him. Today, he is dressed in a deep blue shirt with a pair of dark trousers and formal shoes. He looks impeccable, and a little strange, I notice for the first time. He is yet to say something that is not out of place, and everything is just so proper and in place that it's almost unsettling. No misplaced snorts. Measured smiles, all at the right places. His perfection kind of bugs me. He's way too . . . immaculate. For someone like me, who has embraced imperfections for the majority of my life, it is new and troubling. I can't help asking myself this question—what does he *really* want from me?

He comes back and tells me that he wants to know all about me, all that we could not cover that evening, when I had to rush home, after spending those heavenly hours with him on the bonnet of his car. No one has ever wanted to know anything about me, so once I start, I just can't seem to be able to stop. I tell him about my parents, my sister and what my plans are. For the most part of the conversation, he listens intently, his chin resting on the palm of his right hand. Only when we talk about Simran does he get a little uncomfortable for a few seconds. But before I can ask, he is back to his perfect self again.

Soon, my phone rings again and I look at my watch. It's seven o'clock and I am sure my mother is freaking out by now. He understands and calls for the bill and pays it, despite an attempt from my side to go dutch.

'I'll drop you home,' he says.

'Oh, that won't be necessary Akshat. I can take—'

'Please, Niharika. I insist.'

'Umm . . . okay,' I reply. The look in his eyes is so sincere that I just have to accept his offer. At least this time.

When we get to the car, he holds the door open for me. No one has ever done that for me! I am flattered. The last guy I dated—Piyush Mehra—didn't even want to be seen with me. I see him make his way around the car and get in. He's perfect. How did I ever get so lucky?

'So? Excited about the new college?' he asks.

'Yes. A little nervous, but excited.'

'Would you mind if I come to visit you some time?'

'Why would you do that?' I ask, and look at him stupidly. I know it's a question I shouldn't have asked, but I want an honest answer to it. I may have got myself a new hairstyle and borrowed some of Simran's personality, but a guy like Akshat can get anyone. Then, why me?

'I think you're very pretty. But that's not it, there are many pretty girls out there, but you're smart and you're funny too. That's what I really like about you. If I were to guess which college you should go to, it would either be NIFT because you carry yourself so well in those clothes or IIT, for you are smart as hell,' he says, and while he does he holds my hands tight and looks into my eyes.

'Typhoid. Right before the tests. I barely even managed to get to the exam hall,' I say, as I struggle to find words. I choke on my words and tremble. 'Just before the exams.'

'I hope you know it's IIT's loss, not yours,' he says and flashes his perfectly white teeth at me.

I like to believe what he says. I'd prepared very hard for the IIT exams. And after two years of dedicated effort and sleepless nights, two days before the exam, typhoid got me. I was so heavily medicated during the exams that I could barely keep my eyes open.

The All India Entrance Examination for Engineering was considerably better, and I got into ICE, Nagpur. After the results came out, everyone promptly forgot about the ailment and my incompetence became the reason why I couldn't crack the IIT examination. I stayed locked up in my room for a few days, but then it became better and I stopped thinking about it. After all, my parents were proud of me and that's what matters.

'They're just jealous,' is what Simran had said. 'They've just seen you succeed all your life. It's obvious they'd love a chance to speak shit when you're down. Bloody losers!'

She, like the painfully good-looking guy sitting in front of me, knows what to say to make me feel good. On the way to the car, he turns on his charm and has me on my knees. I can't call it flirting, because he makes everything sound so genuine and from the bottom of the heart. It's like his eyes see right through me and he knows just what he needs to say.

'I'll see you, then,' he says as I get out of the car. He's holding the door open for me. I wonder if people even do that these days. I look at his perfectly sculpted jawline and I am amazed at how perfect he is.

'I had fun.'

'Yes. It was the nicest evening I have had in the longest time.'

As I turn to leave, he catches my arm and turns me around. He is strong and I find it hard to muster the strength to resist as the distance between us closes. Before I can take a deep breath and say anything, he pulls me towards him and his lips touch mine. I am surprised at first, dazed, but then I start to like it. It's not really a kiss, it's more like a peck, only with a lot of love and tenderness. The way he's holding my face and the way his lips touch mine . . . I like the feeling.

We break the kiss and he loosens his grip on me. I sway back and stagger to the stairs of my apartment.

He smiles, walks away and gets into the car. I stand there and see him drive off. It's something right out of a romantic movie! I turn around and make my way to the house. It's a good thing it is so dark. Mom could've seen me otherwise or worse still, my nosey neighbours.

I change into my pyjamas and wash my face. I think about calling Simran. She'd said that she wanted me to find a guy. She'd said she'd like to see me happy. I'm happy now.

But I decide against calling her. I want to be alone with the thoughts of what happened just now and earlier today. My phone vibrates and my heartbeat quickens. It's a message. Please let it be him. Please let it be him. It is him. The message says:

'You're sweet. Take it in whatever sense you want. Good night. Kisses.'

I smile as I turn on my side. I never thought I would say this after my first date but I liked it that he kissed me.

I look at Akshat's message again. The hidden meaning gives me tickles. *I'm sweet.* My head still tingles and it feels like his lips are still on mine. I'm dazed. I reply to his text.

'I hope your dreams are sweet too.'

Chapter Seven

'I Didn't Want To Lose You.'

I don't take his call. My phone has been off the hook all day. I know Akshat wants to talk to me. But I ignore all his calls and don't reply to any of his text messages. This morning, I think I saw a big, red car hovering around my apartment building and I think it was him. He has been trying incessantly to get me to talk to him, but I don't think I am ever going to do that again. I'm leaving for Nagpur today and I hope that he never comes to my college. I never want to see that perfect face or hear the perfect things he says to me.

As it begins to annoy me, I pick up my cell phone to turn it off. 19 Missed Calls, it says. And 8 Unread Messages. I don't check them. They would all be the same.

I really wanted to tell you.' 'I was going to tell you.' 'I didn't know how to begin.' 'I didn't want to ruin things between us.' 'I didn't want to lose you.'

Well. He lost me.

Two days ago, I woke up in bliss. I had been on the perfect date, with the perfect guy and it had ended with the perfect kiss. What could be better? *What could be worse?*

It took just ten minutes to get from the first question to the second and in the process, all my silly, stupid, rosy dreams were crushed. From the best possible date a girl like me could ever get, it became a complete disaster. If only I had known. If only I had known, I wouldn't have been so torn right now, cursing myself and thinking about what could have been. No matter how angry and dejected I am, I still find it hard to push his gorgeous face out of my head, and I feel terribly guilty about it.

After my last date with Akshat, I had spent the night tossing and turning in my bed. I had spent countless hours thinking about everything that had happened and playing it back repeatedly in my head. Not being able to keep the excitement to myself any longer, I had called Simran, first thing the next morning.

'Hello?'

'Hi Simran,' I said, grinning from ear to ear.

'Hey. What's up? Tell me if it's important. Else I've to get to class. This stupid college schedule, extra classes on Saturday! It's almost like they are paying us to study and not the other way around,' she muttered, more to herself.

'Oh. You're busy. I'll call you later then?'

'No, no. What is it? I think I'll bunk the lecture. I can't seem to find the other shoe . . .'

'Umm . . . something happened.'

'Hmm?' She still sounded distracted.

'Leave it. I will tell you later.'

'Would you just tell already?'

'I . . . I met someone,' I said. 'I met a guy. He's nice and we went on a date. And it was perfect. He is gorgeous. We went to—'

'Wait, wait, wait! Hold on. Who is he? Where did you meet him? When did this happen?' she shot a volley of questions at me. I could tell that I finally had her undivided attention. And I could hear the excitement in her voice.

'I met him at Barista a few days back. He was so amazing. And then he asked for my number. When I got home, he called to ask me out. We went on our first date today. To watch—'

'You went to a movie with him?'

'Yeah. Why? What's wrong with that?' I asked. The movie was the most irrelevant part of the whole deal. Why was she stressing on it then?

'Did something happen?'

'What? No, Simran, don't be silly. He didn't do anything silly! And anyway, it was *I* who suggested watching a movie, not him. He was the perfect gentleman.'

'Oh. If he didn't get physical, it's okay. What happened next?' she asked, getting excited again.

'Umm . . . actually . . . we did get a bit physical.'

'As in? What did you do?'

'He kissed me. After he dropped me home,' I told her. 'More like a prolonged peck than a kiss, on the lips.'

'Okay. Never mind,' I could feel her shrug it away. 'What next?'

'Yeah. After the movie, we went to the Plaza for dinner. I had an awesome time there. He's just so well behaved, you know? Polished—' I said, but she cut me off.

'Okay, now he sounds boring.'

'Akshat is NOT boring!' I said, and I was surprised at my tone. Just one date and I was already defending him?

'Akshat?'

'Yes. Akshat Verma. He is like a big businessman or something. He's very rich, but I somehow feel awkward about it. He drives these big cars which draw a lot of attention and I don't really like it,' I ranted.

'*Niharika!*' she shouts. 'You're *not* going to see him any more. No matter what happens. You have met him the last time. You have talked to him the last time. *You're not going to meet him again.*'

'But—'

'I have to go to class now,' she said and disconnected the call.

I couldn't do anything until she called again. I had put two and two together and I had guessed that either Akshat had something to do with someone close to my sister, or worse—my sister herself. It made me sad to think that my fairy-tale was going to come to such an abrupt end. I wondered what it was that he had done. Simran's reaction seemed kind of extreme. What had he done to deserve that?

She called me a couple of hours later and I got the answers to all my questions. I was told not to talk and just listen. She went on to tell me more about Akshat and what he had done. I could not believe that he was the same guy who I had dreamt would give me my happy ending. I knew it was too good to be true right from the beginning.

She told me that everyone in Jaipur knew who Akshat Verma was—a rich, spoilt womanizer who would stick himself inside anything that moved. He was a number one bastard and Simran warned me against going anywhere near him. I asked her meekly if she knew him personally, and she said that I didn't need to know. It became obvious that there used to be something between Akshat and her, but I didn't want to probe too much into it. I know Simran and I know that there are times when she doesn't want anyone to talk back to her, and this was one of those times.

She asked me repeatedly to stay away from him and the sheer desperation in her tone made me pause. She was behaving as if Akshat was a real threat to me. At one point, she even suggested that I get a new cell number and discard the old one, since I was leaving for Nagpur anyway. I thought she was getting paranoid, but I did not question her. I had already decided not to see Akshat again. I guessed that they were once in a relationship, and I would never date someone who had once been with my sister. One of the basic unspoken rules of sisterhood.

I assured Simran that I would stop seeing Akshat. I wasn't angry at him, but then Simran wasn't really the irrational kind either. Whatever that happened three or four years earlier must have been serious enough for Simran to hold a grudge for so long. So, no matter how hard I fought to get his perfectly shiny hair and gorgeous jawline out of my head, I knew I had no choice but to do it. I had to end it.

I had called him right away.

'Hey Niharika,' he said. 'What's up? I have been missing you.'

'I wanted to talk to you about something . . .' I began, getting straight to the point.

'Yes?'

'I, uh, we can't see each other any more,' I laid it out straight.

We stayed silent for a while. And then, what he said shocked me. He asked, 'Is this about Simran?'

'What . . . what do you mean . . . ?' I stammered. He knew? *He knew?*

'Did she ask you to stop seeing me?'

'Akshat . . . you knew Simran is my sister?'

'Not at first. But yes, I realized soon,' he replied, as if nothing was wrong.

'Then why didn't you tell me?' I asked.

'I was going to . . . but it looks like she beat me to it. She asked you to do this, right?'

I was baffled for a moment, but not for long. I rushed to say all that I had to say, before things got out of hand. 'Yes, she did and I am going to do just that. I don't know what happened between the two of you, but I don't want any part of this. I don't want to hurt my sister. So, it's better that we end this right now. Please don't call me or text me and please don't try anything stupid. It won't work; I've decided.'

'Come on. This is just unfair and you know that,' he said. Simran had just told me that he was a player and womanizer, but somehow, as he said those words, whatever she had said had started to take a back seat. But I had to be strong and concentrate on the job on hand.

'No, it's not. My sister doesn't want me to see you any more and I respect that. And you knew that I was Simran's sister and you didn't feel like mentioning it to me? You knew I wouldn't talk to you, didn't you?'

'No, Niharika. Yes, I do admit that I should have told you. But the first day when I met you, I had no idea who you were. It was only the second time we met that you told me about your sister. I didn't want things to get weird between us. I really like you and I didn't want to screw this up,' he said, every word more sincere than the other.

'You know what? This is exactly what my sister warned me against. You and your pathetic lies. Why me, Akshat? Go and try it with some other girl whose sister you might not have pissed off before.'

'I didn't—'

'Shut up, Akshat. This is the end of the conversation. And this is the last time we are talking. Don't try to contact me ever again.'

'WOULD YOU JUST LISTEN TO ME ONCE?' he suddenly shouted. That shut me up immediately. I was taken aback. That was it. I hung up and vowed to never take his calls again. Almost instantly, his frantic calls started. And the messages, which I stopped reading after the fifth one. I have to admit that it was a little tough for me to do. Even when I broke the news to him that I knew about his past alliance with Simran, he wasn't thrown off his feet. He, instead, was extremely calm and wanted us to talk about it. How could he be so calm? And perfect?

I flop on the bed and dig my head in the pillow, silently hoping to *not* see his perfect smiling face in front of me when I open my eyes again. I hope I will not see his outstretched hand waiting for my hand—I hope I will forget the two most beautiful days I spent with a stranger, who ended up being a devil of a person.

I doze off a with huge *why* on my mind. I was happy with people not knowing about my existence.

~

I have been sleeping for the last four hours, but still, the moment I wake up I can almost smell his cologne on me. I feel pity for myself now. How can I be so into him when I don't even know him?

My mother shouts from her room and asks me if I am done with my packing. I am, and it just adds to my already crushing pile of misery. I look around the room one last time. I have spent my entire childhood here and I am going to miss it. I grew up here. I shared this room with Simran till the time she turned fifteen and wanted a separate room for herself. She was growing up and I wasn't old enough to understand why my sister wanted to sleep in a separate room. Three months later, my father turned the balcony into a room and Simran shifted there.

For more than a month, I used to knock on Simran's door and apologize for whatever mistakes I had done. She never let me in and I never understood why. I slept next to Mom for the entire next month. And for the next three after that, in my room, with the lights on. I feared that my sister had stopped loving me, but eventually, life crawled back to normal. This is just one of the million memories that my room holds.

As a family, we have been very close and very loving. Hugs and kisses, birthday celebrations, anniversary celebrations—we have never held back from any of those. We, as a family, celebrate everything. I still remember the days when Dad got our first car—a second-hand Maruti Esteem. Simran and I were so happy! We used to pester Dad to take us on a drive every day, and even used to fight for the front seat. The car still stands proudly in our driveway and it looks good for an old car. Dad says it has character.

Leaving this house feels like a huge chunk of my life is being cut off. Being a girl, I know that I might never come back to actually live here again. After graduating, I would probably go to some other city for a Master's, then to some other for a job and would probably get married after that.

Just thinking about all this makes me sad. I check my luggage one last time, remove my cell phone from its charging point and put in it my pocket.

Akshat Missed Call (23)

As if I don't have to deal with enough, I have this awfully good-looking and sweet monster to forget. Did he really like me so much that he couldn't tell me the truth, fearing he would lose me? I don't know. I don't want to think about it. But whatever the answer, I can't see him any more. Because the fact remains—he probably once dated Simran. I know it will take me a long time to find a guy, but I'm not that desperate. I would prefer being single than dating Akshat.

'Mom. I'm ready!' I shout.

'Tell Dad. He has been waiting for you.'

I pick up a few bags and make my way to the car.

'All done?' Dad asks as he opens the boot of the beloved car that had once dropped Simran to her college. Now, it is my turn. I think of my parents and I wonder how hard it is for them.

'Yeah, Dad,' I hug him and he hugs me back. I can see he is trying very hard not to cry. Yes, he is very emotional and he cries during movies too. I love him for that. At least, it lets us know that he cares and we are his world.

We load everything in the boot together and I try to hold back tears. I will miss home. The last three months have been amazing—doing nothing, lazing around with a book as Mom shouted at me to learn to cook something, watching cricket matches on TV with Dad. Sometimes even discussing politics—something he is passionate about and I know nothing about.

'Go check your room. See if you forgot something,' Mom says, not looking at me. I am sure she is about to cry too.

'No, Mom. I have checked. I have packed everything,' I assure her.

'Would it hurt to just check once more?'

'Yes. I'm way too lazy.'

She glares at me angrily and goes to check for herself. It's all an act. I know she wants to avoid spending too much time with me. We, the Singhs, are bad at farewells. When Simran had left for college in Delhi, literally a five-hour drive away, we had cried like someone had died. But we are not embarrassed by it, we love each other and we like to show it in the precious life that we have. I know of friends whose dads beat up their moms, or their sisters or them, and I feel lucky to have a family that is perfect. We might live in a house with rotten plumbing, and drive around in a fifteen-year-old car, but we care about each other and I am very proud of that.

Dad gets into the driver's seat and I get into the back seat of the car. My phone is really irritating me now. I turn off the ringer and the vibration.

'See? I told you,' Mom says triumphantly as she locks the door and comes towards the car.

'What?' I ask.

'You left your mobile's charger. I asked you to check once again. What if I had not checked?' Mom says. Don't moms just love the I-told-you-so regime? I make a face at her as she takes the seat next to Dad.

'Leave her alone. She's leaving for such a long time,' Dad comes to my rescue.

'Yeah . . . I don't know when I will see her again . . . When are your Puja vacations?' Mom asks me.

'I don't know. I'll have to check the schedule.'

'Okay. Do that and let me know. I don't like it here . . . without you. The house seems so empty . . . especially after Simran . . . I don't know what I will do . . .' her voice breaks and she turns her face away, towards the window.

And then start the tears. It's going to be another tearful farewell.

Chapter Eight

A New Search

The train journey is long and boring, and I spend most of my time tucked inside the blanket with earphones stuffed deep inside my ears. Suddenly, I don't want to leave any more; I already miss my parents and my old room. The excitement of joining a new college has given way to anxiety, and the Akshat incident is still not behind me. I just close my eyes and hope the journey will be over soon.

I get off the train and look for a taxi outside the dusty railway station. Strangely enough, there are no taxi drivers clamouring to get my attention, like it usually happens at railway stations. I get myself a pre-paid slip for a taxi, read the number on the slip and look for the taxi.

'Hey!' a voice calls from behind.

I turn around to find a guy with cute Harry-Potter-style round spectacles walking towards me, struggling with the huge bags behind him. He is really lean and not actually short, but his face (*oh, his face!*) gives him a very innocent and child-like aura.

'Excuse me?' I ask. He looks lost and barely keeps from tripping over his suitcases.

Mom had asked me not to talk to any strangers but I'm sure she meant dangerous-looking ones. The guy in front of me looks like an eighth grader and is cute beyond measure.

He reminds me of my neighbour's four-year-old son whom I used to cuddle to bits.

'Are you going to ICE too?' he asks. His voice matches his child-like face. I notice beads of sweat on his brow and that he is panting.

'Yes, why? Are you going there too?' I ask him. I resist an urge to ruffle his hair, which falls droopily on his forehead and partially covers his spectacles.

'I am. I was wondering if we could share a taxi. I was standing right behind you in the queue,' the kid explains to me, and I can barely suppress a laugh.

'Sure,' I say and the taxi driver loads up our suitcases and bags on the top of the cab and binds them with a rope. The kid gets a little paranoid about the bags falling down during the journey, but the driver assures him that they won't. The college is barely a ten-minute drive away from the railway station and for the first five minutes, we don't talk. The kid is too busy trying to catch his breath and I don't want to put extra pressure on him.

'Tanmay,' he says and thrusts his hand out.

'Niharika. Are you joining this year?' I ask, even though it's kind of obvious.

'Yes, Electronics,' he says.

'Oh, really? I am in Electronics too!' I say and he smiles. We talk for a bit and we tell each other about our engineering preparations, and how and why we couldn't get into IIT. That is one topic every engineering student can use as a conversation starter. *How and why I could or could not make it to the IITs.* Soon, we reach the college and ask for directions to the hostel. The boys' hostel is closer to the main gate of the college and Tanmay gets off there. He tries to offer me money for the taxi we just shared, but I refuse, saying that we will meet again soon and he could treat me then.

The campus is huge. As I look around, I feel a little lost. There are loads and loads of people moving around, and I am just one of them. Remember the times when you stand on a beach and look at the never-ending expanse of water that stretches in front of you? And you feel like the world is so very big and you are such an inconsequential part of it? Well, this was one of those times.

I enter the Administration Building and ask for the way to the hostel. The hostel warden, an old lady, takes down my details, checks the payment receipts, cites a few basic hostel rules, and hands over the key to me. It takes me three trips to get all my luggage to my room. Once I get everything there, I'm just too tired to do anything. But I'm too excited to relax either. The room is at a bare minimum, but thankfully, I had prepared myself for that. I arrange the lamps, the curtains and the bedsheets and the room starts to look a lot better than before.

It strikes me that *I'm finally in college.*

I look around the room—now much smaller after I unpacked my stuff. It's not too small, actually. My room in Kota was way smaller, but then, I lived there alone. I have a roommate here. Which makes me think—where is she? Who is she? I hope she's not too messy. I've never had much patience with dirty roommates and that was the reason I lived alone in Kota.

After admiring what I have done to the room, I lie down and fall asleep as soon as my head hits the pillow. My last thought before sleeping is one of Simran and Akshat, and I find it hard to push it out of my head.

~

It's already eight in the evening when I get up and hear frantic footsteps outside the corridor. It takes me a few minutes to get accustomed to the new surroundings. I recall the words of the warden who had said that dinner would be served till eight thirty in the common mess. I get into half-decent clothes, splash my face with a little water and start to look for the common mess.

It's a five-minute walk from the girls' hostel and my stomach has started to growl. I have hardly eaten anything since the long and tortuous train journey and I need to eat. I find my way to the common mess and I can hear a clamouring noise from far away. I enter the mess to see table after table filled with students—mostly guys—eating and chatting rather loudly.

At one end of the room, I spot a long line of students with big, steel plates in their hands. I pick up one too and stand in the line. I wonder where the juniors are, since everyone seems to know each other. I start to feel a little lonely and curse my roommate—who hasn't yet turned up—because had she been there, I wouldn't have been alone at least.

The line moves at a snail's pace and I have barely reached the salad counter when I hear a voice behind me.

'This is like the worst day of the year. All these freshers with big stomachs lining up for hostel food. But at least the girls are better this time. Good for all the juniors who have found their way to this shithole,' the voice says from behind. There is a certain careless disdain in the voice. I wonder if he's talking about me because it sounds like he is right beside me. I raise the plate up to waist level and look at his reflection in it. I can't make out much of him, just that he has slightly longish hair that curls at the ends.

He keeps talking and I no longer listen to what he is saying. I can feel him towering over me. For a moment, I feel like hitting him for objectifying women, but his demeanour is one of such nonchalance that I don't think he would even care.

More people join in the conversation and they talk to him with a certain respect in their tones. Maybe a senior, I think to myself. This guy has hooked everyone's attention as he goes about bashing the authorities, the hostels, the infrastructure and the like. It's not out of frustration, neither does it sound like he is complaining. It's very strange, because he doesn't himself sound interested in what he is saying, but everyone else is.

Maybe, it's the voice. It's a little . . . a sort of . . . it's very smooth, like satin, but with very rough edges to it. I can't put it in words, but the carelessness and the friendly-yet-rude attitude in his voice—husky but not cracked—is alluring. It's like music to my ears, like the kind not everyone can enjoy.

I'm totally and completely enchanted, even though I really want to hate him. He starts to talk about more girls and teachers and bashes them to the boisterous laughter of other students around him and I still find it hard to dislike him. My gaze is transfixed on whatever is visible of him. I stand here, spellbound and confused, wanting to see the face of the owner of the voice. But I also don't want to turn around and make my interest—or whatever it is—obvious to him. Lost in my thoughts, I feel a warm breath on my neck, followed by a whisper in my ear, 'The line has moved.' It's the same voice.

I stagger ahead, and I can still feel the warmth of his breath on my neck and hear the timbre of his voice in my head. I hear the rustle of feet on the concrete floor behind me and I wonder how far he is from me. I put dollops of rice and daal on my plate mindlessly, as my face flushes red and I breathe unevenly.

I take a deep breath, leave the line, and stride towards a seat in the corner of the mess, not looking back even once.

Chapter Nine

The Guy with the Dark Eyes

I rummage through my bags for clothes as I look at the wall clock from the corner of my eye. I find it hard to believe that I am late on the first day of college, when I haven't ever been late for any of my classes till now in my whole life. I blame that voice in the mess, and the loser back in Jaipur. I couldn't sleep well last night as conflicting thoughts of the phenomenal date with the near-perfect guy, Akshat, and the guy with the magical voice in the mess flooded my mind and kept me awake.

I drop the idea of taking a shower, dress quickly, and step out of the room. It takes me another fifteen minutes to find the building and my class amidst the maze of concrete buildings and workshops. The door is closed and I can see a lot of students through the little glass window. After wasting two more minutes standing outside, I knock at the door.

'Excuse me, sir?' I say softly, to the short, balding man standing in the class.

'Yes?'

'May I come in, sir?'

'Oh yes. Come in, come in. Welcome to the class,' he says. I struggle to figure if there is sarcasm in his voice. Why does he sound so happy to see me and how come he is so comfortable with me being late to class?

I bow my head a little and silently make my way into the class.

'Got lost in the campus? It happens to most people. I remember my own first day here, as a student . . . confusing corridors . . .' he babbles away happily.

'Yes, sir. I got kind of confused there,' I say and smile at him.

'Well, never mind. You didn't miss much. I was just introducing myself to the class. Please take a seat.'

I look around to find a seat. The classroom looks full and the first few benches look especially overflowing. On each of these benches are new, sparkling pens and registers. No matter how old you get, the charm and excitement of a new class never fades, though it's likely that those registers will never be scribbled upon and the pens will not be used till the first set of exams.

I, too, look for a seat in the front rows, but I can't see one. Being studious is a part of my identity and I can't run away from it, though I was never too much into writing notes. As per my new plan, I wouldn't be too much into studying either. The day I got the admission letter to ICE, Nagpur and I ripped it open, I had decided that I wouldn't study as much any more. I was angry that I couldn't get into IIT, but more than that, I realized that I have been missing out on a lot of things.

As I look for a seat, someone waves his hand frantically from the last bench. It's Tanmay. I flash him a smile and climb up the steps to take a seat with the other backbenchers.

'Good morning, class. Welcome to Indian College of Engineering. I hope you find the love of your lives here, because that's what matters more. Everything else, be it education, jobs or careers . . . they just come and go. Love stays. I am Sudeep Wadhwa. I have been a teacher here for the last nineteen years. I'll be teaching—'

'Did he actually say that?' Tanmay says. He looks a lot more relaxed today. No sweat, no panting and puffing. 'He's a professor here. And he said *that* in the introductory speech?'

'Cool, right? I think things are pretty casual here.'

'I hope so. Or he just might be one of the lenient teachers,' he says and adjusts his funny spectacles. He carries them off really well. Anyone else would have looked downright crazy. He just looks immensely adorable!

Prof. Wadhwa tells us that he would be teaching us Mechanics of Solids and jumps right into some basic problems and formulas, even though people have already stopped listening to him. But it does not look like he minds that much. Two minutes into the class and I can tell he is used to talking to the walls.

'Tanmay Srivastava,' my new friend says. 'Just in case you forgot my name.'

'Niharika Singh,' I reply. 'Just in case *you* forgot mine.'

'I remember.'

We stay silent for a while after that and try to listen to what Prof. Wadhwa has to say, but it's just way too boring.

'Are you taking notes?' I whisper to Tanmay, who is staring intently into his notebook and scribbling something. He occasionally adjusts his spectacles and smiles stupidly at the notebook.

'No,' he whispers back and pushes his notebook towards me.

'Oh my God!' I almost exclaim as I peer into the notebook.

On his notebook is an elaborate caricature of the entire class, the professor, a few students in the front row, him and me. It's just like those comic strips from the newspapers and magazines! I am amazed.

'That's me?' I point at the girl who's wearing the same clothes as mine. The girl has frizzy, unmanageable hair that is all over the place. 'Is my hair that bad?'

'Umm . . . actually, when doing caricatures, you have to magnify the good or bad features to make them resemble the person more. And yes, that's you.'

'No way! Are those *my* eyes? Are they really as big as footballs?'

'Yes,' he says and smiles shyly.

'This is amazing,' I say and look at it more closely.

He starts to tell me that he has been doing this for over ten years now. He tells me that a lot of people have asked him to pick it up as a career, but he has never wanted to do it for money. He shows me a few more sketches he has made, and each one is more impressive than the last.

'So, where are you from?' I ask as I look at the caricature again and wonder if my hair is really that bad.

'Barwaha. It's a small place in Madhya Pradesh. You could not have heard about it.'

'Yes, I haven't. Was it nice there?' I ask.

He looks at my face for a second, as if judging if I'm making fun of him. Satisfied that I'm not, he replies, 'Yes, it was nice. It's a small town, but it's beautiful. We have the Narmada river like one mile away from my home. It was fun . . .' I can clearly hear the nostalgia in his tone.

'Nice. I'm sure it's lovely there. I am from Jaipur. I've lived there all my life. I spent the last two years in Kota though.'

'I thought you were from Delhi. Or Mumbai or Bangalore,' he says and adjusts his spectacles that drop below his nose-bridge.

'Why would you say that?' I ask.

'You look like you are from there. The clothes, the way you talk . . . you know? The style . . . I don't know,' he says, and it looks like he regrets saying it.

We start talking about our home towns and he tells me

more about himself. He tells me his father has a small factory
that makes parts for electronic calculators and his interest in
electronics started from there. He looks like someone who
comes from a background without a lot of money. His
complexion is darkish, his looks are average, his clothes are
regular and his hairstyle shouts that he belongs to a small
town. And that is what I find most appealing about him.
He is just a kid, from a small place, from where he must
have always wanted to go out and study. But the best thing
about him is that after he completes his studies, his plan is
to go back to his home town and work with his father. He
dreams of taking his father's small business to heights some
day. He wants to go back to where he was from, and do
something there.

'So you always wanted to be an electronics engineer?'
I ask.

'Yes. There are a lot of things I have wanted to do with
my father's business that he can't. So I thought I would get
a Master's degree in electronics and join my father's business.
I had started studying all our subjects in my twelfth class
itself. What about you? You always wanted to be an electronics
engineer too?'

The kid's sincerity and the innocence in his voice make
me feel a little ashamed and worthless.

'Me? Not at all. I just wanted to get into IIT to make
my parents proud. I didn't mind studying and I didn't know
what else to do. I have not really thought about what I want
to be,' I say, at the risk of sounding stupid.

'Oh, that's okay,' he says and there is a silence.

We listen to what the professor is saying, but he has gone
off on a tangentially different topic and we are clueless.
I break the silence and start telling him about Kota and what
it was like there. I tell him about my classes there and my
only friend—Navroz.

'Navroz. Is he your . . . I mean, are you committed to him?' he asks and I don't blame him. I guess I was talking too much about Navroz, so I had it coming.

'What? Navroz? Oh, no. He used to have a girlfriend there. Priya. But then they broke up—'

'Because she thought he was going out with you too?' he asks.

'No. Because of other reasons.'

'Hmm. I thought they broke up because of you.'

'No, they didn't,' I say, exasperatedly.

'Are you sure he didn't secretly love you? Maybe he did. And his girlfriend got to know. That's how it always happens,' he continues, quite irritatingly.

I don't say anything. *What just happened to the cute kid?* I don't understand why he suddenly started acting so weird. It was getting a little awkward, so I decide to shut up.

'I'm sorry,' he whispers after a while. 'I just wanted to keep the conversation going. But I didn't know what to say. I was nervous.'

'Why would you be so nervous? You're so . . . you know . . . lovely . . .'

He looks embarrassed. And I think that's kind of sweet too.

'I hope you're not mad,' he says meekly. 'I just thought it would sound cool if I talk about relationships and break-ups. My friend said that's what people do in the cities,' he explains.

'That is the silliest thing I've ever heard,' I say and we burst out laughing.

I suddenly remember that I didn't put him through my Three-Minute Test. But then I didn't need to. There are a few people who come into your life like sunshine on a gloomy, winter morning, Tanmay seems exactly like that. I have met him twice and it seems like I know him for a really long time. I don't know if I ever talked to anyone like this in the second meeting itself. I really like Tanmay, the shy kid with Harry Potter glasses.

The class ends and Tanmay tells me that the next class in not until two hours from now. He looks at me blankly for a while before I tell him that we should hang out in the college canteen. As we leave the class, we hear a few murmurs behind us and sense a few eyes on us. I wonder what that means.

The canteen is a good five-minute walk from our building and the sun overhead is not pleasant. There are groups of students everywhere interacting with college seniors. Ragging has reduced in the last few years, after the college authorities came down hard on it because a student killed himself after his head was dunked in a toilet and flushed in front of many of his classmates.

We reach the canteen and Tanmay fights the twenty-strong crowd in front of the counter to get us sandwiches.

'Hey, juniors!' A tall guy in his pyjamas comes our way and sits in front of us. A few more of his friends join him. All of them are in dirty T-shirts, faded pyjamas and stink of hostel filth—a weird smell of sweat, smoke and alcohol. Simran has often told me horror stories about how dirty guys are in the hostel and now I see a few examples in front of me.

'Hi,' I mumble back, and look at Tanmay from the corner of my eye to find that he has the fear of death writ across his face.

'Which branch?' the guy asks rudely.

'Electronics,' I say.

'Names,' another guy shouts out.

I don't like the look of these guys—rude and very gruff. They are certainly not the kind of people I would have liked to meet on my first day in college.

'Niharika,' I say clearly, trying not to let my fear show.

Tanmay isn't that good at masking his feelings. Blood rushes to his face and he shuffles his feet uncomfortably. 'T-T-Tanmay,' he stammers.

'So, T-T-Tanmay,' the senior—the one who is sitting down—points at me and asks, 'do you like her?'

'Huh?'

'I asked you—*do you fucking like her?*' he repeats, with apparent anger in his voice, which I clearly don't like.

Tanmay just looks at him and sweats. The senior waits for an answer and asks again, 'Open your mouth, you son of a bitch!'

'I . . . I . . . don't know her. N-not r-really . . .'

'Then get the hell out of here,' the senior says and the other two laugh loudly. I think they are overdoing the evil-villain-laughter, but it sounds scary nonetheless. I see Tanmay freeze, his scared eyes on the three laughing seniors. I know it's me who is going to get into real trouble once these seniors make Tanmay leave, but I still feel sorrier for Tanmay. The poor kid, he looks lost.

'Didn't you get it?' One of the two standing seniors comes close and stares down angrily at him.

'I . . . I won't go,' Tanmay says.

'Do you even know who you're talking to?' the senior who was sitting down stands up and glowers down at Tanmay.

Tanmay shakes his head and looks down.

'*GET THE HELL OUT OF HERE!*' the senior shouts and I see people from the adjoining tables look at us.

I steal a glance at Tanmay, who is looking down and away from these guys. He still doesn't budge. But I can see that he is shivering quite badly by now. I feel bad for him. I can't stay silent any more.

'Excuse me—' I say but I am cut off.

'*CHETAN MEHTA* is the name. *I AM THE COLLEGE-FUCKING-PRESIDENT,*' the senior thunders. He now turns to me and continues, 'And I don't want this guy in the canteen. You have a problem with that?'

He looks at me with his bloodshot eyes and I have to admit, I am a little scared. Before I can get hold of my senses and say something, I see a hand creep up the college-fucking-president's back and pat it.

'You're creating trouble again, aren't you? How many times have I told you not to get drunk in the morning?' the guy says.

Strangely enough, the voice seems familiar. It comes back in a flash—it's the one from the college mess yesterday. The satin-smooth voice with the rough edges to it. I look up and I can finally see the face of the guy who had objectified girls—and probably me—just yesterday in the college mess. I notice that he has deep black eyes, partially hidden by a mop of wild curly hair. I know I should not be, but I am instantly attracted to him.

'You guys can go,' he says, looking at me.

His dark, deep black eyes stare right at me and I can't tear my gaze away.

'*YOU*,' he repeats, when he notices that I haven't budged.

'Huh,' I come out of my trance.

'*Leave*. And don't find trouble again.'

Tanmay is already on his feet with his bag securely slung across his shoulder. I grab my bag and start walking away with him, my eyes still on the guy who saved us, as he stares right back at me, his lips tilted upwards in a smirk. I break eye contact and walk silently behind Tanmay.

'Hey, you?' he says and points to Tanmay.

'Uh, yes?' Tanmay answers uncertainly.

'Come here.'

Tanmay hesitates and then, with unsure steps, walks up to where the four seniors are standing. The guy with the deep, black eyes puts a hand on Tanmay's shoulder, turns away from me and asks him, 'Did they trouble you?'

Tanmay nods like a schoolkid. The guy asks him, 'Is there something you want to say to them?' Tanmay shakes his head, but the guy prods him again. 'This is the only chance you might ever get.'

'I . . . umm . . .' Tanmay struggles.

'Say it, man.'

'Fuck you. And don't ever come near her again . . .' Tanmay says with a strange attempt at anger. He points a finger at the college president whose expression changes within a split second.

'What the hell did you just say? You pathetic son of a—

'Don't you dare abuse me!' Tanmay suddenly shouts.

Before the college president and his two cronies can react the guy with the dark eyes turns to them and holds down the three of them. He asks Tanmay to leave and I follow him with quick footsteps, even though half of me wants to turn around and see what happens. As we leave the canteen, I can see the college president swinging his arm wildly and pointing in our direction. The guy who saved us is still smiling, patting his back, holding him back and laughing, without a care in the world.

~

We walk in silence for a while. We get to know that our classes have been suspended for the day because there is a conference on Automotive Robotics being held in the auditorium and every professor is supposed to be present there. We learn that suspensions like these are very common in this college. A part of me is happy, but another part of me wants to attend a class or a lecture or whatever can distract me from what happened at the canteen. I don't feel too good, and Tanmay's mortified face keeps reminding me of it.

'I am sorry,' Tanmay says after a while.

'Sorry? Why?'

'I couldn't stand up to them. I got scared. I don't get into fights,' he says, finding it hard to even look at me.

'Are you kidding me! I think you were very brave.'

'Brave, how? I couldn't do anything in front of them . . .'

'You *were* brave. And you did shout at them! You didn't even know if the guy who saved us today will save you tomorrow. So what you said to them was really sweet. I really liked it.'

'You did?'

'Most certainly, Tanmay,'

'Do you think they will come after me?' he asks, frowning.

'I don't think so. They looked too drunk to remember any of what happened today,' I try to assure him.

'But what if that guy hadn't come to our rescue?'-

'Relax. We would have been fine,' I say.

I know I am lying, but I have no idea what would have happened. With the way things were going before that guy with the dark eyes interfered, those seniors would have probably hit Tanmay and gotten away with it. Thank God that guy interfered! I am pretty sure he was the guy from the mess yesterday. The same voice, the same lean frame—this time more visible—and the same charming rudeness in his voice, there is no doubt in my mind that it was him. I hadn't caught a proper glimpse of his face, his eyes demanded too much attention, and I gave it to him. But I did notice the strong jawline and the long, unruly, curly hair.

'You know what will be best for us, Niharika?' Tanmay says and looks at me through his round iron-rimmed spectacles. 'If you date that guy from the canteen. Then we'll be safe always.' I don't know whether he is serious or not.

'What? I don't even know him. I didn't even look at him properly,' I say, turning a little pink in the face. I don't know what it is about this guy. I don't even know his name, and I am trying to fight the feeling, but I have to agree—at least to myself—that I'm strangely intrigued by him.

'Then, please do. Or are you already dating somebody?' Tanmay says and flushes. 'Oh, sorry, I shouldn't talk about relationships.'

'No, no, you can. And no, I'm not dating anyone. Are you?' I ask, and feel a little weird about it. It's hard to picture Tanmay with a girl. He looks eleven years old.

'Umm . . . I have never had a girlfriend. I was just not that kind of a guy. I mean—why would anyone date me?'

'Oh, shut up, Tanmay. Look at yourself. You're so adorable! Like a teddy bear. I would have loved to date you . . . if I was eight years old.'

'Thank you,' he says, fake-offended.

'I was kidding. Never mind, now that we are friends, I will find you a nice girl in this college. We have four years, right?'

He blushes and asks me about the guys I have dated.

'I don't have much to tell,' I say. And almost immediately, thoughts of Akshat cloud my mind. I am suddenly reminded of his perfect white teeth, his perfect mannerisms and how perfect he made me feel. I have tried telling myself that it was just one day, one date and I shouldn't feel the pain—almost physical in its manifestation—that I am going through. I miss him. I know it's irrational, but I do. I tell myself it's more because of the way we broke up than because I had to lose him.

'Just two?' Tanmay asks, shocked at my admission that I have dated just two guys. I nod. 'But at least you have kissed someone! I wonder what that is like.'

'It depends on who you kiss, really. So now, not only do we have to find you a girl, we have to make sure you get to kiss her too,' I say. 'Not that I have too much experience in that area.'

'Or we can remain losers forever,' he says and smiles.

There is something very warm and fuzzy about Tanmay that makes me want to hug him and never leave him. Unlike Navroz—who is, and will always be, my best friend—he isn't the smart-ass guy who will joke around and make you feel at home. He is different and has a child-like air around him.

We pick a spot on the stairs of the physics laboratory to rest our aching legs. It's surrounded by buildings and is substantially cooler than the rest of the campus. He takes out his red and silver laptop and puts it on his lap.

'Let's watch a movie?' he asks me.

'Sure! Neat laptop, by the way,' I say.

'I know. My dad got it for me when I got into ICE. He had promised me he would get me one when I start college,' he says with a glint in his eye, and starts talking fondly about the laptop, like a child does about a new toy.

'It's nice,' I say after he is done explaining the high-end configuration and the confusing buttons on the laptop. 'It's red, after all. It looks like a panel fell out of a spaceship.'

'Thank you,' he says and offers me one earpiece of the earphone.

We fight for a bit about which movie to watch. He chooses English sci-fi movies while I pick up the chick flicks. We have a short disagreement after which we finally decide—on a baseless premise that we are in college and we need to watch a movie set in college—on watching *Dil Chahta Hai*. The movie came out quite a few years back, but the charm still hasn't died down. All the stars were fifteen years too old to play the characters they were playing, but somehow, they had managed to pull it off.

We watch the movie and hide our faces whenever there is an emotional scene. It's embarrassing to cry in front of someone you have just met. At least not while watching a movie. Some bits of the movie are hilarious and we laugh our heads off, too. Two hours into the movie, we realize that we need a break. We are both ravenous.

'Let's get something to eat?' I ask and he nods. He pauses the movie and we walk back to the canteen. The last couple of hours made us forget about what had happened in the canteen this morning.

'What if . . . ?' Tanmay asks as we are about to enter the canteen.

'Nothing will happen,' I say, even though I am a little scared myself. We are both a little nervous and don't look around while we order a lot of sandwiches and French fries. We wait nervously at the counter for our order to be served. From the corner of my eye, I check if those hooligans or our rugged saviour are anywhere near. Strangely, I want to see him again. If not anything else, at least to thank him. But none of them are anywhere in sight.

As soon as our food is put into little polythene bags, we turn on our heels and rush out of the canteen. We don't exchange a word till we reach the stairs again.

'Relax, Tanmay. Why are you so afraid?' I ask him.

'I have never been in fights before, and I definitely do not like it now. They won't hurt you, you're a girl. I wish I was a girl too, if only to prevent rowdy seniors from beating me up,' he says and we laugh. It's been only a few hours since we have been together but I can feel the pretences melting away. We are like two old friends who never got a chance to meet again. We start the movie again and munch on our sandwiches. We shed a tear when the movie ends and laugh at each other.

'What now?' he asks.

'I don't know,' I say. It's already five in the evening and the sun is coming down a little. We are not hungry really but we start walking back to college canteen. The fear has subsided a little now and I don't think of those seniors when I enter the canteen this time. I just look around for the dark-eyed guy.

'Even he is not around . . .' I think aloud and Tanmay hears it.

'Oh, you want to meet that guy, don't you?'

'Just to thank him.'

'Yes, why not? I can thank you on his behalf. You really don't have to meet him, what say?' he jokes.

'Whatever. Go do that, I don't care,' I say.

He laughs. We sit facing each other and start talking. There are plenty of people hanging around in the canteen now. All the classes are over and it seems like the entire campus is in the canteen. Tanmay tells me more about himself and his school days. Though there is nothing interesting—and I can totally relate to it since I have led that kind of life too—it feels like I can listen to him talk for hours..

While he was describing the incident where he was caught bunking his class the first time when he was in the eighth standard, my phone starts to ring. It's the hostel warden. I wonder what it is. I take the call and she tells me that my roommate—Pia, she says her name is—is about to arrive and I should drop an extra key at the office or stay in my room to receive her. I had changed the locks earlier this morning and had forgotten to leave one key with the hostel warden.

'What is it?' Tanmay asks.

'I have to go back to the hostel. My roommate is about to arrive so I have to stay in my room,' I say.

'Okay, then. See you at the mess for dinner?' he asks.

'Sure,' I say and pick up my bag. 'Or . . . you can come to the hostel with me too? Maybe you will like her. How cool would that be?'

'Umm . . . no . . . Am I even allowed? It's a girls' hostel . . .'

'Yes, yes,' I assure him. 'The rules changed last year. Guys are allowed at the girls' hostel till seven p.m., but some girl has to sign for it.'

'But, I . . . it will be strange.'

'Oh, c'mon! It won't be strange. We will watch another movie? This time it's your choice,' I try to convince him.

But no matter how hard I try, he doesn't agree. He is a lot shyer than I had imagined him to be, and I quite like that. I have burnt my fingers talking to a smart-ass stranger in Barista and I don't want that to happen again. I sling my bag on my shoulder and he does the same.

'Can I walk you back to your hostel?' he asks shyly.

'I would like that,' I say.

We both walk silently and I wonder if he is thinking what I am thinking. I thank my stars to have found someone who I can talk to, on the very first day of college.

'Thank you,' I say as I turn towards him at the foot of my hostel stairs, 'for today.'

'Thank you,' he says and drops his bag on the ground. He takes his notebook out, flips to the page on which he had sketched my caricature, tears it and hands it to me. 'No matter how your hair is, here or for real, it looks amazing.'

I smile at him.

Chapter Ten

Love at First Sight

It's been half an hour since I have been back in my room and my roommate still hasn't turned up. I am getting a little anxious now. I tried sleeping a little while back, but it didn't really work and I am still wide awake. It's almost seven when I hear a commotion out in the corridor. It sounds almost like a landslide and I go out of my room to check.

Just outside my room is a pile of at least ten suitcases and I see two men carrying four more behind them. The skinny men drop the suitcases where the others are lying and then stack them next to each other—exactly fifteen suitcases. One of them leaves while the other stands at attention, looking down the hallway like someone important is coming. Is this my roommate? Is she some kind of a princess or something?

From the far end of the hall, I can hear the sound of heels clicking against the mosaic floor, taking quick and determined steps towards where I am standing. The girl turns the corner and I see her brownish-black hair bounce around her face, a pair of sunglasses perched firmly on her forehead, a white T-shirt clinging to her slender body tucked into skinny navy blue trousers held up by a thin brown belt. The heels making the noise are white too, and are at least four inches tall.

'Hi,' she says as she comes and stands right in front me.

She is as fair as snow, her lips are amazingly pink, and her teeth blindingly white. She is not very tall and even with her heels, she is only just as tall as me. She looks like a dainty fairy and smells of freshly picked roses. My guess was not that wrong, after all. If not a princess, she is at least a fairy.

'Niharika,' I thrust my hand out, but she hugs me instead. And it's not a pretentious hug, it feels like she is genuinely happy to see me. I can only wonder why.

'I am Pia,' she says. She looks at her maid standing next to her and says, 'Didn't I tell you that a girl with a name as nice as Niharika can't be bad? Oh, Niharika, this is Didi. She used to take care of me back in Delhi. And she is really sad that I have come to Nagpur.' Pia hugs the old woman and the old woman look like she will never let Pia go.

'That's sweet. But Pia . . . I don't think we can fit all your stuff in,' I say as I open the door.

'Don't worry. Didi will handle everything,' Pia says and flops on the bed opposite to mine. 'The room was given to you like this?'

'No, it was bare. It just came with furniture and the mattresses. I put up the curtains and the posters and shifted the furniture around a little bit.'

'Oh, nice. I like it,' she says, smiles at me and looks at all the little things I have put here and there.

The skinny guy and the old woman open suitcase after suitcase filled with clothes, shoes, toiletries and everything one can possibly need and start to stack them neatly into Pia's cupboard. The cupboard seems to have expanded, as it swallows everything that is in those fifteen suitcases. Pia actively directs them and rejects stuff that she doesn't think is important any more. Time and again, she looks at me and asks if she would need a certain piece of clothing or a set of bedsheets and takes my suggestions seriously.

Finally, after an hour, all the suitcases are empty (or filled, with whatever we thought was not needed). Pia hugs the old woman—who is in tears now—and bids both of them goodbye. The old woman just doesn't want to let her go. Pia assures her that she will be back soon and asks her to take care of herself and her mom and dad. She closes the door behind them and drops flat on the bed with her face down on her pillow.

'So,' she says as she looks up, 'how do you find the college?'

'It has just been one day and half the classes got cancelled. So, there was nothing much to do.'

'And how is the crowd?' she asks me, her eyes filled with curiosity.

'It's okay. Though, ragging is still quite prevalent in this college. Tanmay and I ran into some trouble this morning,' I say.

'Tanmay?' she asks and I narrate the whole morning incident and also tell her all about Tanmay and how we met. She lets out a few shocked gasps and some radiant smiles every few minutes. She has a really expressive face and it gives me a feeling that she doesn't really do a good job at hiding what she is feeling. She tells me that she is from Delhi, and has passed out from Delhi Public School, R.K. Puram. She also tells me that her dad is in some kind of business that she herself doesn't understand. She asks me about my background and as I tell her, she listens intently and bobs her head. The minute I tell her that my sister studies in Delhi, she freaks out and announces that we have to go on a girls' night-out there soon.

I feel a little strange, seeing her here. She is a rich, pretty brat from Delhi. Well, she does not actually come across as a brat, and if I go by first impressions, she is really sweet, but it really doesn't look like she belongs here. She belongs to her big castle back in Delhi, with all her expensive clothes and a line of servants; she is too pampered to be here and to be pursuing engineering. Why would someone so happy and cheerful come to destroy her life in engineering? I ask her exactly that.

She says, 'I know why you are asking this. A lot of people think I am good for nothing—'

'I didn't mean that.'

'No, I didn't take offence. I know I spend a lot of my dad's money on clothes and shoes, but I have always been good at studies too. Actually, I wanted to do fashion designing, because I love clothes! And shoes too.' Her eyes light up. 'But I realized when I took the entrance examination that you need to be really talented to get there. I did way better in my engineering entrance examinations, so I came here. People were shocked, but that was fun too!'

I laugh. 'But then—were your parents okay with sending you here?'

'Actually, my parents were the most shocked. They never cared about my marks. When I told them, they had no idea what I was saying. Now, they are proud,' she says with a huge smile on her face. 'Oh! And I love your top.'

'Thank you,' I say and blush. I have to take her word seriously—she almost became a fashion designer.

And then, it strikes me! A little late, but better late than tomorrow. *Tanmay and Pia!* They would make an amazing pair. The cute kindergarten couple. Harry Potter and the little fairy. How perfect was that?

~

'Where are we going?' Pia asks, as I hold her hand and pull her to the common mess. 'Let's go outside and eat today? Mom said hostel food is really bad,' she chirps.

'I want you to meet Tanmay,' I say. I can't be blamed

for thinking that they would probably have the cutest kids ever born.

'Sure! But we can still go out to eat, right? We can ask him to come along?'

Pia's mom has called ten times since the evening to remind her that she shouldn't eat the hostel food for at least the first few weeks. Apparently, she has a weak stomach, which takes time to adapt to new surroundings. It's obvious; she is a little princess after all. But Pia isn't that insistent on it.

'Let's ask him,' I say and drag her inside the canteen.

A lot of people start looking in our direction. I would give Pia's bright pink attire, with USA 64 written in bold silver letters, the credit for it. Her spaghetti top, too, is a little too skimpy for a hostel mess and I realize it now.

'Why is everyone looking at us?' she whispers under her breath, her perfectly shaped eyebrows in knots.

'Just stick close to me,' I say.

We look for Tanmay and I am furious that he is not here. I shouldn't have mentioned in the text I had sent him that Pia is this amazing. He makes us wait for fifteen minutes in the crowded mess, and I don't see what took him so much time. In his checked pyjamas, a cartoon-embellished T-shirt and his Harry Potter glasses, he looks just the same.

He smiles on seeing me, but his smile automatically disappears as his eyes move from me to the girl at my side. My eyes follow his and I see how cute Pia is. She has left her wavy hair open and it hides half of her snowy white face. By the time Tanmay is standing in front of us, all the blood from his body has rushed to his face and he is bright red.

'Hi, Tanmay. I am Pia,' she introduces herself, smiling brightly at him. Tanmay responds with a silent *Hi*.

He stretches out a hand to shake hers, but by that time Pia has already moved forward for a hug. There is an awkward moment of something between a hug and a handshake and

I'm glad it lasts just for a few seconds. I make a mental note to tell Pia later that around here not everyone is used to getting hugged.

'Where are you from, Tanmay?' the bubbly, cheerful girl asks.

'Barwaha. You must not have heard of it . . . a small town in Madhya Pradesh . . .' Tanmay mumbles, looking everywhere but at her.

'No, I have heard of it. One of my Dad's partners has a farmhouse there. I have been there once. It's a beautiful place,' she says and Tanmay turns to look at me with love-struck eyes. I think he has fallen in love just because a girl as pretty as her even knows where Barwaha is, let alone having visited the place.

'So Tanmay, don't you think we should go out and eat? My mom just messaged me,' she shows us her spanking new iPhone with a pink cover, 'that there is a McDonald's just outside the college campus. I think we should go. But I don't know, it's really your choice,' she says and makes a face kids make when you don't take them out for an ice cream. Tanmay looks at me like I am their mom and they are waiting for me to decide.

'Fine,' I say. 'Let's go.'

Pia shrieks and hugs both of us, grabbing some more attention from the hostellers in the mess. I think I have to be quick with that talk I have decided to have with Pia about who to hug and where.

~

We ordered burgers, fries and Coke for ourselves. Our table is now filled with transfats, mayonnaise and cholesterol! But Pia gave me another thing to like about her. She wasn't finicky about eating only low-calorie food. In fact, she ridiculed me when I asked for a burger without cheese. I notice that she has the perfect body—neither too thin, nor too fat.

'How's the burger without cheese?' she mocks me.

'I don't want to get fat!' I say to defend myself.

'You can't get fat. You're already too thin,' Tanmay says.

'Are you on my side or hers? You just met her, Tanmay.'

'You could have had the extra cheese,' Pia says. 'We will go to the gym together, what say?'

'Gym?'

'Yes, there is a beautiful gym here, don't you know? I passed it on my way to our room and I stepped in to check it out. It's very nice, actually. All the equipment looked new too, maybe because I think no one uses it,' she says and takes a huge bite out of the burger, 'You can join me there. Tanmay, why don't you come too?'

'Me? Gym . . . ? I, uh, no thanks . . . I'm not really a gym person,' he says shyly.

'Come on! You can start now. I could be your trainer? I have been doing this for a long time now,' she says with a wide-eyed expression and I know Tanmay has no option but to take up her offer.

'Fine,' he says and turns beet-red again.

But slowly, Tanmay gets slightly better and stops stammering, though I do notice him blushing every now or then. His behaviour is not too shy; he is just very decent and childlike. Sitting with us, he is comfortable talking to us and is neither too cocky nor too guy*ish*. He is like perfect best friend material. I already like him. He is like those gay men whom you instantly like. There is nothing to not like.

'Hey,' Tanmay says and nudges my arm.

'Ouch! What?' I ask.

'Look,' he says and points to a guy sitting on the corner table, working furiously on his black, weathered laptop. 'Isn't it him?'

I look in his direction, and for the first time, I am not staring at his hair, or his eyes. I look at his face and the rest of him. He is sitting alone, his back straight as an arrow, nerd glasses in front of his eyes and a brooding expression on his face. He looks much older now.

'Are you sure it's him?' I ask, though I am pretty sure.

'Yes,' Tanmay says.

'Who is he?' Pia asks and Tanmay fills her in. 'Oh. Then why don't you go say thank you to him?'

'What? No!' I say.

'Why? He saved both of you from God-knows-what. And I think he is hot!' she says and takes another bite of her burger and wipes the dripping mayonnaise with a tissue.

'He is *not* hot. He is just average,' I say. I think of Akshat and his perfection and this guy is nowhere near him. His hair is a crumpled mess, his jeans are worn out and his black t-shirt looks like it's what he has been wearing for many days now.

'But he helped you! You should say thanks, it'll be rude not to. Go talk to him,' she says.

'I think we should,' Tanmay says.

Just as I am about to give a serious thought to going over and thanking him for the morning, I see him flip down the laptop cover. He takes off his spectacles and his smouldering eyes look up. I realize that he looks different when his eyes are not looking directly at you, because when they do, it's all you can look at.

He drops his spectacles and the laptop in what looks like a gym bag, gets up and winks at the guy at the counter at McDonald's who smiles back at him. He then takes out his iPod, plugs the earphones in and heads towards the exit. He is quite tall, I notice. He shakes the hand of the guard standing at the door and moves out. All this while, we three stare at him unblinkingly.

'He really is hot,' Pia says once he is out of the door.

'He is not,' I protest. Even if he is, he is not my kind. He is too dirty and too . . . *rough* for my taste. Not that I have dated much to have a type. But, I like guys who are . . . like Akshat. My mind wanders off to thoughts about him again.

'He *so* is. You're blind! I wish he had saved me, and not you,' Pia says and laughs out loud.

We finish our burgers and I can see Tanmay steal glances at Pia every now and then. I don't blame him, because I find myself doing the same. She is such a nice little girl—cute as a bug and pure as an angel.

Just as we are leaving McDonald's, my phone rings. I don't recognize the number, but I still take the call.

'Hi?' I ask. 'Who's this?'

'Hi, Niharika. I am coming to Nagpur,' Aksaht's voice says from the other end.

Chapter Eleven

The Wild Chants

I look at my phone, it's not ringing. Obviously, it's not. I had destroyed my phone's SIM card the day Akshat had called. I had to replace the Jaipur SIM card with a Nagpur one anyway. Right after the call, I had gotten myself a new number and he has not called ever since. I don't know whether I want him to call or not, but I find myself staring at my phone every now and then.

It's been a week and I remember my entire schedule by heart, but Pia and I still stick a huge timetable on my cupboard to remind us. The classes have been easy and none of the professors are really strict. It's been one week but it feels like we have been doing this for months. Classes, canteen, copied assignments, classes again, an odd movie, late night gossip, sleep and the same thing the next day.

'Don't forget the apron,' Pia reminds me as I pack a lone register in my bag.

She has turned out to be a perfect roommate. I had thought that after having been surrounded by servants cleaning up after her all her life, she would know nothing about doing it herself. But I soon found out she is a neat freak and has no pretensions. I had expected her to be a spoilt brat, but apart from the expensive clothes that she wears and lets me borrow, she is a very nice girl.

'Oh yes,' I say. 'But maybe you should forget yours and let some guy sacrifice his for you!'

We both laugh. Pia has been getting strange phone calls, letters and text messages from scores of guys, all trying to ask her out. I have received my share, too, but the number is nothing in comparison. Tanmay says everyone thinks that he and I are dating. I don't mind that, because I have seen Pia getting disturbed in the middle of the night by the incessant ringing of her phone.

'Oh, c'mon, he was really nice,' Pia says, referring to the guy who offered her his apron the last time. He was thrown out of the class and he had not protested.

'I never said he was not nice. Didn't you look at his poor face when he kept staring at you from outside the class?'

'He did? That's creepy,' she says and locks the room behind us.

'And don't you think it's high time you told me more about Vishal?' I ask, as we start walking towards the workshop, which is a ten-minute walk away.

It had not taken me long to discover that Pia has a boyfriend. On the very first day, when we came back from our dinner, she had started crying on the phone. I had assumed that it was her boyfriend, which she confirmed later. When Tanmay got to know about it, his lips did curve downwards, making him look even more adorable, but then he said he never had a shot anyway. I marvel at how clean at heart he is.

'Okay. I met Vishal when I joined a new school in the eleventh standard. Vishal wasn't a science student; he was in the commerce section. So I didn't notice him in the beginning, but we had our maths tuitions together, so I slowly got to know him, and we fell in love. He is a very nice guy and we both love each other. We've been together for two years now . . . And you know what? Every year on my birthday, he gives me twelve poems written by him—one for every month,' she says fondly. 'They are really, really bad, but it's so sweet of him, no?'

She laughs and I laugh with her.

'That's very romantic! You're a lucky girl,' I say, and ask the next obvious question. 'So, now? Where is he?'

'Bangalore. He's doing BBA from Christ College there.'

'Oh. Long-distance relationship . . .' I trail off.

'I wonder if it will work,' she says exactly what I had been wondering. It is one of those rare moments when I don't see her smiling or laughing. Nagpur is hardly close to Bangalore. And in this case, it's a minimum of three years of separation, till Vishal completes his course. How will it last?

'It's not impossible . . .' I answer vaguely. What else could I say?

'Hmm. We love each other a lot. I hope that's enough,' she said, sounding a little sad.

'Relax. It will work out, then. Love answers a lot of questions.' I try to cheer her up. She smiles. I send a silent prayer to God—*Please make it last. Please prove me wrong.*

'Where is Tanmay?' she asks.

'Oh, there are football auditions today, for the college team. Tanmay has gone there. I don't think he will attend classes today.'

'Tanmay plays football?' Pia looks at me, her eyes wide in shock.

'Yes, he does. I was shocked too. And he has this whole football kit with him—shoes, shin guard and everything. He showed it to me yesterday. He seemed very excited about today.'

'*Haw!* Why didn't he show me?' Pia makes a sad face.

'You were in the gym,' I say. 'And I think he is a little shy in front of you. He likes you.'

'He *DOES NOT!*'

'He does. It's at least a crush,' I say.

'It's not like that,' she says. 'Whatever. So, can we, like, go and see the auditions?'

'I think so,' I say and we decide to drop the classes and go to the football field straight away. It is at the opposite end of the college campus and by the time we reach there, I am out of breath and the excitement to see Tanmay play has totally drained out. We climb over the railing, which Pia does with surprising ease, and walk towards the football field.

'That's why you should go to the gym,' she mocks me when she sees me out of breath. She has been waking up at six in the morning every single day and comes back at eight, sweating and looking sexy, while I sleep my head off.

'I can't get up that early and after college, I am just tired,' I defend myself.

'It's your loss, really. Many good-looking guys come to the gym. You would be surprised that our college has them,' she says and winks at me.

'Good-looking guys, eh? I think it's time we call Vishal!'

'Oh! No! I was saying—for you, not me. And there aren't a lot of them there anyway. It's basically empty. But that guy from McDonald's? The rough, hot guy? He does come there every morning, with his girlfriend.'

'Girlfriend?' I ask. I hadn't realized that he had a girlfriend.

'There is always a girl with him who keeps falling all over him, so I assumed that they were together. I don't know for sure. But why are *you* so interested in that, anyway?' she winks at me and smiles naughtily.

'I am not. I was just asking generally,' I say.

We turn to the football field—which, too, is nicely maintained—and find that we are not the only people there who had no intentions to audition for the team. The stand looks pretty full. There are a lot of people loitering around, bunking classes to be here. Most of them are girls. Tanmay **had** told me that our college's football team was one of the best in the state, but we have not won in the last six years. He seemed quite pumped about the team, because the tournament is due to start in a month's time and he desperately wants to make it to the team.

'There he is!' I shout out and wave at him.

He is surrounded by a bunch of guys and they are just practising. There is still some time for the auditions to start and the seniors are nowhere to be seen.

'He looks different,' Pia notes.

She is right. The spectacles are off and he is in a football uniform—probably his school's jersey—and looks athletic. His comparatively dark and skinny legs stretch out from his shorts and you need to just look at him to know that he really knows his game. His brand-new shoes shine brightly and if anything, look out of place. After seeing him in his geek glasses, and getting used to his nerdy behaviour, this was a change.

A little later, a group of guys—around thirteen of them—walk on to the football field in their dirty blue and white uniforms. Clearly, this is the famed football team of our college. Tanmay had told me stories about the ten-year-long winning streak—the highest in the state—and then the three-year drought. He told me that the seniors really wanted to win this time.

'HEY! LISTEN UP, EVERYONE!' a tall guy with a slightly heavy build shouts and the juniors assemble in front of them. 'WE WILL GIVE YOU ONE CHANCE AND ONE CHANCE ONLY TO MAKE IT TO THE TEAM. PROVE YOURSELF!'

He signals to them to huddle around another guy, a shorter one, who explains the rules. There will be a match between unequal teams. Five juniors against eleven seniors—a five-minute match. The juniors are asked to split themselves into teams of five. They form six teams, but Tanmay and two frail-looking kids are left out. No one picks them.

The shorter guy announces that the rules will remain the same and they will have to go up against the eleven seniors. I think it is highly unfair and I see Tanmay's face droop. I know how badly he wants this. But there is nothing he can do about it.

Soon, the matches begin. The first team takes the field and the five minutes that follow are painful to watch. After the first five goals scored by the seniors, the juniors give up. The seniors make fun of them mercilessly. The juniors crawl on their knees when they return. The score of the next match is 13–0 and of the one after that, 14–0. It continues thus.

The score cards of the matches don't reflect even the tiny bit of humiliation the juniors have faced. The senior football team looks like a bunch of arrogant assholes. Or it's the wounded glory of losing the state title five years in a row that shows on the field. They take out their frustration on the poor kids, and we feel sorry for them.

I dread Tanmay's team's turn. They have been sitting on a bench right opposite us on the stands, and when it's their turn, they get up together and make their way to the centre of the field. We try to catch Tanmay's eye to wish him luck, but he doesn't look up even once. I can feel his fear. I feel sad to see their dried-up faces and dampened enthusiasm.

The ball is kicked to Tanmay, who stands at the centre line, with the ball under his feet, and his teammate standing next to him. There is just one guy on his side, since his only other teammate guards the goalpost. On the other side of the goalposts, there are eleven ravenous wolves waiting to taste blood again.

Tanmay kicks the ball to his teammate, who kicks it back to Tanmay in a split second. And then does it again. We can

see by now that his teammate is a wimp. Tanmay looks ahead
and weaves the ball through the first five seniors, who are
befuddled, but then he is soon surrounded by more seniors.
He tries to keep the ball, but ends up losing it to the seniors.
I can see him struggle to prove himself, but none of what he
does seems to help. There is something wrong with his kick
too. The ball never ends up where he intends to send it. He
panics and swings his kick wildly. The ball bounces high in
the air, drops to the ground and rolls over outside the playing
area. The seniors snigger and the entire crowd—which consists
of girls who have been looking at the athletic, rude seniors
and sighing—knows where this match is going.

'25–0?' Pia asks and bites her nails.

'I hope not,' I murmur.

The ball is still outside the playing area and one of the
seniors is walking towards it. Obviously, no one is in a hurry.

Just outside the playing area, someone kicks the ball into
mid-air, balances it on his head, bounces it a few times on
his forehead and shifts it back under his foot. One hand on
his side, his head cocked the other way, the intruder says,
'Now, now. This is *not* fair play!'

'BUZZ OFF FROM MY FIELD!' the captain shouts and
walks angrily towards the guy who just walked in.

'Here is he again,' Pia points out, as if I have not already
realized that it's the dark-eyed guy—the guy from the mess,
the canteen, McDonald's and from Pia's early morning gym.
The guy with a girlfriend.

'Oh, really, Mandar? So that you can gratify your sadist
selves by defeating these juniors? Look at them—they are just
kids!' he says with unabashed authority. Somehow, I notice
that apart from the hostile stance of the team's captain, the
rest of the team is smiling and even seems pleased by the
new entrant's presence.

'IT'S NONE OF YOUR FREAKING BUSINESS!' the

captain—whom the dark-eyed guy refers to as Mandar—shouts again.

'Oh, I get it. Beating these kids will inflate your ego, won't it? That too, outnumbered three against eleven? But let me tell you what—*it still won't give you a bigger dick!*' he shouts and the crowd greets this with a wild roar of laughter. The captain, Mandar, looks seriously offended.

'Fine, you asshole. You can join them and see us beat the shit out of you.'

'We'll see,' the dark-eyed guy says and walks up to the team of three already beaten down juniors. I see him wink at them as he walks close. He is the only guy in the field in a plain black tee and jeans, and sticks out like a sore thumb.

Tanmay's eyes light up when he sees him. The guy hugs him and the other two juniors. I see Tanmay say something to him, before making his way towards us. When he gets to us, he swiftly removes his shoes and starts to pull off one of his socks.

'What are you doing?' I ask, baffled.

'I can't play with these shoes on,' he murmurs, not making eye contact.

'What do you mean? Are you changing shoes?' Pia asks. We cannot see a spare pair of shoes anywhere in sight.

Tanmay says something very softly, that we both do not understand. 'No . . . without shoes . . .'

'Tanmay, what is going on?' I ask, now concerned.

He folds both his socks and stuffs them into his shoes, before pushing them under my seat. He looks up at me, and meets my eye, carefully avoiding Pia's eye, before saying softly, 'I have played football barefooted all my life. No shoes used to last more than a few weeks and we did not have enough money to get a new pair every month. So I have always played without my shoes on. Now, it seems like I cannot aim with these on.' He points to the brand-new pair of shoes he had bought out of his savings, now lying useless under my bench.

I nod silently and whisper, 'Good luck.'

'Go get them,' Pia says, and I see Tanmay blush slightly before turning around and running to the field.

Pia and I cross our fingers. The match starts, and the seniors miss a goal. They are already a little disturbed by the new guy's presence and one of them shoots the ball outside nervously, seeing the guy in front of him.

The dark-eyed guy puts his hand on Tanmay's shoulder and tells him something animatedly. They run to opposite directions after he pats Tanmay's shoulder. The next few minutes seem fast forwarded as the two of them criss-cross between the seniors, leaving some of them looking for the ball in a smoke of dust, and almost score a goal. They miss it, and the crowd lets out a sigh. The new guy still goes running to Tanmay and celebrates as if they scored. He looks at the crowd and prods us to make a noise. He clearly has everyone's attention now.

Another attempt by the seniors is foiled and we can see the tension rise. The juniors make another decent attempt at the senior's goalpost. The ball rebounds from the pole. The crowd is now fully behind the four-man team led by this ridiculously arrogant dark-eyed guy on the field.

Third minute into the game, every senior is shouting abuses, the dark-eyed guy is running with the ball, dodging seniors on his right and left, when the captain, Mandar, comes from behind, grabs him by his T-shirt and pulls him down to the ground. The guy falls and a dust ball engulfs them both.

'FUCK YOU!' Mandar shouts at him as he is lying on the ground. The crowd boos.

The dark-eyed guy gets up, clearly hurt, bleeding from his mouth, his T-shirt torn and hanging from his waist. He tears the rest of the T-shirt, wipes the blood off his mouth and throws the t-shirt on the ground. As the dust clears and he runs to his part of the field, I can see his ripped upper body. There are hushed whispers amongst all the girls sitting outside, all of whom notice the thick veins on his arms, the clearly cut lines of his chest and the perfectly rectangular abs.

The smile is no longer there in his face. The charm in his eyes is replaced with anger and his eyebrows are creased. He takes a long run-up to take his kick for the foul. He hits the ball with brute force, which makes it go flying across every senior on the field. The ball misses the post by an inch. No one could move while it happens and there is a sigh again. The mood changes to a very sombre one, almost like the guy in the field decided it to be.

Last minute into play, Tanmay and the guy pass the ball to each other for a very long time, much to the frustration of the opposing team. Slowly and steadily, they penetrate the offensive and mid-field cordon of the senior team. Once in, the guy dashes in with the ball, with knife-like precision and amazing speed. Every player in the seniors' team is chasing after the dark-eyed guy, without paying any attention to the other three players of the juniors' team. Twenty metres from the goal, he hits the ball hard and gestures something to Tanmay, who is magically in a spot with no seniors around. Tanmay jumps and hits the ball in mid-air, sending it crashing to the right-end corner of the goalpost.

The crowd explodes in excitement! Tanmay is on his knees. The guy just pumps his fist and his face accommodates a wry smile. The three guys come running to him and they hug him and pat his back repeatedly.

Seconds later, the crowd bursts out in rhythmic loud chants. *'KARTHIK! KARTHIK! KARTHIK! KARTHIK!'*

The dark-eyed guy smiles, picks up his torn t-shirt from the ground, stuffs it into his pocket and walks off the field in a cloud of dust.

Chapter Twelve

A Cup of Tea

It's been a couple of weeks since that match, since the loud chants of *Karthik*, and since the time Tanmay was inducted into the football team of our college. He is a lot busier these days, and he has started to get a lot of attention from the girls of our class. Just last night, Pia said that she thinks Tanmay looks cool in his football uniform. To me, though, he still looks like an overgrown kid in round-rimmed spectacles.

Akshat has not called after that day. I think he was just bluffing to see how I reacted. But strangely enough, I think more about Karthik these days than Akshat. It's strange, because I don't really like that guy, but I don't exactly hate him either. But I can't fight the feeling that there is . . . *something* about him. I think that, like every other girl in the college, I too have developed a minor crush on him. Ever since that match day, I wake up whenever Pia is getting ready for the gym and feel like joining her. But I am afraid I would make my reason for going there too obvious, and I am in no mood to answer Pia's questions. So I have waited to tell her that I want to go the gym too.

What's worse is that I haven't seen him in the college ever since that day. I had asked Tanmay but he didn't have any idea either.

I check the watch. It's 5:45 a.m. and in another ten

minutes, Pia's alarm will ring. I struggle to keep my eyes open and not fall asleep. Exactly ten minutes later, her alarm chimes. She immediately sits up straight as a ramrod and I do the same.

'You're up so early? What happened?' she asks as she stretches both her arms in the air. She is in an old, long T-shirt—of her boyfriend—and I can see her gym-toned legs.

'I just couldn't sleep well,' I lie.

'So you want to come today?'

'Naah, I don't. I'll maybe just . . . watch a movie, or . . . something. And I have never been to a gym in my life,' I say.

'Oh c'mon! I will tell you what to do,' she says and starts to tug at my hands to pull me up off my bed.

'Alright, alright, I'm coming,' I make a show of disinterest and yawn dramatically.

'Now get up,' Pia kisses me on my cheek and looks for her toothbrush.

I act highly uninterested, but when she looks the other way, I clean myself up, brush my teeth, comb my hair and put on a little bit of lip gloss, just in case. When we are ready to go, Pia looks at me strangely and says, 'You look . . . fresh.'

I smile innocently and hope she doesn't notice the lip gloss.

The gym is in the sports complex, another ten-minute walk away from our hostel. As soon as we leave the hostel, she asks me to jog and I go 'what!' After much prodding, I do so and realize that it's not that bad. The weather is nice and the wide roads of our campus are empty.

'Okay, so I will take two more rounds and join you in the gym in five?' Pia asks when we get to the gym.

'Huh?' I say, with both my hands on my knees, panting.

'Unless you want to run with me too?' she smirks, as she knows my answer.

She doesn't wait for my answer and starts running, her sexy little butt wiggling away from me. I want to ask her if *he* would be in the gym right now, but she has already gone quite a distance from me. I start to get a little nervous as I climb up the stairs to the gym. I take a deep breath to calm myself, write my name down on the register and push open the door.

I run my eyes quickly over the gym floor and I spot no one. For a moment, I forget about him and admire the gym. It's huge and has millions of strange contraptions and equipment. Sadly enough, it seems like not many people use them. I walk around when I hear murmurs from the other end. Could it be him? My heart almost stops.

I walk gingerly, taking care not to be heard or seen, towards the voice. It's a girl's voice. I go closer and cross some more treadmills, cross-trainers, benches and weight racks to see two people standing very close to each other.

What I see stuns me. I know I should not be here. I know I should not be seeing this. My mind orders my feet to turn around and leave. But it's like I'm glued to the ground beneath me. I can't move my feet, or any other part of my body, for that matter. My eyes are transfixed to what there is in front of me. Luckily, I am behind a huge contraption with big weights hanging from it, so I am completely hidden.

Not that there is much visible, but I can still figure out that there is a guy with his back pressed against the wall and he is breathing hard, with his head tilted back. I recognize him. How can I not? The tall frame, the curly hair, the strong jaw and the voice that has anger in it. The unmistakeable voice—satin with rough edges and a careless rudeness to it. I've heard it before . . . so many times now.

Karthik.

There is a girl pressed against him. All I can see of her is her long dark hair that is totally covering her face and

I recognize her too. I have seen her in college. One of her hands holds him against the wall, with her mouth on his neck. The other hand is inside his T-shirt and creeping down slowly.

'You like that?'

'No. Stop,' he says and tries to jerk her away.

'Really? I don't think you mean that,' she says in a fake husky voice.

'No, I do. I don't want this. I told you this has to end,' he says, frees his hand and pushes her away.

'You don't know what you're talking about. You still want this. Just like you still want me, Karthik.'

'No!' he shouts but she doesn't listen. He grasps both her hands and pushes her away.

'Let me go,' she says, authoritatively.

'Stop. I told you I don't want this any more. This is not going to help!' he shouts.

'Stop fooling yourself. You say you don't want me? That's not how this looks.' She smiles and presses herself against Karthik.

'Niyati. Go away—'

My phone rings. I un-freeze. It rings louder. I see them turn to look at me, but I don't think they can see anything. Where I am standing is way too dark or so I hope. I turn around and run, sweat trickling down profusely from my forehead. I keep running haphazardly in all directions, till I find a way out of the building. I leave the building behind and find myself lost after five minutes of running. Instead of going close to the hostel, I am even further away. I look back and find no one following me.

For some reason, I feel sick to the stomach and feel a bad taste in my mouth. I don't know why, but I found it gross. And I felt a little . . . cheated. I try to find my way to the hostel, my breathing still ragged and strained, my mind still replaying images of what I just saw.

I have barely walked a few meters, when a voice calls out from behind, 'HEY!'

I look behind me to see my worst nightmare staring at me. *Karthik.* He starts running towards me and within a few seconds, is standing right in front of me. He towers above me, all six feet of his muscular frame. I can barely speak, and I don't know what to say anyway.

'I am sorry you had to see that,' he looks at me and says.

'It's okay,' I say as I collect myself. In my thoughts, I had imagined what it would be like to talk to him, and this beats everything. This is the first time he is looking right at me, and talking *only* to me, with nobody else around. The impact of it is overwhelming. I hate myself for liking it.

'I have to go,' I say and turn away from him.

'Hey, listen—you can't just go like that,' he says and starts walking next to me.

'Why not? You get back to your gym and do . . . whatever it is that you do there,' I say and I am surprised that I sound pissed.

'I work out. What you saw wasn't something that happens daily.'

'I don't care. Go work out and impress girls. Why should I care? By the way, thank you for that day in the canteen. And for helping Tanmay out in that football match.'

'You're welcome,' he says, still walking beside me.

We walk silently and it has started to bother me. In a good way, and in a bad way.

'You can go,' I say.

'Do you really want me to?' he asks.

'Why would I not?'

'I thought you wanted to say something more to me. On that day in McDonalds, on the football field? Or maybe the day you were trying to see me in the mess? In the reflection of your plate, Niharika?'

'What? What are you talking about?' I ask, almost shocked as I stop in my tracks. My mind tingles with the knowledge that he knows my name.

'What? You were, weren't you?'

'But how do you know my name?' *He knows my name!*

'Tanmay told me, that's how,' he says matter-of-factly. His lips curve into a small smile and I look directly at him. Like every time, he is still unshaved and his hair is all over the place. His eyes look directly at me and I try to look away from his piercing gaze. I find it impossible to do so; his eyes demand attention.

'Fine,' I say and start walking away from him.

'So, now that we know each other's name, we will not talk to each other?' he says, and throws up his hands in the air.

I don't answer and keep walking away from him. After a few steps, I can't feel him following me and I wonder if he's going back. A part of me wants him around so bad, I want to go back and chase him. The other part hates him and what I just saw. When I can't handle the curiosity any more, I turn around. He is standing there, his arms crossed on his muscular chest, his head tilted cockily to one side and a lopsided half-grin on his face. I can't help but smile grudgingly, before turning away from him. He runs up to me and it surprises me how quickly he reaches my side.

'Why did you talk to Tanmay about me?' I ask, as he walks with me at a safe distance.

'It was hard not to.'

'Why was it hard not to?'

'That's something you're not supposed to ask,' he says and there is a silence. I realize that there is a slight nip in the air though it's not too cold.

'Tea?' he asks, and points in the direction that leads outside the college.

I am taken aback. I know I should say *no*, because I hate him so much, but I still find myself whispering a *yes*. I have no idea why. Everything about Karthik and my reaction to him is way above my level of understanding. Since when have I started drinking tea?

He points to his bike that is parked just at the college gate. It's something I have never seen on the road before. It's a huge cruiser bike, but not like the ones I have seen on television. The exhaust pipe has rusted, the body looks like it has been patched up, the seat has an army leather covering and it doesn't look in a working condition. It looks at least twice as old as Karthik himself.

'This?' I ask, a little scared. He just smiles at me and puts on his helmet.

I see him get on the bike and a shiver of fear runs up my spine. But I somehow know that he would not let anything hurt me. I get on the bike and I have no option but to hold him around his waist. He clutches my hands and makes me hold him tighter. He kicks the bike and it makes an ear-splitting thundering noise before moving with a jerk. Throughout the journey, I am glad that I held him tight, because the roads are empty and he clearly doesn't believe in driving slow.

A few minutes later, he parks the bike on an open field with a few other bikes and cars around his. We walk, not exchanging a word, to the little chai shop about five kilometres away from the main gate of the college. Pia calls and I explain—in as few words as possible—what happened and where I am. She freaks out and shouts excitedly on the phone, leaving me with no other option but to disconnect the call.

Karthik calls for two masala teas and the little boy smiles at him. It seems like they know each other. Karthik asks the kid about his school and studies, to which he answers gleefully, and gets us the teas. As he sips on it and reads the newspaper that lies in front of him, I wonder if he remembers that I am sitting right in front of him. I take the time to notice him closely, though. The stubble, the strong jaw, the veins in his hands and the long ruffled hair—all still there, all amazingly appealing.

'So, what made you come to the gym today?' he asks, as if he knows why I really went there.

'Pia. She has wanted me to join her in the gym ever since she came. I didn't want to come . . . but she forced me to,' I say. He smiles knowingly and I try to change the topic. 'You know that your bike makes an awful lot of noise, don't you?'

'I thought girls liked bikes that make a lot of noise.'

'I hate it.'

'I could see you crinkle your nose when you got on the back seat,' he says, and adds, 'I thought it was adorable.'

'So . . . the noise is intentional?' I ask, wondering if I am blushing.

'Not really. This bike is my father's and is a 1954 Harley classic. It rotted in our garage for thirty years before I started to restore it. The silencer is the tricky part, because there are no drawings publicly available and the real one is expensive. With import duty, it should be around a lakh and a half,' he says.

He talks passionately about everything he has changed in the bike and how. He tells me about the special permission he has from the dean of the college to work in the college workshop and use the induction furnaces. For a person not particularly interested in bikes and cars, I am strangely intrigued. I think it has more to do with images of Karthik inside my head, forging red-hot molten metal into bike parts, in his dirty t-shirt and eye-protection gear on his head. Interestingly, I was never interested whenever Akshat started to talk about his cars.

'So you're a mechanical engineer? Which year?' I ask.

'I'm flattered, but I am not an undergraduate student any more. I am doing a PhD in cloud computing,' he says. 'I am twenty-four.'

I almost burn my tongue with the hot tea. I always thought he looked older, but not six years older than me. Six years is a lot.

'Oh,' I say.

'Too old?'

'No, no. Just that I am eighteen. But you don't look that old.'

'Thank you again,' he says and sips the last of his tea.

'But Computers and Mechanical? What's the connection?'

'I have been into a lot of things. I flipped a coin and decided between mechanical and computers. Actually, I always wanted to teach. I know you find yourself asking—*teach?* Yeah, but there are so many things that I want to do and the only way I am going to find time to do all of it is by becoming a college professor. Plenty of time and freedom to do any bloody thing I want,' he says with a smirk.

'What do your parents say about this?'

'They don't care and I try not to care about what they think either. I've got to do what I got to do, right?'

'And that includes beating kids at football matches?' I ask.

'Oh! So now that you know my age, they become kids? I saw you cheering for me that day. Just because they are younger doesn't mean they can't be awesome footballers. Especially Mandar, their elephant-like captain, is a good player.'

'Why was he so angry at you?'

'The girl you saw in the gym? That's Niyati, Mandar's ex-girlfriend. They broke up a couple of years back, and he thinks that was because she likes me. So, that's that. And that's why I was thrown out of the team,' Karthik says.

'That's unfair.'

'I really don't mind. With a captain like that, they will never win.'

'Don't you want them to?'

'Never gave it a thought,' he says rudely. It's as if nothing bothers him. What he does in life, what others think about him or do to him, he cares about none of that. To think he asked Tanmay my name seems a little odd now. To know that he cares about my existence seems out of place.

He talks a little more about the college and soon we realize that we should get back to college. Though he is in no hurry, he says, since he is done with his thesis and he is just taking his time to submit it.

We get back on the bike again and this time the explosive sound is more bearable. He drives me back to the college campus. As I hold him, I feel a lot closer to him. It feels like a barrier between us is now broken, and I know him. I don't know why my heart beats faster and the world narrows down to him. I am still confused about my feelings for him. I am still unsure whether I like him or not. Maybe I do, and I am just fighting that feeling God knows why. Maybe.

Way too soon, we reach the college. He stops the bike just outside my hostel, and I get down carefully, holding his shoulder for support.

'It was great seeing you today,' he says. 'You look even better from up close.'

'Thank you,' I smile and wave him a goodbye.

When I turn back, I see a familiar face standing with a suitcase and a bag slung across his shoulder.

'Hi!' he shouts out to me.

As I stand there frozen, I hear the bike's engine explode again and Karthik drives off.

Chapter Thirteen

The Stalker

It takes me a little time to recover from the shock of seeing Akshat standing right in front of me. His crisp white shirt, black trousers, the perfect shoes and his sheer *beauty* shocks me. And then, reality sets in and I remember—I am supposed to be angry.

As I try to stalk past him, he blocks me and says, 'Hey! At least talk to me.'

'What do you want?'

'I want my time with you. I came all the way just to see you. You can't just walk away from me like that,' he says.

'I can and I will. What do you want?' I ask.

'Oh, please. Just—' his tone is getting sharper, which I don't like. I cut him off.

'I am not interested in seeing you ever again, Akshat Verma. And I've already made it very clear to you. So stop all this that you're doing.'

'Please listen to me—'

'Speak!' I shout, suddenly losing patience. With every second that I talk to him, I feel like I'm betraying Simran. I want to get this over and done with as quickly as possible.

'Okay. If this is the way you want to do this. I know I should've told you that I once dated Simran, but there's more to the story than you think. Why do you think we broke up?'

'I don't know. I already told you—I didn't ask her. I didn't feel the need to.'

'Maybe you should have,' he says.

'I don't know whether how you guys broke up has to do with anything,' I say irritably.

'It has *everything* to do with *everything*. Niharika, I don't know how you could just leave me like that . . . without even listening to my side of the story. And you don't even know her side! I really liked you. From the first second I saw you, you were all I thought about . . . but you turned out to be so . . . so irrational. You didn't even give me a chance to explain. Okay. Whatever. If this is what you want, I'll stop bothering you.'

I've never heard him use that tone before. Not that I know him well, but he has always come across as such a gentleman. I'm amazed to see that he shouts too. As I stand here, running the scene through my head, I feel strangely disturbed. It's not like I haven't thought about him in the days gone by, but I certainly do not appreciate him using that tone with me.

'I am leaving,' I say and take long strides towards my hostel gate.

'I WILL WAIT RIGHT HERE TILL YOU COME OUT!' he shouts after me.

I ignore what he says and charge back to my room. A part of me knows that he will actually go through with that. He is going to wait. There is just an hour to class and I find it's been two hours since I first met Karthik.

Maybe I should just listen to what Akshat has to say, because he so clearly wants to say it. And what do I have to lose, anyway? Just a few minutes of my time? At least this way, we can end things on a better note. If not anything else, I will know why Simran hates him so much. I still remember the tone she used when she asked me to stop

seeing him. So, I'll never see him again. Just this once. He
gets his meeting, I get rid of him forever. I will never see
his gorgeous face again.

Just as I am thinking about what to do with Akshat, Pia
walks into our room, wrapped in a short pink towel, water
dripping from the tips of her hair. I look at her and wonder
how her boyfriend must feel about dating someone so perfect.
He is a lucky guy.

'Tell me EVERYTHING!' she shrieks as soon as she notices
me in the room.

'There is nothing to tell,' I say, my mind still partially
on Akshat.

'Oh yeah? Guess what—we are not going anywhere till
you tell me everything that happened with Karthik! You do
not have an option.'

I look at Pia, who is standing in front of me in her
pink towel, with her hands stubbornly on her hips and eyes
looking piercingly into mine, and I realize that there is no
way I can get out of it. Giving up, I narrate every bit of it
to a sometimes shocked, sometimes ecstatic Pia.

'So he actually drives that thing?' she asks excitedly, drying
her hair with a towel.

'Yes,' I say. 'Oh crap! We are late for classes again.' I rush
to change into decent clothes.

As I lock the door behind me, I wonder if Akshat is still
out there. It's been an hour since I saw him. Nervously,
I step down the stairs, and outside the main gate of the hostel
with Pia by my side. He is still there, sitting on his suitcase,
tapping on his phone. On seeing me walk out of the hostel,
he gets up and waves at me.

'Who is he?' Pia asks and adds, 'He is so pretty!'

'That's Akshat. I told you about him, remember?' I say
and walk towards him. 'You go to the class. I will join
you later.'

'It's raining men on you!' she says nudging me, and leaves for class.

'I need you to go,' I tell Akshat, who looks at me and smiles.

'Can't we just talk before I do?' he says.

'Five minutes. I am late for class.'

He nods and we walk towards my class, though at a way slower pace. He looks at me and tells me that I look good. Somehow, I choose to believe him. And I feel guilty when I feel all the anger against him melt away. I feel like I am betraying Simran. I think I was never angry at him, just uncomfortable and feeling really weird.

'How have you been?' he asks.

'Fine. How are you? Things have been good?'

'Well, frankly—no. Things haven't being going well since you left. Or rather *because* you left . . . Why, Niharika? What we had was so beautiful . . . Why did you end it like this? I have been thinking about that day every day.'

'Akshat . . .' I begin, not knowing exactly what it is that I am going to say.

'Did it mean so little to you—what we had? Did *I* mean so little to you?' he asks with such hurt in his eyes that I cringe. Until now, I hadn't realized it meant so much to him. After all, we had known each other for only a very short time. And we had met just twice, though they were two of the best days I have ever spent. After meeting him, I remember having felt a strange happiness in my heart.

'I didn't have any other option. You lied to me,' I say.

'I didn't lie . . .'

'You hid the truth knowingly. It means the same thing.'

'I didn't know what to say,' he says.

'The truth. What else?'

'It's not as easy as you think. There is a lot more to it than meets the eye. Whatever happened was way back and things have changed since then. I have changed.'

'Tell me,' I say, bracing myself to face what's coming next. This has been too much of a mystery. I just have to know now—*why did they break up?*

'Okay. I met Simran when I joined her school in tenth class. I liked her instantly. And I told her so. But she didn't pay any attention to it. Months passed and she finally started to notice me. This time, when I asked her out, she said yes. We went out for a couple of months. Did she tell you about it then? You were in the same school as us,' he asks.

'No. I didn't know she was dating in tenth class. We never used to talk about all that, anyway.'

'Hmm. Not really a surprise for me. She wanted to keep it a secret and said it won't reflect well on us, in case the school's staff members get to know. I agreed. How could I not? She used to rule my world back then,' he says. His sensitivity surprises me. A far cry from the carelessness with which Karthik speaks. Careless, but charming . . . I shake myself back to *now*, away from thoughts of Karthik.

'But then why did you break up?' I ask.

'She left me. I agree that it was my fault . . . I was stupid. I lied to her a couple of times and went out with a family friend's daughter. I apologized for days but she didn't listen. Nothing happened between me and the other girl. I didn't even like her. It was a stupid mistake and I regretted it. Simran believed me, but after seeing me cry and cringe, she said she wanted her revenge and she never came back.'

That does it. I am angry at him now—not because he hid it from me—but because he hurt Simran and that's something I can't take.

'But that was a long time ago...' he says as his eyes fill with tears, 'I am no longer that person. I learnt my lesson back then. I meant no harm to your sister. I really loved her and I cared about her a lot.'

'Whatever happened has happened, Akshat. I am sorry,' I say and get up to leave. I am glad I took the decision that I took. He is not worth my time; he cheated or whatever on my sister and he doesn't deserve her.

'Wait. This is not why I told you this,' he lets out, 'I called you to meet me because . . . Niharika, I like you. I *really* like you. When I first saw you, I had no idea you were Simran's sister. I shared a table with you by pure chance, but then when I saw you properly . . . I just couldn't take my eyes off you. You're so . . . But it didn't take me long to realize you were related to her. You look like her.'

'What are you trying to say, Akshat?'

'I like you. And I want to be with you. I know I should have told you about me and Simran before, but I couldn't. That doesn't mean I didn't try. I was just afraid of the way you would react. And see? That is exactly what happened. You left me. Without even giving me a chance to explain,' he says.

I stay silent for a while and ask, 'What do you want?'

'You,' he replies simply.

'This can't happen,' I get up to leave. 'I won't betray my sister like that.'

'Betray?' he stops and takes a deep breath. 'Are you listening to what you're saying? I told you it was a long time ago. I have changed.'

'Akshat, please—'

'Listen to me, Niharika—'

'No!' I shout and a few heads turn to look at us. '*You* listen to *me*. I cannot do this. So, please. Just leave me alone,' I say and storm off.

As I leave, he doesn't say anything. I don't turn back to look at him. Though I wonder if he is still looking at me.

Chapter Fourteen

Football Stud

'Do you like her?' I ask Tanmay. 'That girl in the pink tee?'

'Niharika, for the last time—I'm not interested in dating. That's not why I came here,' Tanmay says.

'Then? Why did you come here? To attend classes? Because I don't see you doing *that* very often,' I snicker.

'Whatever. I am not interested in girls, so please stop selecting them for me. Plus, I am really busy with the football practice and the lab work and assignments,' he says and adjusts his spectacles.

'I just . . . I still think that girl is quite sweet.'

'I don't think so,' he says and gets back to completing his assignment. I don't understand his rush. We still have a week till the last date of submission. Pia is not around and I assume she is on one of her long, long-distance calls with her boyfriend, Vishal. So I concentrate on staring unblinkingly at Tanmay instead. I am not in a mood to complete the assignment just yet, and so, I don't want to let him do it either.

'*What?*' he asks, irritation etched across his face.

'I think your specs are cool. They make you look sexy,' I tease him.

He's caught off-guard. For a moment, he stares at me. I wink at him. We laugh. It's true that over the last few days—ever since he made it to the football team—he has been getting substantial attention from the fairer sex. Football is like an obsession in this college and at first, I was shocked to see it. The seniors in the football team—a bunch of good-looking, arrogant seniors—are very desirable in our college.

Now they have another boy in their team. But Tanmay is not just one of them. In fact, he is nothing like them. He is way different. In a team full of huge, bulky, cocky players, who spend half their time on the football field and the rest getting high on weed and alcohol, Tanmay definitely stands out. He is not one of those rich, spoiled brats, who have lots of their dad's money to spend. Even though he is wearing the same uniform and shoes as the rest of them, Tanmay stands out. He, instead of using his weight and attitude on the field, concentrates on adroitness and speed. A typical small-town boy that he is, he does not believe in playing dirty. He is just plain talented; he does not need cheap tricks to win.

After getting into the team, he was instructed that playing without shoes on is not allowed as per the sport's rules. So Tanmay has started practising with shoes on, and he is getting better by the second. He just needs to get used to them, and the day isn't far when he would be a better player than every other guy on the team. And, surprisingly, the rest of the seniors on the team do not hold a grudge against Tanmay. In fact—they all love him! He makes the team stronger, and that is what matters the most. I feel proud of him.

'So, football stud,' I say as he scribbles on his assignment sheet in his beautiful, girlish handwriting.

'Let me work,' he says.

'What's your problem? Why are you so irritated today?'

'I am not irritated, I am just a little concerned about Pia.'

'Concerned about Pia? Why? What happened to her?' I ask. I didn't know that there was anything wrong with Pia.

'We have to submit this assignment by today evening and she has not even started it. I have called her thrice and her phone is on waiting. I don't know when she will do it.'

'Excuse me? I am sitting right here and I haven't started it either. You're not pissed off at me?'

'You're responsible, she is not,' Tanmay says.

'You have hardly known us for two weeks! How can you say who's responsible and who's not? You're just making stupid excuses. You just care about her, not me.'

'But—'

'I am just kidding, Tanmay. I was just checking. You're so much in love with her. Aww! That's so sweet,' I say and hug the life out of him. I imagine the two of them together, and the picture in my head looks like one from those cheesy greeting cards.

'I am *not* in love with her. And she has a boyfriend anyway,' he says and keeps scribbling with unnecessary intensity.

'But you like her. And you like her *a lot*. Don't you think I have not noticed your eyes behind your ridiculous glasses? The way you look at her! It's so obvious.'

'You think my glasses are ridiculous? But you just said that they are sexy! Should I get lenses? Did *she* say anything about it?'

'Will you stop freaking out? No, she didn't. And I love your glasses. They are the cutest thing about you,' I laugh.

'Oh. Okay,' he says, looking clearly relieved.

I don't know what to say to him, so I just reassure him, 'If she were single, I think you would make a great couple.'

He smiles a little sadly and I feel bad for him. I change the topic. 'So—about this assignment—did you say we are supposed to hand it in *today*? I thought we had another week!'

'It's today. I have been telling you since the morning, but you seem to be in some other world,' he shakes his head and takes out the first few pages of his assignment and passes them to me to copy from. Life has been easy for the first two weeks here. The college professors are taking it easy on us. We try not to make a lot of noise in class and stay out of trouble. There are piles of assignments and laboratory manuals to be filled up, but Tanmay socializes with anyone and everyone, so he has a few studious friends, too, who help us out. As an added advantage, he himself is very studious.

'Niharika, who's the fair guy who keeps following you around?' he asks.

'Oh. Don't look his way. He is Akshat. I told you about him, didn't I?' I ask and look at him from the corner of my eye. For the last so many days, he has been following me around college. He did disappear for a few days, but then came back for good. As he had said earlier, he does know a lot of people from this college, most of them M. Tech students. They look nothing like him; they are way bigger in size and scary looking. I think I even saw him chatting with Chetan Mehta—the college *fucking* president who had harassed me.

I have been avoiding Akshat, though. He has not been intrusive; he doesn't call or sit right next to me, but he has always been around. I can feel him looking at me, and at times I start to look at him too. During the three days when he had disappeared, I had even missed him slightly.

'Oh, the guy from Jaipur?' Tanmay asks.

'Yes,' I say.

'He is creepy! Why don't you date Karthik instead? He is so cool! He helps me out with football practice, you know? Since the rest of the players don't practise that much and leave early. He said he will let me drive his bike one of these days,' he says.

I have not talked to Karthik since that day we went out for tea. I have not gone to the gym either. I don't know why, because I had had a really good time that day. I think if

Akshat hadn't been haunting me all these days, I would have. He has crossed my path a few times in the last few days and has smiled at me. I have smiled back. I don't know, but the moment I see him, I feel guilty. Like I am doing something wrong with Akshat. I don't know whether I like Karthik or not, but he is so intriguing, like there is an endless ocean of secrets behind those hypnotic eyes.

Plus, it's very hard to talk to him. We had not exchanged numbers and he is constantly surrounded by juniors or professors. On a few mornings, I have wanted to go the gym but I don't want to look desperate. Even though I actually am desperate to sit behind him on his noisy bike and go on a never-ending drive.

'I don't even know if he likes me,' I say.

'I am sure he does. He keeps asking me about you all the time,' Tanmay says.

'Are you serious? He does? What does he ask?'

'Everything about you. Like what you like, what you don't, whether you have a boyfriend or not?'

'Oh my God. I don't believe this! What did you tell him?' I ask. I try hard to hide my excitement but I fail quite miserably.

'I was kidding, I just wanted to check . . .' he says and starts laughing loudly, during which his spectacles slip down right to the tip of his nose.

'You're an idiot.'

'But you like him! That's cool. By the way, he does ask about you. Not in great detail, but he does,' he says and starts writing again. 'We spend a lot of time together for the football coaching he gives me. I wish he could be on the team. We would be so unbeatable. But our stubborn captain!' his face flushes red in anger.

'Aren't you taking it a little too seriously? I know it's

important to you and I know that it's fun to watch, but it's just a game,' I say, glad for the change of topic.

'We haven't won a match for the last five years. I desperately want our college to win. You know I lead the team to my school's first district victory? It was the best day of my life,' he says with nostalgia and passion in his voice.

'I have seen you play and I still think it's so odd. You really don't look the football kinds. You're too polite for this game.'

'Every player is a different player,' he smiles at me.

'Hey! What are you guys doing?' Pia asks, coming back from her long phone call. She looks a little disturbed but I don't ask her why. Long-distance relationships have their own pitfalls. Only yesterday, after getting off from a call to Vishal, she almost cried because she was missing him and Delhi so much. Thank God I had my Mom's home-baked chocolate cake to distract her.

'Pia, I have been calling you for so long. You need to complete this assignment, quick,' Tanmay says. 'We need to submit it by four in the evening.'

'Which page are you on?' she asks.

'Sixteen.'

'Oh shit!'

'Never mind; Niharika has just started. You can copy it with her,' Tanmay says and hands over the assignment to Pia whose hands are full—a plate of fries in one hand and a Coke in another.

Pia gives me a questioning look and I acknowledge it. She knows that Tanmay has a huge crush on her. But there is nothing we can do about it. We just sit silently and keep scribbling, not even bothering to understand what we are copying down.

By the time it's four, only Tanmay has finished. He gets his assignment photocopied and hands it over to us to copy it down.

'I will go and submit mine. Call me when you guys finish it. I will talk to the teacher and get you a time extension,' he says, opening his bag and stuffing his assignment in. He takes out his football shoes and ties the laces.

Pia leans over and whispers in my ear, 'That's one thing I really love about him.'

We both laugh and Tanmay looks at us strangely. 'I've got to go. Karthik is waiting. The match is in five days and the last time we played against NITE, Nagpur, he scored three goals,' he says and leaves. I suppress an urge to go with him and see Karthik play, as images from that day cloud my head. The strong arms, the muscled chest and the protruding abs muscles—very distracting.

'He likes you so much, I feel bad for him. It is *not* funny.' I look at Pia.

'I know, and he is such a nice guy. I wish I could just turn him into a teddy bear and keep him. We don't see guys like that any more, do we? Everyone tries to be such a stud,' Pia says and smiles.

'Do you like him?'

'How can anyone *not* like Tanmay? I don't know how he would be as a boyfriend, but we are so lucky to have him around, aren't we?'

'We sure are,' I say, still unsure about Pia's feelings for Tanmay.

'Plus, I like the football part of him!'

'Pia, tell me! Do you like him? Like, *really* like him? I am getting all kinds of signals here,' I say.

'No, I don't like him in *that* way. He is good as a friend,' she says and smiles at me. 'But you tell me? What's going on with Akshat? Seen him today?'

'Second table to our left. But don't look!'

'Why don't you talk to him? He is so pretty. Have you looked at his lips? So pink! I wish my lips were like that,' she says. I thought her mood was off, and here she just can't shut up. And I don't even know if it is a compliment or an insult to Akshat. Though, Pia isn't someone who is capable of insulting people. She is way too sweet for that.

'You think I should talk to Akshat?' I ask.

'Yes, that way at least it would end. At least he will go away from here,' she says and I nod.

'Fine, I will meet him.'

We get back to our assignments and it's six by the time we finish copying everything. We call up Tanmay, who is still busy with his football practice, but says he talked to the teacher concerned and we can slip in our assignments inside her room.

He is such a sweetheart.

Chapter Fifteen

The Drunk Confession

I have not seen Akshat in the last six days. The very day I had decided to talk to him, he had vanished. I have thought about calling him, but have refrained till now. If he doesn't come back, I think it makes sense not to talk to him.

We have been waiting for an hour for the match to start, but there are no signs of the players of NITE, Nagpur. Tanmay had told us that NITE is one of the strongest teams of the competition and we were hoping not to have our first match against them. Our team hasn't had the time to practise and two of our key players are injured. Tanmay said he had tried to convince Mandar to bring Karthik back, but he had turned a deaf ear.

'Do you think Karthik is going to come?' Pia asks.

Over the past one week, Pia has not gone to the gym. She says that the equipment is being replaced but I can feel that something is wrong. She has barely slept and kept awake throughout the night, talking to someone on the phone, often crying. I met her only six weeks ago, probably that's why she doesn't want to share her problems with me, but I am sure it's about Vishal.

'I don't think so,' I say. 'Tanmay told me that Karthik hates the football team and wishes that it would lose.'

'He hates the team? Then why does he train Tanmay?'

'He likes Tanmay, that's why.'

'Maybe he likes Tanmay because Tanmay is *your* friend,' Pia suggests with a naughty smile. I ignore it.

'There he is!' I point out.

Tanmay, along with the rest of team, comes running inside the football field, surrounded by the 300-people strong crowd that has turned up to support both the teams. The match starts shortly and things immediately look bad for our college. Within the first ten minutes, we concede the first goal. Tanmay is not in the playing eleven yet, and I can see him getting restless on the benches.

At half-time, our team is behind by two goals and the players are already discouraged; I can see their shoulders drooping. The opposite team, on the other hand, looks ecstatic. As soon as the seniors sit on the bench, Tanmay goes up to Mandar and says something animatedly. Mandar says something, and by the look of his expression, I can tell that it cannot be anything pleasant. Tanmay doesn't relent and still keeps talking.

One of the seniors gets up, puts an arm across Tanmay's shoulder and walks him away. From where we are sitting, it looks like Mandar is bitching about Tanmay to the player on his left. After a ten-minute break, the match starts again and this time it is no better. We assume that the whole matter is about Tanmay trying to get into the playing eleven, and Mandar not letting him in.

Pia and I look at each other with downcast faces. The crowd from the other college has now gone ballistic and they are shouting the name of their college at the top of their lungs. We can hear the chants of *'NITE, NITE, NITE'* roaring in our ears, and it discourages us. Tanmay is still walking on the side-lines, pacing about the line, kicking dirt and muttering something angrily to himself. Minutes later, NITE scores again. Tanmay throws his hands up in the air and shouts something at Mandar again.

'I think he is in trouble. He is messing with the captain,' Pia whispers, as we see Mandar running towards Tanmay.

Once there, he points a finger at him and then presses it against his chest, and shouts something. Mandar substitutes a striker as a favour to Tanmay and this inclusion displeases the other senior players. They are clearly unhappy about the decision.

'He'd better do good,' I say nervously and Pia clutches my hand.

Tanmay, on the other hand, looks confident as he runs up to where he is supposed to play from. He does a few stretches and Pia shouts out loud, 'GO, TANMAY!'

There is muted laughter from behind. I look behind to see who laughed. There is no one. But something tells me it was Karthik. The whistle is blown; the match starts and Tanmay's eyes are fixed unwaveringly on the ball.

I close my eyes and say a little prayer.

~

AMAZING.

We must have said this word about a million times by now. The loud cheers of the name 'TANMAY! TANMAY!' is still fresh in our ears as we munch on the pizzas Tanmay has ordered for us in our room.

The match ended at six, 4–3 in our favour with a spectacular hat trick from Tanmay. He was like a kid on steroids in the field. The opposition was zapped, and I am sure they must be thinking now that it was all part of a plan. Concede three goals, give some false confidence to the opposite team, unleash the secret weapon 'Tanmay', and win the match.

Even though he did not look like how Karthik did that day, Tanmay did end up with a similar fan base for himself. No one expected anything from him; he was just a short, skinny junior, eager to play for his college team. Who would have imagined the kind of talent he hid within himself? He dazzled everyone and I will never forget the image of his teammates picking him up on their shoulders and carrying him off the field. The match ended at six and we had to rush back to the hostel while Tanmay went off with his teammates to celebrate. He was back in the campus by eight and had ordered pizzas for us, to treat us for the win.

'It was brilliant, wasn't it?' Pia says for the zillionth time this evening.

'Yes, it was,' I agree.

'Where is he anyway?'

'I think he is out with Karthik. The last time he called, I could hear Karthik in the background.'

'What's the deal with Karthik? I will not be surprised if he transforms into some Batman or something like that. He is always so mysterious and stuff. Don't you think?'

'A little bit, yes,' I say.

'You haven't talked to him after that day, have you? I am amazed he didn't try to get in touch with you. I thought he liked you . . . anyway, what happened to Akshat?'

'Argh. I don't want to think about all this. Akshat is missing. I don't know what or who Karthik is and I don't know if I care! Let me just concentrate on the pizza,' I say, now irritated by all this boy-talk. I seriously don't know how I got myself into all this.

Our conversation dries up after a little while as she keeps on texting her boyfriend, and I keep on refreshing my profile on a social networking site, hoping for something exciting to come up. Bored, I put on a movie that seems interesting. Tanmay, with his strange laptop and scores of other computer hardware accessories, had transferred a good stock of movies on my laptop. A lot of them are superhero/mindless action movies, but there are a few good romantic comedies as well. I put on one and get lost in the handsome guy's wonderful words in the movie.

A little later, I see Pia wave her hand at me from her bed. 'What?'

'Someone's outside!' she says.

I pluck out the earphones and try to listen. I am pretty sure that someone is shouting our names. It doesn't take me long to realize that it's Tanmay, a different Tanmay, a *loud* Tanmay! We both run to the window and look down.

'*HEY! PRETTY LADIES!*' he shouts and waves his hands at us. He is swaying from side to side.

'What the hell!' Pia shouts back at him.

'PIA! I'M *NOT* DRUNK! Or maybe I *am*. *Shhhhhhhh . . .*' he shouts and turns to look to his right. Our eyes follow his and we see Karthik sitting on his bike, smiling back at him, from a few feet away.

'You need to go. Right *now*,' I shout. The warden could come out any time and report him, and that's the last thing I want happening to Tanmay. I wonder if it is Karthik who made Tanmay drink.

'*I ain't going nowhere!*' he shouts in a fake twang and starts laughing maniacally. He can barely stand straight now. His spectacles are all wrong and tilted to one side, his hair is ruffled and windblown, his clothes are dirty and he looks like shit.

'GO! Go back before someone complains about you. NOW!' Pia shouts, clearly concerned.

'But I LOVE YOU!' he says out loud and flashes a smile at her.

I do find it a little funny, but I also know what will happen if someone catches him doing this. I ask him to go to his hostel, 'We can talk about that tomorrow! You need to go now.'

Pia, meanwhile, has started to blush.

'I LOVE YOU! I LOVE YOU! I LOVE YOU! YOU'RE SO BEAUTIFUL! YOU'RE MY SUNSHINE!' he starts singing totally out of tune, but totally cute. He keeps tripping over himself as he sings the self-written, self-composed song.

'KARTHIK!' I shout. He is sitting quietly on the bike and enjoying the show. 'CAN YOU TAKE HIM BACK?'

He throws his hands up in the air and drives close to Tanmay. He pulls him and forces him on the back seat of the bike while Tanmay is still singing his 'I LOVE YOU' song.

'Goodbye, ladies!' Karthik shouts out as his bike roars away.

'AND I LOVE YOU, PIA!' Tanmay shouts.

When we see the bike turn around the corner we come back inside our room. We are both too shocked and bewildered to say anything. There is a pause in which we try to digest what just happened.

'Tanmay drinks?' I ask.

'He loves me?' Pia asks.

'*Crap!*' we both say.

Chapter Sixteen

The Morning After

'Is it just me or do you too think that it was adorable?'
Pia asks me as she gets ready for class the next morning.
It amazes me how she can wake up early, go to the gym,
take a shower and get dressed every morning by the time I
struggle to get my eyelids open. Willpower like hers is hard
to find.

'What was cute?' I croak, my head dug deep into my pillow.

'What Tanmay did last night? I thought it was kind of cute.'

'It was stupid. I know that he does not drink and I don't
want him to start now, just because his friends think it's a
cool thing to do. He is *not* that guy,' I say and pull the pillow
over my head. 'And I hate chemistry labs.'

'Will you please just get up? We are already late!'

'I don't think I am going.'

'Please? You have ten minutes. And you can't ditch me
today. Tanmay is going to be there. I don't know what he
will say or what I should say!' she starts freaking out and
turns red in the face.

'What is there to say? You have a boyfriend you love.'

'Exactly. I love Vishal and I plan to keep loving him
for life. I know that Tanmay has . . . *something* for me, and
I think it is sweet. But I cannot let it develop into something
more serious. You don't understand. I can't give Tanmay false

hope, only to let him down eventually. I can't do this to him. And I need you to help me in this. I need to make him understand!'

'Woah, woah, woah. Just relax, Pia. We'll figure it out,' I say, trying to calm her down. She is in a a full-fledged panic attack and I am left with no other option. I get up, wash my face, brush my teeth, try to look presentable and walk the long walk to the chemistry lab.

'Do you think he will remember?' Pia asks.

'I have never had friends who drink, and I really don't like people who do so. So, I have no idea. For all I know, I may not be talking to him for the next few days,' I say. I am majorly pissed at him. Not for saying the things he said to Pia last night, nor because of the way he shouted it from outside the girls' hostel. But because of drinking. He really doesn't have to drink; he is such a kid. He should still be subsisting on milk and Cerelac—why did he have alcohol?

We enter the chemistry lab, and it smells of ammonia, and I instantly feel sick. Just the look of yellowed bottles, beakers and test tubes makes me want to run away and never come back. Pia, on the other hand, loves chemistry and knows more about benzene rings than any sane person should. It is kind of creepy.

We are the last ones to enter the class and the students have already huddled near the lab in-charge's table to take down the procedure and requirements for today's experiment. While Pia finds her way to the front, I hide behind the taller guys to avoid being asked a question.

Fifteen minutes of instructions and the experiment is the same, to add something into something, at a certain temperature, till it starts smelling funny and the colour changes. I don't see the sense behind anyone wanting to do that. Pia breaks through the crowd and looks at me with the widest and silliest grin possible and says, 'Guess what!'

'What?' I ask and hope it's not about chemistry.

'Look at who's going to assist us,' she says and points to someone standing right next to the professor.

It's Karthik. In his black T-shirt, blue jeans and sneakers, he looks just like us. His hair is all ruffled and it looks like he has just gotten out of bed. He is surrounded by a lot of girls from our class and uninterestedly answers the questions the girls ask him between foolish giggles. Even the few guys around him giggle. He has that effect on people.

'Whatever,' I say and accompany Pia to our table.

She starts picking out chemicals and bases and whatnot with alarming accuracy and determination. Like they are all just different shades of lipstick or something.

'You're so good at this!' I exclaim.

'We all have our strong points,' she says and smiles at me.

I stand in a corner and look at Pia while she goes about the experiment excitedly. I don't even pretend to hide my boredom. I wonder what Tanmay is up to. Maybe suffering from a terrible hangover. A little later, Karthik—who I have been unintentionally staring at for quite some time—walks up to us.

'Hi,' he says and Pia smiles at him.

He looks at me and I don't acknowledge his look or his smile.

'I am sorry for yesterday. I should never have asked him to drink. He created a problem for you guys, didn't he?' Karthik says. 'But at least he was better than the guy who keeps following you like a creep? What's his name . . . Akshat?'

'You asked him to drink? Why would you do that?' I ask angrily. *And Akshat? How does he know about all that?*

'We needed to celebrate, that's all. The team won. That doesn't happen a lot, you know? And he was awesome on the field yesterday. He deserved to drink and celebrate, right?'

'But he doesn't drink and you did not need to make him.'

'I did not *make* him. You make it sound like I *forced* him to drink, like I'm some kind of a villain or something here. And I know that he doesn't drink, but he will some day. If not yesterday, it would have happened sooner or later. He's a man, he can handle a drink,' he smirks.

'Oh, yeah? He can handle a drink? Why do I have a feeling that what happened yesterday suggests something different? You're such a typical guy,' I say, not appreciating what he just said.

'What? So? He went a little out of hand last night? And I suggested a drink? What the hell is so wrong with that?'

'You totally don't get it, do you? This is how it starts, this alcohol business. And I really don't like it.'

'But apparently *he* does,' Karthik smirks again.

'You have no concerns about how you may affect his life, do you? He really looks up to you. Please don't influence him in all the wrong ways,' I say.

'Fine, Mom. I won't. But I think he is old enough to take his own decisions,' he says, his arms locked stubbornly in front of his chest.

'Whatever,' I say. 'And if you don't mind, we have an experiment to do.'

'Of course,' he says and walks away.

'What was that?' Pia asks, shocked. 'Why were you fighting with him?'

'I just didn't like that he made Tanmay drink.'

'But you saw him drunk yesterday. You were okay, then, weren't you?'

'I didn't know that Karthik made him drink. I thought it was his own choice,' I say.

Pia gives me a strange look.

Frankly, even I don't know why I am so angry. I am concerned about Tanmay, but I didn't think I would be so angry. I have always been uncomfortable around people who

drink, but I am more disturbed by Tanmay's drinking because
he is such a kid, and so different from the others.

~

A little later, Tanmay walks in to the Chemistry lab, and joins
us, unnoticed by any of the lab assistants or the teacher in-
charge. His eyes are bloodshot and he's still in the clothes he
was wearing last night. He is smiling stupidly as we walks
up to us.

'Are you okay?' Pia asks and puts her hand on his elbow.

'Never better,' he smiles goofily.

'Where are your spectacles?' I ask.

'I think I broke them somewhere . . . last night. I have
a spare pair back in my room. I will use them for now,'
he says.

'So, how was last night?' I ask and he keeps smiling stupidly.

'*AWESOME!*' he says and laughs. Half the class turns to
look at us and Tanmay fiddles with the beakers to fake that
he is working.

'What happened last night?' Pia asks.

'I went out with the team and we had a party to celebrate
the win against NITE. Everyone drank but I didn't. After the
party, I met Karthik and forced him to celebrate with me,'
he says, his speech still slurred. 'He was not happy about the
team winning. He never is. But I pleaded with him so he
took me out drinking! Then, we drank a lot and drove around
the city. Then, the next morning, I found myself sleeping in
Karthik's room, on the floor. Crazy night!'

'Are you sure that's all you did?' I ask, forgetting all about
being mad at him for drinking.

'Yes, why?' he asks stupidly.

'Don't you remember coming outside our hostel?' Pia asks.

'Outside *your* hostel? No. Why would I come to your
hostel?' Tanmay looks puzzled.

'You don't remember?' I ask. 'You don't remember the song? I LOVE YOU! I LOVE YOU! I LOVE YOU! YOU'RE SO BEAUTIFUL! YOU'RE MY SUNSHINE!' I start singing out of tune, just like Tanmay had sung it.

'Oh.' Tanmay's face goes blank, and I guess he can now remember bits of it. The colour from his face disappears and he freezes. 'Oh. I sang that . . . I don't really . . . I . . . did I do anything else?'

'You proposed to her, you fool,' I say, and note that Pia is almost blushing.

There is an awkward silence, during which Tanmay and Pia try to look at everything else other than each other. Tanmay just stands there and looks at his feet and shuffles them uncomfortably. He looks highly embarrassed, and so does Pia. I feel like running away and giving them some time alone. I can see Karthik a few feet away from me, instructing some students. Maybe I should go to him and apologize. I feel bad about what I said to him before. Tanmay had a good time last night and there was no harm done. I should not have lashed out at Karthik like that.

'Umm . . . I'll be back in a minute,' I say.

'Where are you going?' Pia and Tanmay ask at once.

'Just to . . . to get some,' I glance at the procedure lying on the platform and say, 'conc. sulphuric acid for the next step. 4.2 ml, right?'

'Do you even know how to withdraw acid from its bottle?' Pia asks.

Now, I really don't know much about chemistry experiments, but this is downright insulting. 'Of course,' I say. 'I'll use a 10 ml pipette.'

'And suck it from your mouth?' Pia cocks her head and asks. I am about to nod my head, because that was exactly what I was going to do, but judging by her stance, it seems to be the wrong answer. I keep my mouth shut. She shakes her head and goes to fetch the acid, murmuring, 'We always use a bubbler for acids. And this is concentrated sulphuric acid we are talking about . . .'

'I knew that,' I mutter. I know that getting the chemical was just her excuse to get out of the awkward situation between her and Tanmay, so I don't protest and let her go.

'Shit. I don't believe I actually did that. What else did I say?' Tanmay completely freaks out, as soon as Pia is out of sight.

'Nothing much. That you love her and she is so beautiful and blah, blah, blah. You just kept shouting the same thing over and over again.'

'Oh, shit.'

'Don't feel bad. You said nothing that was not true,' I say.

'But she . . . she must be so mad at me. That was so out of line. I shouldn't have . . . I should apologize to her.'

'Relax, now. I don't think she will bring up the topic again. So just let it be. Or else it'll get awkward.'

He nods and gets a little lost in thought.

'Why doesn't he like it when our team wins?' I ask after a while.

'Who? Oh, Karthik. Umm . . . when he was kicked out of the team two years ago, people had ganged up against him to throw him out. I told you about the girl, didn't I?'

'Yes, I know about it.' I remember it from when Karthik told me.

'So, no one believed him. Plus, no one ever understands him. By the look of him, people feel he is a bit of a loner. But he talks to a lot of people and everyone knows him. It's all very strange. Someone told me that he used to miss practice, get drunk and kept sleeping in his room for days. Also, I think a lot of people in the team were really jealous of him. He used to be a really good player and hogged all the limelight.'

'Like you did yesterday?' I smile.

'Oh. Thank you. Anyway—so, basically, it had ended up in a fight and it is said that Karthik had beaten up half the team before someone came from behind and knocked him out.'

'Half the team?'

'He is a little bit of a *goonda*, isn't he?'

'Maybe,' I say, as images of Karthik taking on six guys and beating the living hell out of them flash in front of my eyes. 'So now he hates it when our team wins?'

'That would be an understatement. Usually, he coaches other teams just before the tournament to take down ICE, but this time he was busy.'

'Busy? Doing what?'

'He is working on his bike,' Tanmay tells me.

'Oh, I know. The silencer right?' I ask, quite proud for some weird reason. I feel good that I know a bit of Karthik too; he had told me about his repair work on his bike.

'Oh, no, not that one. That bike is always under repair. But I was talking about another bike—he is making a bike from scratch. No one has seen it, but he says it's awesome. I saw a few drawings and they looked out of the world,' Tanmay says excitedly.

'What? Are you serious? He is actually *making* a bike? Where does he do all this? And when does he do all this?' I shower him with a barrage of questions.

'Oh. You don't know? He has plenty of time; he completed his thesis way back. Now, all he does is this. He is a freaking genius. I hope I can see the bike some day,' Tanmay says wistfully and tells me whatever he knows about it.

'Cool,' I say.

Pia comes back a few minutes later with the acid. God knows how someone needs so much time to get something from twenty feet away. Once back, she keeps muttering things about how I need to concentrate more on how the experiments are performed and the general safety rules I should know about. I stop paying attention to her blabber, my mind still on Karthik.

'Tell Pia that I'm sorry,' Tanmay whispers to me when the bell rings and he is about to leave.

'I don't think that will be necessary. But try not to drink again,' I say.

Chapter Seventeen

How Life Changes

A few weeks pass and life's a routine even though things are changing slowly and steadily and aren't exactly the way they were before. The more things change, the more they remain the same.

'Good morning,' Tanmay croaks from the other side of the phone.

'You're still sleeping?' I ask.

'Yes. I am sorry. I will just sleep today. Terrible headache,' he says, sounding barely coherent.

'Did you drink again?'

'Huh? Me? No?' he says, unconvincingly.

'Don't lie. You did, didn't you? After all that I said, you still went ahead and got drunk?'

'But the whole team was there! I had no choice,' he defends himself.

'You always have a choice. You have three more matches left. Why are you doing this?'

'It doesn't affect my performance! I practise five hours a day. I can afford a little fun,' he says, almost angry now. 'And you need to stop being a mom! Every first year guy is trying it out. I think you should too.'

'What? I am trying to ask you to stop drinking, and you are asking me to try it too? Don't you have any shame?'

He doesn't say anything.

'Look—I am just saying—you don't have to drink so much,' I say.

'Fine. I am sorry,' he says and hangs up.

I disconnect the call. He didn't sound convincing at all. I know he will give in if his new football friends ask him to drink again. Seven matches, six wins, thirteen goals from Tanmay, and ten drinking binges left him unreachable for days after the match. It's been a month and I have seen less and less of him. The time we spend together is usually spent in copying assignments. Other than that, he is usually practising on the field, hanging around with Karthik or playing his matches. Or sleeping when he gets too drunk!

I understand him being busy, but I don't endorse his consumption of alcohol. Of late, he has even started hanging out with his teammates and drinking. He claims he doesn't drink much, but I can see his bloodshot eyes and tell what must have happened the night before.

I had initially blamed Karthik for it, but I think Karthik was right when he said, 'It was just waiting to happen.'

I don't know what is wrong with him. Life has taken a turn that's not much fun. Exams are just around the corner and panic has started to set it. No matter how much I show I don't care, I do want to score well. And with Tanmay and Pia busy with their own lives, I have absolutely no one around me. Pia sleeps through the day and talks through the night, often crying on the phone for hours. I don't have the heart to ask her why, because I know it's regarding Vishal.

Today, I saw Akshat drag his suitcases to the guys' hostel in the morning. He didn't notice me, but I think he will start following me again soon. And this time, I am going to talk to him and put it to rest. Things have started to take shape in my head. Maybe Akshat isn't that bad at all. He has been persisting for long enough. It's been close to a long time

now, and he wouldn't have hung around if I did
anything to him.

On the other hand, I don't really like Karthik,
realized that. He is too brash and too reckless for me.
the last few days, I have heard about more than a few n
brawls he has been in. Though, surprisingly, no one rea
says a bad word about him. But he is the kind of guy who
throws his life away. I am not too sure that I want someone
like him around me. Not that he likes me back anyway.

Moreover, I blame him for Tanmay's new-found love for
alcohol. I know that it's not he who is at fault here, but
I can see that Tanmay has started to ape Karthik. The clothes,
the mannerisms—he is fascinated by a lot more than just
Karthik's football skills.

'Are you coming for class?' I ask Pia, who is sprawled
across the bed like a corpse. She has been up all night talking
again. She shakes her head.

I call Tanmay again, but he says he is not coming, this
time even more forcefully. He says he needs to practise when
he gets up.

There are just three matches left for us to win the title
and he is doing everything to get us there. It seems like a
lot is riding on him. And since we are winning, everyone
has started taking even more interest in the matches. Even
people who are not interested in football turn up at the
matches and cheer till their lungs give up. Needless to say,
Tanmay is the most popular junior in our batch. No one
even remembers who won Mr Fresher, the annual title given
to the most impressive junior after a series of talent rounds
and what-not.

I walk to the class, head hung low, already dreading the long
day that is ahead of me. I haven't even started studying for
the exams. I was thinking Tanmay would teach us everything
but he now says he will not start studying till two of his

v. Luckily, the final, if we make it,

...g a terrible day, when I get to
...at it's a chemistry class. I am bored
...n the first fifteen minutes. I try talking
...g next to me, but he just freaks me out by
... the impending examination and how he has
...e syllabus only thrice.

...ored, tired and pissed off, I look out of the window
absent-mindedly when I see someone waving at me. It's *him*.
Akshat, in all his morning glory and carefully chosen clothes,
is standing right outside my classroom and waving at me. I
don't even think twice before I come up with an excuse
and sneak out of the class.

I walk towards him determinedly and stop right in front
of him.

'Is this for real? All I had to do was wave to get your
attention, I was following you around for a month and you
didn't notice,' he says.

'Sometimes doing what you need to do is all it takes. Like
saying the truth,' I say.

'Are we going into that conversation all over again?'

'We—'

'No, don't even answer that. That topic is closed. I have an
idea. Let's get out of here? I am sick of this college!' he says.

'Where?'

'Some place nice. Come.'

As I walk behind him to the parking lot, I realize how
easily I am back to the day when he held my hand during
the movie and kissed me thereafter. Or am I just bored and
needy enough to want whatever company I can get? With
Tanmay busy with his being-cool stuff, and Pia crying her
heart out for that bastard back in Bangalore, perhaps I don't

know what to do with myself. I think I should have made more friends in college, but it's not that we haven't tried. Tanmay, Pia and I have taken others along on our walks once in a while—mostly guys—but nothing actually worked out. The guys hit on us, and the girls kept saying Tanmay is so-sweet, so-sweet and I don't think either Pia nor I liked it. We like to keep Tanmay for ourselves.

'You have a car here?' I almost gasp when I see the car. I know by the logo that it's the German-made BMW and I don't know or even want to know anything beyond that.

'Since you weren't talking to me anyway, I thought I should see the city a little,' he smiles and holds the door open for me, quite a contrast to how Karthik had asked me to jump on his bike and hold him tight. I am surprised I am still thinking about Karthik.

I sit in the front seat, and for a moment, I am dazzled by the interiors of the car. It looks brand-new and has a million lights and LEDs that stare back at me. The leather I am sitting on is smoother than velvet and every surface shines like granite.

'So, how's college?' he asks once he gets into the driver's seat.

'It's okay. Exams from next week, so it's going to be a hectic time. I haven't started studying yet. Let's see how it goes.'

'Oh, but you're smart. You will do well.'

'I hope so,' I reply shortly. I still do not know why I decided to come with him or where it is going to take us. Akshat, however, acts like there has never been anything wrong between us.

'And how are your friends? Pia, right? And Tanmay?'

'You have done your fair bit of stalking me, eh?' I say, a little appreciative of him being abreast of what's happening in my life.

'I can't stop thinking about you.'

'I wonder why,' I say dryly.

'Can you stop being so mean to me? I agree that I once did some things that I am not particularly proud of, but I have changed now. You need to understand that. What happened with your sister is something I regret.'

'I want to believe you. I think I do, too. But I can't be with you; it's just wrong.'

'Fine. But we can be friends, right? We can call, text and meet up sometimes? That's all I want,' he says, sounding exceptionally sincere.

'Don't be that sweet. And I will think about it,' I say, almost blushing.

He smiles at me and drives into a plush hotel's parking lot, and I feel guilty that I won't be able to split the bill. He lets the valet park the car, hands over a 500-rupee note—an amount that I spend in a week—and opens the huge door for me. Somehow, the way he acts and behaves makes me feel like an ill-behaved, immature, underdressed college student. Wait—I am *meant* to be that!

'What place is this?' I ask as he leads me into the restaurant. This place doesn't even have proper tables. There are huge couches—in bright colours—and people are dressed up. I am still in a yellow T-shirt, which has a Superman logo on it. I thought it was nice, but now it looks like I am extremely inappropriately dressed.

'Can't we go to McDonald's or Dominos? Or something like that?' I ask. He laughs. 'I am serious. Why do we have to come to a place like this? I feel so out of place.'

'You will get used to it. And you deserve the best in life.'

'I think the burgers at McDonald's are nice. Here, I won't even know what to order!'

'It's not that bad,' he says as he smiles again.

A waiter—handsome and tall in his black and red

tuxedo—walks up to our table and hands over the menu
to both of us.

'Order for me, and it better be good,' I say.

'Fine,' he says and summons the waiter again. He orders
something from the menu, asks the waiter to add a few things,
not add a few things and to make it quick. Once the waiter
excuses himself, Akshat turns to me and asks, 'Are you going
to tell your sister that you met me?'

'Sooner or later, I guess. But that doesn't matter; I don't
think we are going to meet that often anyway.'

'Because your sister won't approve?'

'Yes,' I reply.

'Okay. Let's talk about something else,' he says, clearly
not happy.

He starts to tell me about his business in Nagpur and how
his father is freaking out about him spending so much time
here. He says he finds it difficult to live with his parents,
with them constantly asking him to get married. Twenty-four
is not an age to get married, he says. He asks me if I like
cars and I shake my head, but nonetheless, he tells me about
the cars he has driven till now. He got his first car when
he was fourteen and it was a Fiat Palio. Soon, he moved
on to a Maruti Esteem when he was fifteen, a Tata Sierra
at seventeen and he was gifted his first BMW at eighteen.
Since then, he has been a fan of European cars, he tells me.
BMWs, Audis, an old Porsche—he has driven them all. By
the time he finishes, I am more interested in the chicken
drumsticks he has ordered than the engine capacity of the
cars he has driven.

'So, cars, huh?' I asks absent-mindedly, still very much
absorbed in the food on my plate.

'Yeah, I love them.'

'What else do you love?'

'Apart from you, I love to travel,' he winks.

'Oh, you do? It must be fun, right? I have never gone out of the country. Not even to Nepal!'

'Never? You definitely should go out . . . *we* should go on a holiday. My treat,' he says.

'Yeah, right. You expect me to just get up and take a vacation with you. I am not sure we will even talk again! You're pushing it too far.'

'Okay, okay, fine. I just thought it would be nice for you and me to go to Venice. Italy is an immensely romantic country.'

'Tell me about it!' I say enthusiastically.

He tells me about his vacation in Italy and everything he did there. Sporadically, the conversation veered to cars and the showrooms and the factories of Ferrari and Fiat and what-not that he visited. There are times when I stop listening to him and concentrate only on his beautiful face or the amazing food he has ordered for me. Though he talks about places he would take me to if I agreed to go with him, he obviously doesn't realize that our worlds are different. And from where I come from, there are no spontaneous international vacations. I can count the number of times I have been inside an aircraft—none of them flew me to international destinations.

'So, what do you think?' he asks.

'About Italy? Great. I would love to visit that place some time. Maybe in the next hundred years, if I get the chance,' I smile wryly.

'You will. Best of luck,' he says and slides his hand towards mine. For some reason, I let him hold it. He has held it before and it doesn't feel odd. But it doesn't feel incredible either, like it did the last time.

'We should go,' I say, looking at my watch.

'Do we have to?' he says, his eyes stuck on me in a deep stare. 'I can sit here for the rest of the day spending time with you.'

Talking about cars?

'I wish I could stay too, but I really have to start studying,' I say, even though I don't feel the need to be sweet to him from the inside. But he has been—or at least tried to be—so sweet to me, so I think it's not fair to give him such a hard time.

He settles the bill; I don't even have the courage to see how much it cost us. I had spotted the price of the mocktail he had ordered for me, and the amount was enough to pay for pizzas for ten people at Dominos. I didn't have the heart to look any further and feel guiltier about it than I already was.

Akshat drives back to the campus really slowly and takes two rounds around the campus before parking the car at the farthest end of the parking lot. Though we had nothing to talk about during our entire ride back to the college, he had been looking at me and smiling, as if he had a secret.

We get out of the car and I, finally, ask, 'What's the matter? Why are you smiling so much?'

'Come here,' he says as he sits on the bumper of the car. Gingerly, I walk up to him and he holds my hand and makes me sit on the bonnet of the car. Strangely enough, unlike my father's Maruti Esteem, the bonnet is surprisingly cool.

'What?' I ask.

And I realize that I shouldn't have. It becomes obvious what's on his mind. He pushes me onto the bonnet and steps forward. I am kind of dazed as he leans into me and I move a couple of inches forward. His lips touch mine and then he moves slowly, kissing my lower lip. I feel all warm and lightheaded. I put my hand on his shoulder for support. I can't make sense of half of what's happening; it's all too quick to grasp. He places his hands on my waist and slowly caresses it. Soon, the kiss turns more intense and I start breathing heavily.

From the little light we have here, I can see him look into my eyes. I stare right back. He breaks the kiss and moves down to my neck. I gulp. He pushes away the neckline of my tee and plants a kiss there. Slowly, his lips travel lower and linger there.

I feel a shiver. Not in a good way. As his hands start to get more exploratory, my breathing becomes strained. *I've to stop him.* But before I can do or say anything, he slips his hand inside my T-shirt and I start to feel even more uncomfortable. I have to stop him.

I jerk back suddenly and he is taken by surprise. He looks at me, his eyes asking a zillion questions. I freeze. *What the hell?* We look at each other, not knowing what to say. This shouldn't have happened. I slide down the hood of the car and he steps back. I turn away, adjust my clothes and walk out of the parking lot, crying, without looking at him at all. He doesn't say anything either.

What on earth just happened?

I find myself asking the question for the next few hours as the tears keep flowing.

~

I keep walking around till my feet are tired, my mind visualizing a thousand worst-case scenarios. I shouldn't have kissed him. Simran has not asked about Akshat yet, but what if she does? I have never lied to my sister and I hate doing that. A harmless date is acceptable, but we almost made out. He had his hands all over me. Worse still, I don't know if I hated it. I was uncomfortable, that's for sure, but I am not sure if I hated it like I should have.

I sit on the stairs, where Tanmay and I had spent the first day of college, and hide my face in my palms. Somehow, the tears don't stop. Seconds later, I hear some footsteps coming towards me. They keep getting louder and more hurried.

'NIHARIKA!' I look up to see Tanmay shout at me, running towards me.

'What?'

'COME. You've got to see this,' he says, sweat dripping down his brow.

'Huh? What?'

'Just come,' he says, takes me by the hand and starts to jog again.

I try to resist, but his grip is way too strong and he doesn't let go. I have no choice but to follow him, even though all I want right now is to be left alone. The episode with Akshat is way too fresh in my mind. My heart starts to race as we walk towards the parking lot I have just come from. As we get closer, I see a crowd of people—at least thirty—standing in a huddle and there are shouts all around.

I look at Tanmay and shout, 'What's happening there?'

KARTHIK AND AKSHAT!' he shouts back.

We push through the crowd and it takes me a second to register what I see. Karthik's hand flies through the air and lands on Akshat's already bloody jaw. Akshat staggers back and falls on the ground. Karthik walks a few steps forward and swings again at his face just when Akshat is about to get up. The fist lands on his inner jaw and he spews a stream of blood out of his mouth before he crumples on the ground. I look at Karthik—his shirt is torn and his nose is bleeding slightly. Akshat seems to be beaten black and blue. He is clearly disoriented and is about to pass out.

'STOP IT!' I shout the minute I gain control over myself.

Before I can move, two security guards come running towards the commotion, raising their batons. The crowd immediately starts to disperse and Tanmay drags me away from the scene. I try, but I can't loosen his grip. We stop some distance away and look back to find the security guards scratching their heads, since the place is now almost empty.

'What was that?' I ask, shocked, my face flushed red and my mind numb.

'I don't know. I just called Karthik and he told me where he was. I was walking to the canteen when I saw these two exchanging blows. Karthik was beating the shit out of Akshat. I heard Karthik take your name so I guessed you would know,' Tanmay explains hurriedly.

'How would I know?' I say and hold my head. The tears start to flow again.

'Did something happen?' he asks and pulls me into a hug.

'No, nothing happened,' I say and hug him back. 'Can you walk me to the hostel?'

'Sure,' he says and helps me to my feet.

As I walk back to my hostel, possibilities of what might have happened a few minutes ago cloud my head. Did Karthik and Akshat fight about me? Did Karthik see us kissing? And me crying? But why would he care? Why would he fight?

I reach the hostel and Tanmay asks me if I need him around. I thank him and ask him to go for his practice. I have half a mind to go and ask Karthik about what just happened but I am too messed up to think clearly.

In the room, I see Pia ferociously marking and underlining parts of her book. She looks at me enter the room and immediately senses that something is wrong.

'What's the matter?'

Almost instantly, I break down and tell her everything that has happened since the morning. She listens to me and like a good friend, she hugs me and tells me that everything will be all right.

'So? Are you going to talk to Karthik about it?' she asks.

'I don't know who to talk to. Karthik or Akshat.'

'I think you should talk to Akshat first. Was he hurt?'

'Much, much more than Karthik .... much more,' I say.

'Talk to him.'

It takes Pia an hour to convince me to call Akshat and ask him what happened and why it happened. Three calls went unanswered and the fourth was rejected. I look at Pia, blank-faced when my phone beeps. It's a text.

Can you meet me in the library? Ten minutes. :/

I show the text to Pia and she says she wants to come along. We both get ready to leave. On our way, Tanmay keeps asking me to keep calm no matter what happens, and despite trying hard to prepare what I would say to Akshat, I draw a blank.

We enter the library and see that it's filled with students picking out huge books from the shelves, scribbling on their pads or peering into their laptops. A few couples hang around here and there, laughing, smiling and holding hands, waiting for a chance to disappear behind the racks for a stolen kiss.

I look around for Askhat on the ground and the first floor and find him nowhere. I guess he must be on the third, where all dusty old scientific journals are kept, since no student usually goes there.

'There,' Pia spots him.

As we walk towards him, I notice that Akshat isn't alone. My eyes widen when I see who he is with. It's *them*—the ones from the canteen. The college-fucking president—Chetan Mehta—and his cronies. They don't look happy, neither does Akshat. His pretty face is all screwed up with cuts and bruises and a bandage stuck across his head. I feel sorry for him and had he been alone, I know I would have cried. But now, I am just scared.

'Sit,' Akshat says and places two chairs for us. I can see Pia looking a little unsettled at seeing seven heavily built guys around us. I am glad she came with me. Akshat smiles at me with his now crooked jaw.

'What happened?' I ask and my voice quakes.

'We're GOING TO KILL HIM!' one of the college president's cronies almost shouts and the rest of them join in unison.

'Calm down,' Akshat tells them.

'But he messed with you!' Chetan argues.

'Let's first try to understand why he did it,' Akshat says and looks at me. His eyes have a strange concoction of anger and distrust in them as he stares, 'Did you tell him . . . something? Did you ask him to?'

'What? Why would I? I had no idea about what was going on until Tanmay told me.'

'Then why?' he relaxes a little.

'Maybe he saw . . . what happened and saw me crying,' I reason.

'Niharika,' he says and takes my hand into his, 'I want you to tell me the truth. Did you or did you not tell him?'

'What the—? I didn't tell him anything. You have to trust me. I was equally shocked,' I say, almost offended at the allegation.

'Fine,' he says and looks at the college president who nods. Then the rest of his cronies nod, and all have devilish smiles on their faces. A few of them even punch their fists into their palms.

'What . . . what are you going to do?'

'We will see,' Akshat says, with a look so cunning that I am a little scared.

'Akshat, look at me, and promise you will not do anything. Please.'

'How can I not? Why would I not? He beat me up, in front of so many people, Niharika! I have every right to destroy this bloody guy's life.'

I have not heard Akshat swear and it's strange to see him do that, although it looks like he is very comfortable with it. But I have to stand my ground, 'I don't want any fights. Not because of me at least.'

'But, I want my revenge,' he says and the rest of the guys nod.

'No, you don't! I am sure it's a misunderstanding. Just let it go,' I say frantically. I look at them and wonder what they will do to Karthik.

'How can I let it go? He needs to know that he was wrong and we know just the right way to make that happen,' he says and looks at Chetan, who smiles gleefully.

'Akshat, you can go have your revenge or whatever. But if I get to know anything about it, trust me, I will never talk to you again. NEVER.'

'What? You're defending him? *He* picked up the fight. *He* beat *me* up! How can you—? Wait. Are you guys . . . ? Is there something between the two of you? Is *that* why?'

'NO! Shut up. There is nothing between us. I hardly know him. I just don't want any fights because of me. And Karthik is friends with my best friend, Tanmay. I don't want anyone to get hurt. Do you get that?' I say angrily and this time he gets it.

'Fine. Fine. I get it, no fights,' he says and the shoulders of the guys around him—who had been warming their knuckles for a fight—droop and they shake their heads in disappointment.

'And I am sorry for what happened, really. I didn't know something like this could happen.'

'Yeah, whatever,' he says and points his finger towards the door. I have never seen him act so rude.

'I am sorry.'

'Fine. You can go now,' he says, his eyes still smouldering with anger.

Pia tugs at my hand and we leave the third floor. As soon

as we are out of hearing range of those guys, Pia says, 'He is rude, isn't he?'

'He is just angry, he is not usually like this.'

'I don't like him.'

'You can't blame him. Karthik beat him up really badly. You should have seen. I feel sorry for Akshat. It shouldn't have happened,' I say as feelings of pity make their presence felt in certain parts of my heart.

'But don't you think it was incredibly romantic of Karthik to beat him up like that?' Pia says, 'I mean I would love it if Tanmay does the same for me.'

'Umm . . . Tanmay?' I ask. She looks shocked. She had said Tanmay . . . not Vishal, but Tanmay.

'Huh . . . Vishal. I mean Tanmay is here, that's why I said Tanmay. And whatever,' she says, her face red with embarrassment.

'Okay, leave it. And I don't think it's romantic, Pia. It's stupid and I will let him know that,' I say.

'Had I been you, I would have kissed him!' Pia says and laughs out loud, back to her normal self in less than fifteen seconds.

Chapter Eighteen

None of Your Business

I have been looking for Karthik for quite some time. His phone has been switched off for the last three days and the only time he shows up in college is when he is practises with Tanmay. Tanmay told me that he works on his bike in his workshop—a workshop that Tanmay and I couldn't find—and when he does that, he really doesn't like phone calls or texts. He told me that Karthik—even on other days—doesn't like people who call or text much and has no love for social networking sites.

Karthik has always struck me as an oddball. The day we had gone out, I had seen him carry a broken old phone with a black and white screen. I clearly remember seeing twenty unread messages on his phone. I had thought about asking him about it, but thought it was too personal and I shouldn't meddle in his life. Actually, his whole demeanour seems to have a board saying 'STAY OUT' stuck on it.

Since he was so out of reach, Tanmay asked me to catch him after the practice if I wanted to talk. I had nodded. I have been waiting on the sidelines for two hours now while Tanmay and Karthik have toiled in the late afternoon sun, running, passing and shooting the ball. They are both pouring with sweat and working very hard.

Finally, Karthik throws his hands up in the air and both of

them lie down next to each other, facing the sun and talking animatedly—I assume about football. A little later, they both get up and start walking towards me. I still haven't framed the questions I want to ask Karthik.

As he walks towards me, he takes off his T-shirt and wipes the sweat off his beautifully muscled arms and chest. I almost blank out. He wears it again and a part of me—a guilty part of me—wants to see him without the T-shirt.

'You guys talk. I need to go,' Tanmay says and runs off, leaving the two of us in the middle of the empty field.

Karthik looks at me, with his craggy face—not a single bruise—and I forget my words. It has been three days since his fight with Akshat happened. In the time it took me to get hold of him, my anger got lost somewhere. Seeing him isn't helping matters either. I try very hard, but can't find it in me to be mad at him. But he is looking at me, and waiting for me to say something. And I certainly do have a lot of things to say to him. I try to sum it all up in one sentence.

'I am here just to tell you that what you did that day to Akshat was wrong. And I don't want you anywhere near me or him,' I say and turn my back towards him.

'That's it?' he asks as I start to walk away from him.

'Yes,' I look back and say.

'What are you doing? I thought you had more sense. Akshat is an asshole! I thought you knew that, when I saw you ignore him for ages even when he followed you around all the time. You're making a mistake.'

'It is none of your freaking business. He is a friend, and I can go out with him if I want. I spend a little time with him once and as soon as I get back, I get to know that you beat him up?'

'I saw you crying . . .' Karthik tries to say something but I cut him off.

'So? You decided to come wipe my tears? By beating him up? Yes, we had some problems, but we could've sorted them out without *your* interference. It was freaking unnecessary. Do you get that?'

'Oh yes? Guess what—I do *not* agree. You don't even know him! He is a piece of shit. He deserves it! Can't you—'

'LET ME FIND THAT OUT FOR MYSELF!' I shout back. I don't know why but all the blood rushes to my head and I find myself very angry at him. 'Let me live my life. Let me make my own mistakes.'

'You will regret it,' he says and looks away.

'Whatever. You're acting like you own me. And that's pissing me off majorly, because you do *not* own me. You do *not* have any right over me. You think you're the smart one here? The smug one? The guy who plays football, but still isn't in the team? The vintage bike? Beating guys up? You know what? That must work on other girls, but *not* me! Please don't even think that. I want you to stay away from me and stop screwing my life over.'

'I didn't mean to. I just—'

'What just?' I ask, now wanting this conversation to end.

'I want you.'

'*What?*'

'I want you. You're who I think about. And I can't see you destroy yourself with that asshole. You deserve better,' he says, sounding strangely sincere.

'Are you kidding me? What do you even *know* about me? And what do you know about *him*?'

'I know enough to tell you that he is not the guy for you. And it feels right, what we have. I know the difference.'

'We have nothing! Feels right? You saw me kiss him and beat him up. That's *not* right. That's crazy. And I love him. I obsess about him. If anything, I will be with him. And

I DON'T CARE ABOUT YOU!' I lie, for no reason I can think of.

'You don't love him,' he says and steps forward, his eyes firmly on me. I step back.

'I do.'

'You don't love him and you know that. 'Cause if you did love him, you would have been with him. And if you loved him and didn't care about me, I would have been lying here with a swollen jaw and a few broken ribs. It's been three days and I have not been touched by his goons.'

'JUST SHUT UP!' I shout and tears start flowing down my cheeks as I find myself running away from him.

'NIHARIKA!' he shouts, but I don't turn back. 'I—'

I stop running only when I reach the hostel. I look back and think—*Why am I crying? Why does he matter? Why did I not want him to get beaten up? Why did I save him?* I get into bed and try not to think about these questions. *What else did he have to say?*

~

My mind is a tangled mess of conflicting emotions right now. Obviously, Karthik's outburst meant something, but he is not the kind of guy I see myself with. A guy who beats up other guys is not a quality I desire in the person I am with. The last few days have been tough, and I have found it hard to concentrate. Akshat has been hounding me to meet him, but I know it will only complicate things. He has started accusing me of having feelings for Karthik, and I don't know if he is right or not. I do feel concerned about Askhat sending some guys after Karthik, but I don't know if it means anything.

It's been three hours since I started studying and my head hurts like hell. I have not told Pia anything about what happened with Karthik. She likes Karthik, and I don't want people to convince me that he is a nice guy and what he did was right. For me, he is an irresponsible brat who has no respect for other people's feelings or privacy. Either that or I just don't want to complicate things.

Tanmay has been pestering us to come for his match but we are in no mood to do so. It's been warm for the last few days, although it does threaten to rain every now and then.

'Do you want to go?' I ask Pia, who has been on her phone texting all morning.

'It's too hot, but I think we should. It's the semi-final, right?'

'Yes, it is. But we haven't studied anything and the match is at Tikaram College. That itself is at least half an hour from here.'

'When's the match? Six?'

'No, I think it's at five,' I say and check Tanmay's message to confirm.

'What? *Five?* Why didn't you tell me?' Pia gets up from her bed and starts putting on her clothes.

'I thought you didn't want to go.'

'NO! I wanted to. I mean—we *should*. It's the semi-finals, after all. He wanted us to come. Let's go! Don't just stand there,' Pia says, in her worn-out yet hot pink track pants and a vest. That was the first thing she could find nearest to her. And it's in no way any better from what she already had on.

'Are you sure you are going like that?' I ask.

She looks at herself and doesn't realize why I said what I did. Pia never goes out of the room until she is convinced that she will be the best dressed person wherever she goes. But today seems to be an exception. She panics and says, 'Yes, why? What's the problem? We need to go. NOW!'

I smile. It becomes obvious that Tanmay means a lot to Pia, more than what he means to me—*a little more than just a friend*. She wants to be there while Tanmay leads our college team to the finals—probably—for the first time in three years.

'Fine, fine. But it's already quarter to four; we will never make it in time.'

'Then let's just hurry up!' she shrieks, now paranoid.

'Or I can ask Akshat to drop us . . . if he is in college.'

'CALL him!'

I don't know why I took his name, but I did, and ended up being pestered and irritated by Pia into calling him. Akshat, the perfect gentleman that he is or tries to be, says that he will be here in five minutes. Pia pushes me out of the room and we wait for Akshat, though the wait is not too long as his big black car screeches to a halt in front of us—in exactly five minutes.

'Hey,' he says, looks at me and smiles. 'Hi, Pia.'

'*QUICK!*' Pia says as she leans into him from the back seat.

'Okay, fine. Someone seems excited!' he says and presses the accelerator, bringing the beast to life. The car leaves the campus and he skilfully starts navigating the traffic. He tilts his head towards me and asks, 'How are you?'

'I am good. The exam preparation is going absolutely nowhere.'

'Is that why you are avoiding me?'

'No, I am not avoiding you. I just have to keep my mind clear for a bit,' I say.

'Are you still thinking about him?'

'No, I am not.'

'If you say so,' he says dryly.

'Why would you say that? I haven't even talked to him after that incident,' I lie and I don't know why.

'I should have taken care of him,' he mutters under his breath. 'That lowlife bastard.'

'Hey, you are doing nothing of that sort.' I put a hand on his arm.

'Why the hell should I not? Don't I get to get back at him for what he did? You don't think that's unfair?' His voice is rising now, he brows are furrowed and his hand is clenched on the gear box. It always unsettles me to see him like that. It feels like I don't know him at all. He turns into this completely different person.

'I don't know what's fair and what's not, Akshat. I just don't want anyone to fight.'

'Whatever. You wouldn't understand what I went through. It was damn humiliating. So many people were there! And that bastard got me from behind.'

'Can you just let it go? Please? For me?' I say, trying desperately to calm him down.

'Whatever,' he says, his forehead knotted. His anger shows in the way he drives. He honks, skips red lights, swears at other drivers, punches fists at them and drives blindingly fast. As soon as we enter Tikaram College, Pia immediately jumps out of the car and runs towards the football field. From the noise, it looks like the match has already started.

'What's wrong with her?' Akshat asks me.

'I think she likes Tanmay.'

'Just like you like Karthik? What's it about him? Football? His stupid stubble? Tell me? What do you see in him?'

'I do *not* like him. Will you stop that? What's *wrong* with you?' I ask, getting more and more annoyed with him. *Why is every guy around me acting like he owns me?*

'What's wrong with *me*? What's wrong with *you*? I still don't get what's between the two of you,' he raises his voice.

'I think you should calm down.'

'I SHOULD CALM DOWN? That asshole hit me. And I should calm down? What the hell! I am sure you made out with him, didn't you?!'

'You are out of your mind, Akshat. I should go.'

'You're *NOT* going anywhere,' he says and grabs my hand. 'YOU HAVE TO TELL ME WHAT'S GOING ON!' he shouts.

'You need to stop shouting first,' I say. 'And let me go; you're hurting me.'

He lets go and I leave the car and walk towards the football field.

'I am sorry,' he shouts, 'but it's *not* my fault!'

I don't answer, as I run to the football field. I hear the car come to life and drive away.

~

'This is so humiliating, isn't it?' Pia shrieks in my ear.

By the time I reached the field, Tanmay had already scored two goals and everyone was chanting his name aloud. He was being a little cocky too, waving to the crowd and blowing kisses. Of all the people shouting his name, Pia was amongst the most vocal. The match progressed and reached its current status—we are leading 6–0 and Tanmay, with a little help from the other team members, has scored four of them. I have been following the matches, and I can see clearly that Tanmay alone can bring in a crowd to a football match. I don't understand football much, but I do understand and recognize his athletic agility and cunning on the field.

I don't know if it's true, but it could be because of Karthik. There is a striking similarity that stares you in the face. And I know that Karthik hates to watch our team play, though somehow, I sense him around.

'It's ended already?' I ask as I see the team crying out in joy and hugging and patting each other.

The other team couldn't even score a single goal, and they are a good team, Pia tells me excitedly. The score line doesn't reflect the opposing team's calibre. Our team does some crazy war-victory dances and runs across the field wildly. It definitely means a lot to them. After that's done, Tanmay comes running to us and almost as a reflex, hugs Pia. The hug lingers on a little longer than it should and they both look at each other, embarrassed, when they realize what happened. Tanmay hugs me also later, quickly and more like a friend. I smile, barely suppressing a chuckle.

'It was crazy. I didn't know you were that good,' I say.

'Crazy, wasn't it?' he says.

'You were AMAZING!' Pia shrieks.

'We should celebrate,' I say.

'Umm . . . I wish I could. But I have to go out with the team. They will not let me bail on them. We made it to the finals, after all! Later, maybe?' he looks with guilt-filled eyes at us.

'We get it,' Pia nods.

'So, will you get drunk again tonight?' I ask, not too happy about it.

'Just today . . . please? Don't be angry,' he pleads.

'And will you come under our window and say good things about her, again?' I poke fun at him and he blushes.

'I've got to go now,' he says, still looking apologetic.

'It's okay! Have your fun. But we need a treat later, okay?' I wink.

Just then, someone calls out his name and he knows he has to leave. He hugs us again. And again, Pia's hug lasts longer than mine and they exchange a smile that says so much more. Pia's eyes follow Tanmay till the time he walks off the field, enters a car and drives off.

'Shall we also leave now?' I ask her, shaking her out of her reverie.

'Sure. And I forgot to ask—what's with Akshat? Things looked kind of tense back in the car . . .'

'Nothing much . . . we had a small fight.'

'Oh, you guys seem to fight more than you talk. And what's his problem? Why was he so agitated?' she asks.

'I wish I knew,' I say and look for an auto.

Chapter Nineteen

Pia

*P*ia walks hurriedly towards the gym. It's evening and she knows
the gym will be empty, like it always is. It's just what she
needs—to be alone. She knows, and she knows for sure, that no one
would understand what she is going through right now. She knows
about all the signals she is sending out to Tanmay and what he
feels for her. It's more than evident on his face whenever he looks
at her; she can see it in his eyes, his clenched fists, and the drops
of sweat on his brow.

Pia thinks Niharika seemed to be happy. But she had no reason
not to be. After all, she knows nothing about her. Or Vishal. But
Pia remembers every single day of every year she has spent with
Vishal. She remembers—clearly, like it was yesterday—the first
time she found a rose on her desk and her friends ridiculed the
mysterious admirer. The next day, it was a letter confessing his love
for her; her friends ridiculed the mysterious admirer a little more,
much to the chagrin of Pia herself. It wasn't until the thirtieth letter
that he revealed himself, and when he did, Pia was glad it was
him—a best friend for seven years, someone who knew everything
about her, someone who understood her inside out—Vishal, the guy
she promised herself she would always be with.

The next two years were blissful. They were always together
and it was as if nothing else mattered. She stayed back to see him
practise for his tennis tournaments after school time, while he always

accompanied her for the numerous shopping sprees. Everything was perfect, it was a match made in heaven.

Over time, their intimacy increased, though Vishal had been very subtle in his advances and never expected—or wanted—anything out of Pia. But, three months before the school term was scheduled to end, they found themselves alone in the school building after his tennis match. Pia still remembers that evening vividly, when she was scared someone would walk in and Vishal had assured her otherwise. She still remembers the touch of his hands on her neck and further down. She remembers every moment of that evening and every detail of what happened.

When Vishal had first tried to move further down, Pia had panicked. She knew that it was not something very unusual and that everyone was doing 'it' nowadays, but she still couldn't see herself doing it. Even with Vishal. She tried to explain to him that she was not ready yet, and in turn, he tried relentlessly to make her change her mind.

'But why?' he had asked, running his hand through his hair, clearly frustrated.

'Because I don't . . . it just doesn't feel right . . .' Pia whispered.

'There is nothing wrong in it. We love each other and we will always be together. There is nothing—'

'But if we are going to be together always, then what is the rush?'

'What do you—? You don't trust me,' he said flatly and moved away.

'No! I trust you. Of course I do . . . it's just that, this is too abrupt . . . I'm not prepared for this . . .'

'When will you be?'

'Just . . . give me some time. I will think about it, I promise,' she said and tried to pull him back close to her. He did come back, but the moment was lost. In his arms, she felt as if they were miles away from each other. That was when the problems between them started.

The growing distance and the way Vishal was taking it made Pia even more doubtful about the idea of bringing intimacy into *their relationship. She did not understand his behaviour. She had never seen him so mad at her before. She did not know what she had done to deserve that treatment. She was an innocent seventeen-year-old girl, who was nervous about her first physical experience. Was that a crime?*

It sure seemed like it was. She could not handle the distance between the two of them, and finally had to agree to give Vishal what he wanted, if only to make things get back to normal. She could not bear to see their relationship suffer because of her stupid fears and insecurities. They made love in his room, the next time Pia went over to complete her maths project. It was everything she had worried it would be, and worse. She had not imagined that the pain would be so intense. Even though the overall experience was far from pleasurable, she took care not to let it show in her expressions. She pretended that it was perfect.

While for Vishal things got back to normal, Pia was scarred for life. She used to spend sleepless nights feeling uneasy and disgusted with herself. Sometimes, she broke down in front of Vishal, but he never understood the issue. Slowly, Pia began to realize it was unfair of her to expect that Vishal would understand what she was going through, since she didn't understand it herself.

The board and the entrance examinations came and went, and throughout, Pia didn't think it would be fair to bug Vishal with her problems. Maybe, it was all her fault, maybe she was thinking too much. But she had tried everything to push it away from her head. It did not work. She often found herself crying in the middle of the night.

The intimacy slowly died out from their relationship since Pia was not very good at hiding her feelings. Vishal had started to get a little cold and she didn't really blame him since she understood that he had his needs too. Though she always wished he understood her better. Time passed and things got better . . . but only to get worse.

Her world crashed when Vishal told her that he would be doing his graduation from Bangalore. They had not discussed it at length before, but Pia always thought it was a given that they would stay in Delhi and study together, even if it meant going to different colleges. There had been fights between them and Vishal had argued that it was what his parents wanted and he had no control over it.

They fought, they cried, they bickered, and they broke up. Only to come together and promise each other that they would be together for the rest of their lives. Pia believed the conviction in his eyes, the touch of his hands, and the warmth of his hug, which told her that they would be together, no matter what, come hell or high water.

Despite the promises, despite the days they had spent wrapped up in each other, they started to change; the people who said those words of togetherness had started to change. By the time Pia shifted to Nagpur, their lives were held together by a thin, tenuous thread of love that could have snapped any moment. That moment came when Vishal landed in Bangalore and immersed himself in a new life, while Pia still struggled to keep it going.

In the days of utter despair that followed, she found comfort in the friendly smile and the nerdish—even childish—demeanour of one who looked like a friend sent from above. Tanmay. The name itself started to bring a tiny glimmer of hope, a spike of joy in an otherwise dead and hopeless heart. Torn between the ghosts of her past and the promise of a new future, she has spent the last few days crying her eyes out. Vishal has slowly started to ignore her calls, turn a deaf ear to her complaints—even when they are completely justified—and has asked her to move on.

Pia looks at her reflection in the mirror and a question keeps haunting her, 'How did we get here?'

Chapter Twenty

The News

My phone rings loudly. At first, I think I am dreaming, but then I open my eyes and realize that it's not a dream. Pia looks at me with confused eyes. I turn to look at the clock which says 3:45 a.m.

'Who's it?' she murmurs, half asleep.

'Unknown number,' I say and take the call, hoping it's a wrong number. 'Hello?' I croak into the speaker.

'Hello? Is this Niharika?' a male voice speaks frantically.

'Yes. May I know who this is?' I ask. My heartbeat increases, just by hearing the tone of the voice. *Something bad has happened.*

'Niharika, this is Mandar. Listen, I need to tell you something—there has been an accident . . . a bike accident on the highway outside the college. Tanmay . . . he is seriously hurt.'

'*WHAT?* When? And . . . how? Bike accident? Tanmay doesn't drive a bike! Where is he?' I shoot out an array of questions at him, barely breathing. I see Pia sit up on her bed.

'It happened a couple of hours ago. Someone took them to the hospital as soon as it happened. We got to know about it and rushed to the hospital too . . .'

'But you weren't with him? I thought he was with you!'

'He was. But then he left for his hostel. And we heard about the accident shortly after. They were on their way back . . .' Mandar explains.

'How . . . how is he?' I ask what I have been dreading the most.

'They are not saying anything yet. He is in the ICU . . . in a critical condition . . . I thought I should let you know.'

'Which hospital?'

'City Hospital,' he replies.

I hang up the call and look at Pia. I am too numb to think clearly.

'Niharika? What is it? Who was that? What happened?' Pia shakes me and asks.

'Tanmay . . . we have to go to the hospital,' I whisper.

'*What?* What happened? Is he okay?'

'Let's go,' I say, as tears overflow from my eyes. Pia's looks at me in sheer horror.

We run.

~

Forty minutes later, we find ourselves outside the hospital. The journey from our room to the gate of the hospital has been hellish. After I told Pia about the accident, we rushed out of our rooms, only to get stopped at the hostel gate. The guard there refused to let us through. We pleaded, we begged, we shouted—nothing worked. When the warden came out, we had to beg her to let us go. In the end, she agreed to, but only if she came with us. To think that she doubted that we were playing her, when in reality, our friend was dying in a hospital, was sickening.

Once in the car, the warden shot questions at us, to which we turned a deaf ear. Pia looked like she would collapse any second. All the blood had left her face and she looked corpse-white. I, on the other hand, had trouble breathing. While

I was already scared shitless about Tanmay, I also had another impending fear . . . *What if Karthik was in the accident too?*

Even in my semi-dazed condition, I distinctly remembered Mandar saying, 'Someone took *them* to the hospital . . .' And knowing about the fascination Tanmay has for Karthik's bike, I can only imagine that it was Karthik's bike that was in the accident. *Who was driving? Does Tanmay even know how to drive that monster of a bike?* There was complete silence in the car, once the warden realized that we weren't exactly in a chatty mood.

Pia had sat in the car, dazed, shocked and staring out of the window blankly. My heartbeat had reached a new high. I could not talk to Pia because she was already on the brink of tears. She seemed to be in shock. Gruesome images flooded my head and I felt extremely agitated. I had closed my eyes and tried to shut out everything. It had not helped. The journey brought me to the brink of a cardiac arrest. I felt as though I was dying.

As soon as the car stops at the hospital gate, Pia and I jump out and start running towards the building. We ask at the reception and take the elevator to the wrong floor. We run three flights of stairs downwards to get to the Emergency floor. We look around and we know that we are at the right place; the whole football team is loitering around here. We spot a door, which says ICU and has a red light above it. We run to it, breathing heavily, sweating profusely, looking like shit.

'Is he in here . . . ?' I ask a guy sitting with his head sunk in his hands. He looks vaguely familiar and his dirtied clothes confirm that he is someone from the football team. He nods.

Pia, who is still clutching my right arm, has started crying a little. We try to peep inside, but cannot see anything. There are drawn curtains on the glass door. I let out a deep, troubled breath and turn around.

'What is going on?' I ask Mandar, who comes running from somewhere and is panting. His eyes look bloodshot, and it is obvious that he is very drunk. But his eyes have a strange alertness too, like someone who is forced to be in his senses, even after consuming barrels of alcohol. Anyone would be shaken back to his senses, by such horrific news.

'Did you see him? Was he hurt really badly?' Pia asks, before Mandar has a chance to answer.

'I . . . his head was bleeding and looked pretty bad . . . I mean—I'm sure he will be okay. I just . . . he wasn't wearing a helmet . . .' Mandar says. He turns to me and tells me that Tanmay's bike hit a divider while he was on his way back to his hostel. He was drunk and must have been driving really fast.

'What are the doctors saying?' I ask. Pia is holding my hand very tightly and has dug her head into my shoulder. I wish I could tell her it will all be okay.

'They are not saying much . . . they are operating, and will take time to figure out the actual damage,' Mandar says.

'They are *operating*? He's into an operation? What kind of operation? Do his parents know yet? Who signed the papers?' I freak out.

'I don't know! Someone from the team, maybe. There was a lot of blood loss . . . they needed to take care of it immediately . . .'

'I . . . this is just so . . .' I try to put it in words, but nothing comes out. My head is filled with a zillion different questions. And the only one who can provide some of the answers is a guy we are not very fond of—the football captain. I look up at Mandar again. I don't know if he's a good person or not, but he certainly does look very concerned about Tanmay right now. That's good enough for me. I take a deep breath to calm myself. It doesn't work. 'I didn't even know Tanmay knew how to drive a bike . . . whose bike was it? Who was with him?' I ask slowly, already dreading the response.

'It was Karthik's bike. But I guess Tanmay was driving . . .' Mandar says and my mind blanks out. 'Don't know why anyone would drive that bike . . . it's a piece of junk. The thing is a bloody death-trap . . .'

Tanmay *and* Karthik. I take support of the wall, as my knees suddenly feel too weak. My breathing gets ragged, as images of Karthik flash through my head. That first night in the mess, when I heard his voice and tried to look at him, using an old, scratched steel plate. The second time in the canteen, when he saved me and Tanmay from that beast Chetan and his cronies. The guy I stole glances at that day at McDonald's, the football match, when he dazzled the entire college, that bike ride with him to have chai at a roadside stall. And then the fights—first for making Tanmay drink and then for interfering between me and Akshat. Last time I met him was at the football field, when he had wanted to say something, but I had not given him a chance, and left him there, waiting for me to turn back.

It suddenly hits me that if something happens to him . . . I did not even give him a chance to say what he wanted to say. My mouth turns very dry and my throat feels parched. I can't think clearly. But I have to know . . .

'How is he? Karthik . . . ?' I manage to whisper.

Mandar looks at me, with a puzzled expression on his face. 'Karthik? He was not in the accident.'

'What? But you said it was Karthik's bike Tanmay was driving . . . ?'

'Yes, it was his bike. But Tanmay had it with him before he got to the party. Karthik was not there,' he explains. He tells me that Karthik apparently had let Tanmay take his bike for the night, since he did so well in the match yesterday. A little after midnight, Tanmay had left with another guy—Ratul,

another player from the football team—and they got the news
of the accident shortly after that.

I let out a sigh of relief. *Karthik is okay*. But almost instantly,
another emotion overtakes me. *Fury*. Why does Karthik
not realize what he is doing to Tanmay? I can forgive him
for trying to interfere with mine and Akshat's matters, but
I cannot tolerate him harming Tanmay. First he teaches him
to drink and now the bike? He knew Tanmay would be
drunk at the party, and he still let him have that bike for
the night? How can he be so careless? If something happens
to Tanmay . . .

'How is that other guy? Ratul . . .?' I ask meekly.

'He is in the ICU too.'

Pia can't listen to any more of it and pulls me away.
I make her sit with me on one of those steel benches lining
the hospital walls. She clutches me tight and keeps asking
me whether Tanmay will be all right.

'He will be okay,' I keep whispering in her ears as she
keeps on crying. After an hour, tired, she goes off to sleep. As
a few more hours pass and the doctors finish their operation,
they come out and one of them walks towards us. It is 8.30
in the morning. Everyone, except Mandar, another player,
Pia and I, have left. Pia wakes up with a jerk and we all
get up and huddle around the doctor, praying silently for
good news.

'How is he, doctor?' Mandar asks.

'We are trying our best, but he is still critical. There has
been some severe head injuries and he has lost too much
blood,' the doctor says.

'But he is going to be okay, right?' Pia asks.

'We can't say anything now. We are thinking about how to
proceed and may need to go in for a surgery immediately . . .'

'*Again?*' Pia asks.

'But wasn't he in an operation just now?' I ask.

'Yes, but we are talking about major surgery here,' the doctor says and looks at us seriously. 'Isn't there an adult here? His parents? Or guardians? In case we decide to perform the surgery, we will need someone to give us a go-ahead . . .'

'His parents will be here soon,' Mandar says.

'Good. We'll be back in a while and let you know what we think is the best way to handle this from here. Ask his parents to be here soon,' the doctor says and leaves.

'Tanmay's parents are coming? You told them about the accident?' I turn to Mandar and ask, as soon as the doctor is out of sight. I had known that the accident was serious, but until this moment I had been thinking that Tanmay will be all right soon. The words 'surgery' and 'parents' now make me realize how much I have been underestimating the turn of events.

'Yes, it looked serious, so we informed them immediately. They must be about to reach anytime now,' Mandar says. 'I don't know how to answer their questions . . .'

'It will be better if we handle all that. They might see you and blame you for it, since you were the ones he went out with,' I suggest.

'Blame *us*? They should blame that asshole—Karthik. It was *his* bike. Why did he even have to give Tanmay his bike? He knew we were going to get drunk. That piece of junk. Drunk or not drunk, anyone could be in an accident in that shitty bike.'

'Let's not think about all that now. You can go home. I am sure we can manage his parents,' I say. After a little more discussion, I convince them to go home. They give me the numbers of Tanmay's parents and leave. I am left in the hospital and my mind goes back to what Mandar just said. It was Karthik's fault. He is right in more senses than he knew himself. Had he not taken Tanmay drinking out on the day they had first won, this would not have happened. Had he not given Tanmay the bike, this wouldn't have happened. Had he not helped Tanmay make it to the team, none of this would have happened . . .

My mind battles with images of Tanmay—smiling, adjusting his funny spectacles and then to an image of him confined to a bed with severe head injuries and multiple broken bones. They do not let us see him, and I dread the moment when we will eventually have to. I don't think I can bear seeing him in the condition that he is in. I close my eyes and pray for that cute smiling face.

I swear to God that if anything happens to him, I will kill Karthik.

Chapter Twenty-one

The Last Resort

I stare at his mother, as she hides her face in her husband's shoulder and cries. They are sitting on the benches right opposite to where I am. Her sobs are heart-breaking, and I feel utterly helpless. I have no idea what to do. I cannot possibly go to her and tell her that it is all going to be okay. As much as I wish that it was true, it isn't, yet. We don't know yet.

I turn to Pia, who is sitting on my right. She looks at me, and tears immediately fill both our eyes. We look away. We cannot cry; we have to be strong . . . or at least pretend to be so. We need to show some strength in front of Tanmay's parents. They are already devastated, and we don't want to add to that. I cannot even begin to imagine what they must be going through.

They arrived here at the hospital about a couple of hours ago, around noon. As soon as they came, they wanted to go in and see Tanmay, but the nurses did not let them in. That's when I realized that the distraught mother screaming for her son was Tanmay's mother, and the man trying to fake strength while tears threatened to overflow his eyes any minute was Tanmay's father. His mother was dressed in an old, dull saree with its *pallu* covering her head and his father was wearing a soiled pale-yellow shirt, black trousers that were torn at the

ankle and worn-out rubber sandals. They both looked equally
disturbed and confused. It had taken me a lot of courage to
go to them and explain everything.

Pia was of no help. Even though I had asked her to keep
a check on her tears, she had started crying almost as soon
as Tanmay's mother had first looked up at us. I had then
explained the whole situation to Tanmay's parents and as soon
as I told them about the possible major brain surgery, they
dissolved into tears again, and I was left with an overpowering
feeling of despair. The sadness I had felt last night was nothing
compared to what I felt then.

Tanmay was their only son. They have always lived in a
small town and his father had worked very hard to send
Tanmay to this college. They had nursed a lot of dreams for
him. He is probably what matters to them above everything.
The possibility of losing him to a careless bike accident
seemed way too bizarre. This is not something he deserves.
This is not something anyone deserves.

After sitting with them for a while, trying to console them
with words we did not completely believe in ourselves, we
took seats a little away from them. They did not look too
comfortable with us around. I feel Pia's hand slowly creep
up and hold mine. I look up at her to see that she is staring
at a group of doctors coming our way. I recognize one
of them as the one we talked to in the morning. We get
up hurriedly.

'Dr Ahuja . . .' Pia whispers, asking a zillion questions with
her eyes, without uttering a word.

The doctor looks at us apologetically. 'You go on, I'll be
there in a short while,' he says to the rest of his team, which
promptly leaves. 'His parents?' he asks.

As soon as Tanmay's parents join us, Dr Ahuja announces
the surgery. 'Due to the impact, he has suffered from
intracranial injury. In simpler terms, we call it TBI—*Traumatic*

Brain Injury. The severity is somewhere between *moderate* to *severe.* His intracranial pressure is very high at the moment, which suggests cerebral haemorrhage. The CT scan strongly suggests so. We need to perform a medical procedure called *decompressive craniectomy.*'

'A *what*?' Pia asks. From the little experience that I have with medical terms, I can tell that the unpronounceable term cannot suggest something good.

'A decompressive craniectomy. It is a neurosurgical procedure. We will remove a part of his skull. There is too much swelling in his brain and not enough space, so that is causing squeezing. We need to take out a part of his skull to provide room for—'

'Doctor, please,' I say to stop him from describing more. I cannot understand half of what he is saying and the horrified expressions on Tanmay's parents' faces tell me that Dr Ahuja is scaring them. I thank God that he is speaking in English. If they are so scared just by the way the doctor is telling us everything, I do not even want to think what they might have gone through if they knew what these doctors are about to do to their son. 'Just do whatever you think is necessary and tell us what we need to do.'

Dr Ahuja motions at Tanmay's parents and says, 'They need to sign the documents. Actually, this is a complicated procedure and is performed only as a last resort. So we need special permission from them to go ahead.'

'What do you mean *complicated*?' Pia asks. 'It is not safe? I mean—is he . . . in danger of . . .?'

'I cannot say right now. We need this surgery,' Dr Ahuja says.

'But . . . but you said that it is used only as a *last resort*,' I say, trying to fight my fear as a shiver runs up my spine.

The doctor pauses and meets our eyes, almost pityingly. We brace ourselves. He turns to look at Tanmay's parents, then back to us. He takes a deep breath and releases it slowly, before he says what we have been dreading all this while.

'This is the last resort.'

~

'Here, Uncle,' Mandar says to Tanmay's father, pointing to the area where he has to sign. Uncle signs the documents with a shaky hand.

As soon as we got the news about the procedure Tanmay is supposed to undergo—*decompressive craniectomy*—we informed people at the college about it, and the entire football team was here in no time. Still hung-over by last night's drinking and the shock of the news, they all looked like a bunch of confused lunatics, roaming around the floor, trying to grasp what was going on and what is going to happen next. I could see that the gravity of the situation had finally sunk into their heads. Till last night, it was just another bike accident, by someone who got drunk after the celebration of winning a football match. Now, it is a matter of life and death.

As soon as the papers are signed, the arrangements for the operation start. We see nurses and compounders rush around the corridors, talking hurriedly to each other, and all this makes us panic even more. Tanmay's mother has finally ceased crying, and we sit with her, trying to maintain outward calm. We wonder if she's trying to do exactly the same thing.

Half an hour later, the operation theatre is all set and we see the door of the ICU open. The next moment, two compounders come out, pulling the stretcher with them. My heart stops.

'Aunty, stop,' I shriek when I see her rush towards Tanmay. I know that it is not going to be a pretty sight. I don't want her to see it. But she doesn't listen and keeps running towards the stretcher. I rush after her, Pia following suit.

The image of what we see next will never leave my mind.

Tanmay's body is covered with a white sheet up to his chest.
I can see blood—lots of it—seeping out from under it and
staining the sheets. The blood looks fresh and the sight is
very scary. But this does not even come close to the scare
I get when I see what is there above his chest. There are tiny
pools of semi-dry blood in the concave portions of his neck.
And his face . . . it is completely disfigured. His whole head
has swollen up to twice its size and is the deepest shade of
red, teamed with the sick blue-green colour of blood clots.
Had I not known that it is him, I would not have believed
it was the same person. His battered face brings a fresh lot
of tears in my eyes.

Aunty pauses, clearly unable to move towards her own son.
Pia takes a step back. No matter how much she tries to deny
it, it's very clear to me that she loves Tanmay with all her
heart. The sight in front of us is unbearable. I have known all
along that his condition is serious, but still, with each thing
that happens, the situation becomes even more difficult for me
to handle. I pull Aunty and Pia back with me, and we stand
a little distance away and see the paramedical staff members
take Tanmay away to another operation theatre. My knees
give up, and I take a seat on the bench, breathing heavily,
my forehead moist with drops of sweat. It's disheartening to
see that even Uncle can't hold back his tears this time, as
he holds Aunty.

I can't take it any more. I suddenly feel the need to get
away from it all. 'Take care of her,' I whisper to Pia, although
I doubt she heard me. I get up and walk down the flight
of stairs, trying to find my way out of the hospital. After
getting lost a few times, I finally see the huge glass doors of
the hospital. I run out and into the parking lot, my
breathing erratic.

Once alone, I let go of the tears I have been holding back
since forever. Those sobs and silent tears I had been letting

out ever since I got the news of the accident were far from satisfying. I needed a good cry, but I couldn't let go with Tanmay's parents and Pia around. Now, in the almost-deserted parking lot, I let them fall. I slide down to the ground and lean against a car, as tears shake my body uncontrollably.

I could see it in the doctor's eyes, that we have little or no hope here. And that is something that just cannot settle down easily. I cannot believe that something like this is actually happening to me. To Pia. To Tanmay's parents. The thought of his parents brings tears to my eyes again. This is just so very unfair. What if he . . . ?

I cannot imagine my life without him. Ever since I came to Nagpur, he has been my friend. He has been one of the very few real friends I have ever had. The selfless way in which he takes care of me, those sweet moments when he blushes and looks away when I tease him by mentioning Pia, the sweet shy guy. And the aggressive football player, the new heartthrob of the college . . . what did he ever do to deserve this? What did his parents do to deserve this?

Between sobs, I try to find out as much as I can about the operation he is going through by using Google on my phone. What comes up is far from encouraging. Two million people suffer from TBI every year, out of which approximately 1,00,000 people die, 5,00,000 more are permanently disabled and 80,000 people experience the onset of long-term disability following a severe brain injury annually. My whole body shakes in terror. When I picture Tanmay—the Tanmay I saw this morning, heavily bandaged, swollen, bleeding, wounded—I cannot help but feel defeated. How can someone whose condition looked as bad as his, come out of such a major injury?

I lose track of the time I spend here, crying my heart out. There is nothing else I can do. I feel completely helpless. Every now and then, I control the volume of my wails, when I hear people move around in the parking lot, where

I sit hidden. My phone keeps vibrating in my pocket, and I finally take it out.

'Yes, Pia?' I ask, my heartbeat elevating even more. 'Is the operation done?'

'Where are you, Niharika? Why were you not taking my calls? I was worried—' Pia's hassled voice says.

'I'm okay. Just outside. Is Tanmay . . .? The operation . . .?'

'It's still going on. We're waiting outside. Please come back . . . Aunty is not feeling well . . .'

'Okay. I'll be there in a minute,' I say and hang up. I wipe away my tears and clear my throat before I get up. I dust myself and make my way back to the hospital entrance.

'Niharika,' someone says into my ears from behind me. I jerk away, startled.

'K-Karthik . . .' I breathe out. 'What the hell do you think you are doing here?'

'I just got to know about what happened. So I came to see *him* . . .'

'Oh. You must be talking about my best friend, right? The short, sweet guy with nerdy spectacles and a smile on his face? The guy who used to worship you and respect you more than anything else in the world? Guess what—that guy is gone. You killed him.'

'*What?*' Karthik asks. 'What are you saying?'

'What I am saying is that you destroyed him. He is in an operation right now with very, very bleak chances of coming out alive. And if he does, he will be a . . . a vegetable all his life. Thanks to you, he will never be the same,' I say. I push my cell phone into his face. 'Here—this is what Wikipedia has to say about Traumatic Brain Injury. Now, as it says here, the treatment starts in the ICU, followed by a neurosurgical ward. That's where Tanmay is *right now*. And do you know what happens after this? *The patient dies.* And even if he somehow magically comes out alive, he becomes a *vegetable*.

Coma, brain death, multiple organ failure . . . and what–not.
I cannot even pronounce half of them, let alone know what
they mean.'

'But Niharika . . . please calm down. We cannot be so
negative. Let's go inside—'

'And do what? Go inside and tell his parents that he
will be okay when it's actually a lie? Do you want me to
do that?'

'I don't mean . . . I am just saying that what has happened
has happened . . .' Karthik says.

'And it has happened *because of you*!'

'I was not even there! How can this be my fault?'

'I'll tell you how this is your fault. You taught him to
drink. You taught him to drive a bike, hell, you even gave
him that death trap of a bike to drive, even when you *knew*
he was going to get drunk!' I let out angrily.

'But he said he won't drink.'

'Maybe he lied. Maybe you taught him that too.'

'Don't be so unreasonable—' Karthik tries to say something
but I cut him off mid-sentence furiously.

'Shut the hell up. I don't want to hear another word from
you. Go away . . . just leave. And never come back. I don't
want to see your face again. Go drive a cool bike and get
a cool hairstyle and work out in the gym and woo girls or
whatever it is you do. Just stay the hell away from me and
my friends. Do you understand?' I shout out, losing all my
calm and patience.

He nods, lighting up a cigarette.

'And another thing—if something happens to Tanmay, please
just know that it's *you* who killed him,' I say and leave.

Chapter Twenty-two

Hope

'Ratul is out of danger,' Mandar tells me as soon as I get back in.

'Ratul?' I ask.

'The other guy in the accident with Tanmay. He is all right now. He has two broken bones in his thigh, and a fracture in his ribs, but the doctors say that he is going to be okay. The fracture in the rib had punctured his lung and was causing internal bleeding or something . . . but he is out of danger now.'

'Where is he?'

Mandar motions to a ward, to my right. I see Pia and Tanmay's mother huddled around the ward's door, peeping in. I walk up to them.

'See? He is okay,' Aunty says happily. 'My Tanmay will be all right too . . . once the operation is done . . .'

I smile a painful constricted smile and nod. What I don't tell her is that the damage her son's body has endured is five times in comparison to Ratul's. I don't want to wipe out her smile. It suits her. I notice that Pia is holding Aunty's hand tightly, as she stares inside Ratul's ward. I am glad that she has been with her all this while, when I was busy losing all hope and crying my heart out.

'The operation? Is it still . . . ?' I ask Pia.

'Yes,' she nods. 'It's still going on. It's been three hours.'

I nod silently and the mood changes back to sombre. We sit outside the neurosurgical ward, and fix our eyes on the small red light above its doors. With every minute that passes, we get more and more nervous. I shift in my seat uncomfortably. I want the wait to be over soon . . . and Tanmay to be okay. If we go by what I read about TBI on the internet and what I said to Karthik, I realize that the chances are not in our favour, but I have to think positive. In my heart, I feel—I *know*—that he is going to be okay. But even if he comes out of this alive . . .

Grotesque images of a paralysed Tanmay flash through my head. The best-case scenario right now is—the operation will be successful and Tanmay will recover over a period of a few months. I shudder to think how he would feel when he gets to know that he won't be able to play in the football league's final match. He would be heartbroken. But never mind. There will be another tournament next year. I am sure he will steal the show again.

Uncle comes back and sits next to Aunty. They begin to talk softly amongst themselves. It is nice to see that they are not crying any more. Things are already looking up. But still, whenever that image of Tanmay in the stretcher comes into my head . . .

'Do you think he will be okay?' Pia asks softly. She looks very haggard, and I suppose I look the same. 'I certainly hope so.'

'But what do you think? What does your heart say?'

'That he will be up and about in a few weeks,' I smile at the picture that thought creates in my head. Pia smiles too. I look at her carefully . . . and say the first thing that comes to my head. 'You love him, don't you?'

'What? Love? No! What are you talking about?' I can tell that she is taken by surprise. I can also tell that she is very much in love with Tanmay. There is no way that she doesn't realize it, she is just not willing to acknowledge it to herself or anyone else.

'You do.'

'I don't. He's a very good friend . . . and I really like him . . . but I don't . . . I have a boyfriend . . . I love Vishal . . .' Pia keeps whispering disconnected half-sentences for a while.

I wonder when she will realize that she does not love Vishal. Her delusion is almost annoying. She belongs with Tanmay. They are perfect together, almost custom-made. They will be the cutest couple on the planet. I hope she realizes that soon. But that should be the least of my worries right now. I know she will one day finally realize that she loves Tanmay . . . but right now, I just pray that Tanmay will be okay.

Just as I look up, I see a group of doctors and paramedical staff leave the ward where Tanmay's operation had been going on. We get up with a jerk and rush towards them. But strangely, they do not even look at us. They just make their way hurriedly towards the elevator. Before we can understand what is happening, they have already left the floor. I turn back towards Tanmay's ward and see Dr Ahuja come out of it, his cell phone stuck to his ear, as he shoots directions to someone on it.

'. . . right now. No! 10 ml. And not intramuscular, administer it intravenously. I'll be there in a minute,' he says and hangs up to find us surrounding him.

'Doctor! Is he okay? Can we see him?' Aunty asks, looking up at him with eyes full of hope and fear. Mostly fear.

'Is the operation over? Was it . . . was it successful?' Uncle asks.

Dr Ahuja looks at the five pairs of eyes looking up at him, and says, 'Yes, the operation is over. You can see him now . . . There is a nurse inside to guide you with that. Now if you'll excuse me, I have to be somewhere . . . there's an emergency. I'll meet you later, as soon as I am done with that. Sorry.'

He walks off before we even get a chance to ask anything else. But we hardly care! He said that we can see him. What can that mean? That Tanmay is out of danger! And probably conscious too. We charge into the neurosurgical ward. The nurse is startled to see us at first but we explain that we have the doctor's permission and she relents, though she keeps murmuring something about it not being a place where visitors are allowed to enter. We hardly care about that either.

We put on those ridiculous white coats, masks and caps and sanitize our hands before pulling aside the curtains and going in. The moment I look at him . . . I feel the breath being knocked out of my body. It is like somebody punched me hard in my gut.

It doesn't seem like Tanmay is any better than he was the last time I saw him. If anything, his head is even more swollen and of a colour so deeply red that it looks almost black. All kinds of equipment beep and blink tiny red lights all around the ward. That is the only sound we can hear. Everything else is absolutely still.

Especially Tanmay.

I can see the medical ventilator, but I can't see his chest rise and fall—he doesn't seem to be breathing. If not for the ECG device, I would have thought . . .

I cannot take my eyes off him. He lies here, in front of me, in complete tranquillity. It scares me no end. What did the doctor mean? I suddenly want to rush to Dr Ahuja and ask him what is going on with Tanmay. To think of it now, we must have completely misinterpreted the meaning of what he had said. He had not said that Tanmay is out of danger.

'*Yes, the operation is over.*' He never said that the operation was successful.

'*You can see him now.*' He never said that Tanmay was conscious.

'*Sorry.*' What else could that word mean when a doctor says it after coming out of an operation theatre?

But Tanmay is not dead. He is very much alive. Artificially supported by every imaginable medical device, yes, but alive nonetheless. Then why are there no doctors around? Maybe . . . maybe the doctors operating on Tanmay, including Dr Ahuja, realized that he cannot be saved. Maybe that's why they left the ward, to handle another emergency, saving someone else's life . . . someone who has a better chance at survival.

My breathing accelerates, as the gravity of the situation strikes me in full measure. *He is going to die.* There is no other explanation. No false hope. No fooling myself and others with a fake positive attitude and forced optimism. I cannot breathe any more. I choke on my tears. My heartbeat elevates to such a level that I feel like it is going to explode out of my chest. My knees give in and I fall to the floor.

I look at Uncle and Aunty. They are both looking at Tanmay with pale faces. It is clear that reality has dawned upon them too. Pia looks like a zombie. She slips down on the floor next to me and digs her head into my shoulder. I have no words to console her.

I will never forget Aunty's wails. She keeps repeating the same sentence over and over again. 'No. Not my son. Not my Tanmay. This cannot happen. This *cannot* happen.' I don't have the strength to even go close to her and . . . I just have no idea what to say to her.

But Uncle still doesn't give up hope. 'He is still alive. There still might be some hope. He still might open his eyes . . .' he keeps saying. It kills me to see him so hopeless, still so hopeful. Maybe he has no other option. Maybe Tanmay is his only option.

Fifteen minutes later, Tanmay's heart stops beating.

Chapter Twenty-three

Darkness

The next few days pass by in a daze. I don't eat, think or even breathe sometimes. I see everything, but comprehend nothing. I see people coming and going. I see Tanmay's parents crying, wailing, and saying things that make everyone cry. Every time a new relative walks in, a fresh lot of tears make their way into their eyes. I hear only the constant crying. But there is nothing anyone can do to lessen their misery.

There are times when I sit and feel that Tanmay is standing right behind me, and will tap my shoulder any second. It feels like I have just talked to him about his matches. Like he is still around, but he is not. It's hard to accept that he is not. Every time I wake up after a troubled sleep, with senseless, confusing dreams, I feel like all of it has never happened. But then I see Pia, lying in her bed, her pillow soaked with tears . . . and I realize that the nightmares have actually happened.

The one thing I remember distinctly is the moment when Tanmay's uncle and aunt arrived, along with their son, Tanmay's cousin. The boy, about three years younger to us, was a spitting image of Tanmay. The exact same features, the cute smile, the stupid hair . . . even the same nerdy glasses. When he spoke, his voice sounded like Tanmay's too. I could not bear to look at him for more than a few seconds. It was

way too painful. Aunty held him close to her and cried her
heart out . . . he was probably the closest to her after her
own son. Her own *dead* son.

Seeing Aunty cry was probably the most difficult thing
I have ever done in my life. No mother should have to face
this. Losing a child is the worst thing that can ever happen
to a woman. If I am this distraught by the death of a friend
whom I met only recently, I cannot even begin to imagine
what his parents must be going through. The first few hours
after Tanmay passed away were the hardest. Even though
I was in no condition to, I had to try and console his parents.
I had no words that could help . . . I doubted *anything* could
have helped. So I just held Aunty and cried softly, as her
body dissolved into convulsions and her wails echoed in my
head—loud and very painful.

After the autopsy, we were allowed to see him. His relatives
arranged for a big vehicle to take him back to their home
town safely. When I saw his . . . *body*, I broke down worse
than ever. I felt a strong jolt. It was like an electric current
shot through my body. It felt like I was floating, away from
everything around me, in some other world, where it's just
me and . . . him—*his body*. How did all of this happen? One
day, I see him as the best footballer on the college field, and
a couple of days later, I see whatever is left of his dead body
wrapped in white cloth, covering everything but his disfigured
face? The cute face, now without the specs, with tiny cotton
balls stuffed up his nose. I have never cried harder. And they
say God exists.

Soon after, Tanmay's parents took his body back to their
home town for the funeral. As soon as they left, there was an
emptiness all around us. They left a void behind them . . . a
void that will never be filled. Even though it had been just
twenty-four hours since the accident, it already felt like a

very long time. Those twenty-four hours . . . they were very long and very exhausting. It felt like we had been waiting and praying for Tanmay to get well soon for ages.

And once he . . . *left*, and his parents took his body away, everything began to seem like a bad dream. I could not believe that at the same time a few days ago, I was on my way back to the hostel from Tanmay's football match. The match he had heroically won. The match Pia had been panicking to be there for. The cheers of *'TANMAY! TANMAY! TANMAY! TANMAY!'* were still in my head. Just that it is never going to happen for real again.

Now, it has been a week since he . . . passed away. It feels weird, the term *passed away*. I still cannot believe what has happened. It feels like we are just sleeping and will wake up to everything being normal once again. But I know that it is never going to happen. Over the last few days, I have realized what has happened, and it has finally settled in—*he is never coming back.*

I spent my entire week either sitting in a corner of my room, wrapping my arms around my knees and pulling them close to me as an armour, or lying down on my back in my bed, staring absently at the ceiling. There has been a constant nagging pain at the back of my head. I haven't slept for more than a couple of hours continuously. Pia has slept even less. Seeing her cry is very painful. She just sits with me, in our room—dark room, actually, with the curtains drawn and the lights off—and keeps crying.

I have not seen her with dry eyes even for a single second; they are constantly filled with tears. She has been staring at his pictures all week. And that is probably the worst thing someone can do. The photographs bring back memories too vividly. Every crinkle of his nose, the specs that rest on his nose a little crookedly, the shy smile . . . everything with double the impact. But she never listens to me when I ask her to stop doing this to herself. Her mourning is painful just to see. Tanmay's death has affected her way worse than I had first thought.

No matter how much she denies it, I can see that she loved Tanmay. In the past week, I have seen her talk to Vishal on the phone just once. She said she needed time to get over this and deal with the pain. But that's not what people in love do. They do not take breaks and lock themselves in alone to deal with their pain. They share it. More than ever, they want to be together to be able to face it. Pia trying to shut him out shows what she has been fighting for a long time—she does not love Vishal. He probably is not even someone who deserves to be loved, anyway. But she never says anything bad about him.

Not knowing what to do, fed up of the darkness, I pick up my phone, and call Simran. She has been calling me every couple of hours, to check up on me. But I rarely take her calls. I had not been in the frame of mind to talk.

'Hello?' she answers the phone.

'Hi Simran,' I say.

'How are you, Niharika? Is Pia okay?'

'I am okay,' I say and look at Pia, who is lying on her bed with her face dug deep into her pillow. Her body shakes and I realize that she is crying. She is not fine at all. 'Pia is fine too.'

'Listen—just come home. Come to Jaipur for a few days. I'll come too. We will spend some time together and it will take your mind off . . . everything that has happened. You need a break. A change of scenery will do you good.'

'I can't leave her here alone. She needs me.'

'So bring her too. I'm sure Pia would want to visit. We all can have fun. I have heard so much about her from you. I am looking forward to seeing her. You both can take some time off and relax,' Simran says in a desperate attempt to cheer me up. It doesn't help. The thought of *having fun* and *relaxing* seems almost funny, given the present situation.

'We have exams in a few days. We cannot just leave . . .'

There is a short pause, after which she says, 'Do you want me to come there for some time? I can come and stay with you, you know? Just to take care that . . . you are doing well. Mom worries about you . . . I am not supposed to tell you this, but she cries on the phone every day. First the news of Tanmay passing away, now your condition . . .'

'I know, Simran. But trust me—I will be okay. You cannot expect such a thing to become all right overnight. Give me some time.'

'Let me come there and help you through this? I know it needs time, but let me be with you in that time. We will handle this together,' she says. I can hear her pleading tone, but I don't want to bother her or Mom with this.

'I am fine! I can take care of myself. I do not need anyone.'

'You do. Look at yourself. Do you even eat? Take a shower? Step out of your room? You are *not* taking care of yourself. You need someone to be there to take care of you. And I don't mind doing that. I prefer being with you and seeing you cry, as opposed to being here and wondering how you are doing.'

'I need to be alone,' I say.

'Don't be so selfish. We are all worried—'

'I am *not* being selfish! Is it too much to want to be left alone for some time? You have no idea what I am going through. And trust me—no one and nothing can make it go away. It's *you* who is being selfish. You can't understand what it is that I am facing and just want to be here as if it is going to help.'

'Niharika, we just care about you. We worry about—' she tries to say something, but I don't let her.

'Stop it, Simran. You are worried about me just by knowing what has happened. *I* am the one who has seen it happen. It has happened *to* me. It was *my* friend who died. So just . . . please. Leave me alone. Let me be.'

I hang up before she can say anything else. I breathe heavily. I know that it was unfair of me to vent my frustration on her like that, but I could not help it. There is a storm raging inside me. What happened to Tanmay was not what he deserved. It was not his fault. It was just bloody wrong.

Karthik. He is the one whose fault it is. I sometimes feel like picking up an axe and bashing him up and showing the cocky bastard what pain is. I want to make him pay for his mistakes. But just blaming everything on Karthik doesn't help either. Even though it is he who began all this, he could not have foreseen such a major accident. I sometimes wonder what he must be going through, knowing that he was—to a major extent—responsible for someone's death. Does he sleep at nights? Can he, ever?

I did see him somewhere in the background a few days ago, when I was making my way back to my hostel from the mess. I don't know if it was him, neither did I turn around to find out. If I did, the urge to kill him would have overtaken me. Though I know I cannot actually kill another person, but I would at least have tried. And a scene in public was the last thing I wanted. Otherwise, I would have been happy to kill him. He doesn't deserve to live. Every breath of his is a curse, a curse that my friend had to pay for. I wish he didn't exist. I wish only the worst for him. I wish *he* had died.

Chapter Twenty-four

Don't Make the Same Mistake

'How was it?' I ask.

Pia shrugs, without saying anything. It was our last exam of the first semester. All of them took place within a span of twelve days, and we did nothing but study in those days.

Three days before the exams, I noticed that Pia hadn't slept in two days and had been studying.

'You should rest. Stop studying,' I said.

'Tanmay would have wanted us to study,' she said with glazed-over eyes. 'And to do well in the exams.'

I nodded. The resolve to complete everything that Tanmay would have wanted to do has taken over our minds completely. That's all that matters now. We studied hard for the exams and covered every single topic on the syllabus, because Tanmay would have taken care of that. We completed the neatest, most original and elaborate projects in class for every subject, because that would have been the case had we copied from Tanmay's work. No one could put together better project reports. We did every big and small thing he would have done, had he been alive.

We leave the department building and make our way to the hostel building. I spot Mandar at a distance and he shoots a sympathetic look at me. I am sure he misses Tanmay too. Who doesn't? There were scores of candles in front of Tanmay's picture kept in the canteen. Tanmay was loved, and always will be. Mandar walks away from us and he is joined by other teammates, all of whom are in their football jerseys. I wish Tanmay was walking with them, talking about how they would win the final match of the tournament. But that can never be now. Tanmay will never see ICE get the title home. He will not be there to strike the winning goal. He will not be carried on the shoulders of his teammates. He is gone. Far away from us and never coming back.

I would hate to see the team losing the final match in his absence, when he had worked so hard for it throughout the series. I know how badly Tanmay wanted that, but there is nothing we can do about it.

'Is something wrong? Did the exam not go well?' I ask Pia. She has been looking a little lost.

'I broke up with Vishal,' she tells me simply.

'What? Why?'

'I don't love him.'

'Pia, please—tell me what happened. I want to know. You don't look so good . . .' I say.

'There is nothing to tell. I just realized that I don't love him, and I told him that. He was more than happy to let me go.'

'No way,' I whisper, more to myself. I cannot believe that someone can let someone like Pia go just like that, without even putting up a fight. The guy has to be nuts.

'Yes way,' she says and smiles sadly.

'What is it, Pia? There is something very wrong, and I know that. Please tell me. I want to help. You don't have to be alone in this.'

Even though I plead and beg her, she does not say anything. I can see tears in her eyes, and they devastate me. What kind

of a person leaves his girlfriend in a time like this? Does he
not know what she is going through? How can someone
be so heartless? When I try and fail to get it out of her,
I finally give up. She is holding back tears, and my insistence
would only make it worse. We have already shed more than
enough tears in public.

We walk back to our room in silence. Our mid-semester
exams are over and we are scheduled to go home for the
semester break after three days, although we both still do not
feel like going home. We have decided to stay back for these
three days and watch the football final, just like we would
have, had Tanmay been playing.

What we are doing might not make sense to anyone else,
but we need to do *something* to keep us sane. Just sitting
around and thinking, remembering everything, was driving us
crazy. So we started to think of things Tanmay would have
wanted to do, and started doing them. Though we could
not find too many of those, we feel a lot calmer doing the
smallest of things. We hope that if he is looking down at us
from wherever he has gone to, he is smiling and is at peace.
We sit together and watch all the sci-fi movies that he had
wanted to see and begged us to watch. We do that on a loop,
over and over again. Just to feel him around.

We spend the rest of the day locked inside, not even going
out to have a meal. If we carry on like this, we will soon
starve ourselves to death. *Which is something Tanmay would
not have wanted*, the thought hits me. I cannot let the pain
of losing him overtake us. Pia needs me; she is even worse
off than I am and now she does not have either Tanmay or
Vishal to take care of her. She is my responsibility right now,
and I feel guilty about allowing her to destroy herself.

I turn to look at her, to ask her to come with me to have
dinner, only to see that she is weeping. She is sitting in the
furthest corner of her bed, and has her head dug into her

knees. I get up from my bed and slip in next to her, holding her tightly. I can feel how thin she has become. Since the past month, she has neither been going to the gym nor eating, and it shows. It saddens me.

'Hush. Relax, Pia. It's going to be okay,' I whisper.

'No, it's not,' she sobs. 'He is never coming back. He has left me forever . . .'

I know her well enough to know that she is talking about Tanmay, not Vishal. My heart aches for her. 'I am sorry. We cannot do anything about it . . .'

'But I miss him!' she cries out. 'I miss him so much! He did not have to go away. Not like this. Not so soon. Not ever. This is not fair. This is *so* not fair.'

'I know. But we cannot be like this. We have to stop thinking about . . . all that.'

'How can I? I have tried, but I just . . . can't. I can't get it out of my head. He . . . do you know how . . .'

'What, Pia?' I ask. She is trying to say something, but her sobs are making her break down.

'He was such a sweetheart . . . he loved me—I always knew, you always knew, everyone knew. But he never said it to me. He did not want to cause trouble between me and Vishal . . . so he never told me how much he . . . I didn't want to hurt him. But there was nothing I could do. I was with Vishal and I didn't want to . . .'

'I understand. It's not your fault.'

'It is! I have been so stupid! I do not love Vishal. Vishal does not love me either. I should have realized it way before. We have been out of love for years now. I don't even know why we were together till today. But because of the stupid feeling of obligation I had with Vishal, I hurt Tanmay so much. If only I had told him . . . just once . . .' she says, crying brokenly. She is having difficulty in breathing.

'Don't blame yourself,' I whisper, crying too. 'You could not have seen this coming.'

'I could not have stopped the accident, but I could have at least . . . he would have been so happy . . . Can you imagine the expression on his face, had I told him that I love him? I have known that I love him, for a long time now. If only I had just . . .'

'You should have,' I murmur.

'Yes, I should have! But I can't, now. He is gone. For always. I denied him something he probably wanted the most . . . and for what? That thing I had with Vishal that I forced myself to believe was love? You know—Vishal probably never loved me. I thought he would learn to love me over time. But it never happened. All he ever loved was my body. I don't know why I even bothered to make it work for so long. I should have just . . .'

I don't know what to say. I can understand her pain, and I know it goes way deeper than mine. I cannot even imagine what she must be going through. I picture Tanmay's reaction, had Pia told him about her feelings. I don't think even a zillion football victories could have matched that happiness. I feel sad for him, that he never got to know. If only . . .

'This is all my fault. Had I told him . . . he would not have been trying to stay away from me and not disrupt things between me and Vishal. He would have wanted to spend time with me. He would have come to me after that football match, not the stupid party. He would never have gotten drunk, never have driven that bike, never have had that accident, never have . . . *died*.'

'No! You can*not* blame yourself. It is not your fault. You could not have known. You could not have stopped it from happening . . .' I say and hug her tightly. The last thing I want right now is for Pia to think that it was her fault in any way. She is already hurting way too much.

I keep holding her, for hours. She keeps crying, and making me cry. The things she says tells me how broken she is from the inside. I wish I could do something to make it better. But when someone dies, there is nothing anyone can do to make it better for the ones close to him. All you can do is be there and make them realize that they are not alone, that someone is with them always, no matter what. I have learnt this first hand. And I would never wish something like this for anyone. No one deserves this kind of pain.

It is almost 2 a.m., and Pia has finally fallen asleep in my arms. I slowly shift and move away, making her lie down on the bed and rest her head on the pillow. As I pull the duvet over her body and tuck her in, she murmurs something incomprehensible.

'What?' I whisper.

'Don't make the same mistake as me. If you love someone . . .' she says and dozes off.

For some very weird reason, a picture of Karthik flashes before my eyes. Before I can decipher my feelings for him, the memory of my last encounter with him comes running back to me. *He killed Tanmay.* I will never find it in my heart to forgive him.

I get under the covers of my bed and roll over. I know that sleep is a long way away. But I will still try. I cannot let this attitude continue any more. Staying in for days, not eating, just thinking about Tanmay and crying is slowly killing us from the inside. It needs to stop. I need to go out, meet people, talk and live. I also have to make Pia do the same. We need to get our lives back on track, and it has to begin now.

I pick up my cell phone and type a text message.

'Let's meet up tomorrow?'

Chapter Twenty-five

—

'She's such a bitch!'

A few kilometres away . . .

A shiny red Audi A6 zips through the streets of Nagpur. The wheels grind hard against the asphalt of the road, and it is obvious that the guy who is driving it is very angry. He holds the steering wheel way too tightly—the veins on his hands are popping out and his knuckles are white. There are beads of sweat on his forehead, even in the air-conditioned car.

'Can you drive a little slow, man?' Chetan, the college president shouts, as he almost falls over onto the dashboard. *He grudgingly buckles up his seat belt and sits back. The expression on Akshat's face scares him.*

'Will you just shut up?' Akshat shouts.

'No, I won't. If you drive like this, you are going to get us killed. What is the problem with you?'

'What's the problem with me? You're asking that, you asshole? You killed him! If I had not asked my dad to call the commissioner and tell him that Tanmay is a friend and it's a drunk driving case, you would be in fucking jail, man!'

'You don't have to repeat it a zillion times to make your point. I get it; I screwed up. And I said I am sorry, man. It was dark and it was Karthik's bike. I didn't know Tanmay was driving it,' Chetan argues. *He has lost count of the times that he has explained this to Akshat ever since the 'accident' happened.*

'What? Are you BLIND? You fucking killed him! I still don't get it. How can you not see it was not Karthik who was driving?'

'It was a mistake, Akshat. Let it go,' Chetan says. He doesn't want to fight this fight again. It's been going on for days, now. He was asked by Akshat to knock over a guy who had beaten Akshat black and blue a few days earlier—Karthik. That night, they had tailed Karthik's bike as soon as it left the party. But that is all they had done—tailed. They did not cause the accident; they did not even touch the bike. They were just following them from a distance of ten feet, honking occasionally to scare them.

Seeing that, the bike had picked up speed and they had also driven their jeep faster, to catch up. But before they got the chance to knock the bike over, it had crashed itself, right in front of their eyes. The bike had crashed straight into the divider, while moving at the speed of over 100 km/hr. Tanmay and Ratul were thrown off, landing around fifteen feet away from where the bike, whatever was left of it, lay. It was not Chetan's fault. He and his cronies had just witnessed the crash and had gotten scared. In the chaos, they accidentally banged the bike with their jeep. And that's how the police came into the picture.

Seeing Ratul and Tanmay bleed, they had panicked and immediately picked them up and driven them to the hospital in their jeep. Later, the police found evidence that the jeep had crashed into the bike. It was Akshat's father who had intervened, to convince the police otherwise. It was difficult to substantiate the fact that the bike crash happened before the jeep crashed the already battered bike, even though it was the truth. By the time the jeep had hit the bike, Tanmay and Ratul had already been thrown off the bike. It wasn't really Chetan's or his gang's fault.

Akshat's father had pulled some strong strings and no one other than a few people in the police department even know of the jeep being involved in any way. And it is never going to come out, they have taken care of that. The policemen's pockets were taken care of very generously.

'I am sorry, man,' Chetan mutters again.

'What has happened has happened. Lucky for you—Tanmay is dead and Ratul doesn't recognize you,' Akshat says. 'But the thing is that . . . we still have unfinished business to take care of. Karthik still does not have any broken bones in his body.'

Akshat hasn't been able to get the image of Karthik beating the shit out of him out of his head. It was humiliating and something like that had never happened to him before. Four years back in Jaipur, a guy had grazed his car against Akshat's newly bought Chevrolet. The poor guy had spent the next three weeks in hospital. Akshat has been after Chetan's life to do something about Karthik and when he failed, he made his life hell with constant taunts. Chetan clearly remembers the night when he tried to talk Akshat out of what he was asking him to do. But he owed a lot to Akshat—the unlimited crazy inflow of cash, the hot women, the rowdy parties, the fast bikes. He just couldn't say no when Akshat told him to knock over Karthik. It wasn't as if he hadn't done it before, but Karthik was a tough guy, and he didn't want to get into trouble with him, just in case something went wrong.

It did. And someone died. The only good part was that everyone knew that Tanmay was drunk and it was assumed to be his fault. What bothers Chetan most is that even after everything that happened, Akshat still doesn't want to back out. He still wants his precious revenge on Karthik.

'I don't know why you're doing this,' he says to Akshat. 'And I am not going to be any part of . . . whatever it is that you have planned.'

'I don't need you to be. You are anyway not efficient enough,' Akshat says with a smirk.

'What are you going to do?' Chetan asks slowly, not sure if he wants to know, but curiosity getting the better of him.

'Take one thing he holds close. What better way to hurt him than attack where he is already hurting?'

'What do you mean?'

'Niharika,' Akshat says with an evil grin stretched across his face.

'Oh. What's with her? Why do you want her so bad? There are like a thousand other girls, you know? I think the first year girls this time are way hotter.'

'I don't know what it is about her. It's just that she rejects me . . . that turns me on. I had made out with her sister and that one was a firecracker. I am hoping this one's better. Can you imagine the odds? I slept with two sisters! I am going to make sure it happens soon,' he says and laughs out loud. There is something very sinister in his laughter which makes even Chetan squirm.

'So, you want to sleep with her just because you made out with her sister?'

'Well, kind of. Plus, she is hot! And the added—and major— advantage now being that it will kill Karthik to see her with me. She wants to meet me. A couple more dates and she is all mine. The death of her loser best friend has already left her vulnerable. Landing her will be very easy right now.'

'Just be careful. Karthik doesn't look like someone who would take this lying down. You might not want to piss him off,' Chetan warns.

'There is nothing he can do. She hates him. This is my best chance. And even if he does something, I am more than eager to take him on. By the way, where is the jeep right now?'

'It's hidden somewhere in the college. No one will be able to find out.'

'That better be the case,' Akshat sighs and thinks about Niharika and her perfectly shaped breasts.

He tries to remember the last time he had taken someone as fine as Niharika to bed and his mind draws a blank. Nagpur has become a fruitful playground for Akshat. Every year, just as the new batch enters he comes to the campus to visit his old friend—the decadent, foolish college president—and entraps one of the many beautiful and nervous juniors. Last year, it was Twinkle Shah—the petite Ms Fresher—and their relationship lasted all of fifteen days, ending once Askhat had his way with her in the parking lot of a movie hall. This year, it's taking a little longer.

He checks her text message again. He is about to get lucky.

Chapter Twenty-six

The Acquitted

I feel bad about having ignored Akshat all this time. Ever since Tanmay's accident, I have seen him around in the background and he has made efforts to talk to me too, but I just wanted to be left alone. I had asked him to give me some time to sort out my emotions, which were all haywire. I am not sure what I feel for Akshat, but I guess I am about to find out.

He had apologized for being rude that day when he dropped us to the football match. He had said some mean things and we had had a small tiff, but strangely, I remembered nothing about it till he mentioned it. I had been so lost in everything that had been happening that there was no time to ponder over a small fight with Akshat. It is all back to normal, anyway. He had been really sweet and understanding all along, waiting patiently for me to come around, being just a phone call away always, so that I don't feel alone.

Last night, when I had sent him that message, I did not know why I had done it. But now, as I walk out of my hostel, I feel that it was probably for the best. I am meeting him in half an hour at a place a little away from the campus. I had refused his offer to pick me up from my hostel; his shiny big cars make me nervous. Using public transport makes me feel like a normal human being.

As I walk towards the front gate of the college campus, I see Mandar coming in, along with a few of his friends. On seeing me, he pauses.

'Hi Niharika,' he says.

'Hey.'

'I have been meaning to call you. You're doing okay? And Pia?'

'We are fine. How's your football practice coming along? Match in two days, right?' I ask, just to make small talk.

'Just two days, yes. We have been practising hard; we need this win. In fact, we were just going for the evening practice.'

'Cool. And how is that other guy . . . Ratul, right?'

'Yes, Ratul. He is fine now. A lot better than before. In fact, we were just returning after seeing him . . . it was so fortunate that he was wearing a helmet . . .' Mandar says, a little lost in his own thoughts. It's like he is in some other world.

'Helmet?' I ask. 'But—why was he wearing one and Tanmay was not, when Tanmay was driving . . .?'

'Oh. You don't know?'

'I don't know *what*?'

'Tanmay was *not* driving that night. Ratul was. He just told me . . .' Mandar says.

'But then . . . why did he not say this before? All this time, I have been thinking that Tanmay was the one driving . . . that it was his fault.'

'How could he come forward? A guy died there, Niharika. It is a lot more complicated than that. The police would have been involved and he got scared. So he never opened his mouth.'

I nod, thinking about it all. For no reason that I could understand, I felt like talking to Ratul. 'Where is he? City Hospital?'

'Yes, but he is now on the ground floor. Physiotherapy department,' Mandar says.

Before I realize what I'm doing and think it through, I find myself at the reception of the City Hospital, asking where I can find Ratul. The receptionist looks into the computer and tells me where his ward is. As I walk towards the corridor to my right, just as the receptionist told me, I wonder what I am going to ask Ratul, and what difference it makes. Tanmay is gone . . . and never coming back. So does it really matter how the accident happened?

Even though it might not make any difference to me, there is one person that will be affected by the news. *Karthik*. I have accused him of killing Tanmay. But if Tanmay wasn't the one driving . . . Karthik must be in a really bad state right now, blaming himself for the accident. Having someone's death on one's conscience is not a good feeling. And I feel regretful about doing that to Karthik. No matter how spoilt he might be, he did have a bond with Tanmay. When he was already devastated by Tanmay's death, I added this feeling of guilt on him too.

If Ratul seconds what Mandar has just told me, I owe Karthik an apology. The two things I blame as being the reasons for Tanmay's death—alcohol and driving that bike—won't any longer be so. If Tanmay was not driving, the accident was in no way Karthik's fault. Though, it still was *his* bike that was in the accident . . .

I have no idea why, but I want it all to *not* be Karthik's fault. For some reason, I do not like being mad at him. He might be cocky, arrogant and all of those things that guys should not be, but I still do not want to hold anything against him. I know it is stupid, but after everything that has happened, I still feel that he is a good person at heart. Guys know guys, and Tanmay had been a big fan of Karthik. I'm guessing that there was a good reason behind that.

Immersed in these thoughts, I find my way to Ratul's room and knock briefly before pushing the door open. I peek in, to see him sitting up on his bed, looking towards me.

'Hi, Ratul,' I say and get in. 'How are you now?'

'I'm fine . . . Niharika, right?' he asks. I'm a little surprised that he knows my name. He reads it in my expression and says, 'There are not that many pretty juniors in our college. It's not too difficult to keep track.'

I smile, but almost immediately, my mind goes back to the reason I am here. I begin, 'Umm . . . actually, I wanted to know something. About the . . . the night of the accident . . . ?'

There is a moment of silence in the room. Beads of sweat appear on his brow almost immediately, and his face closes up. He looks everywhere other than in my direction, and it tells me exactly what I wanted to know. The first feeling I get is that of relief. *Karthik is not to blame for anything in any way.*

'So, you really were the one driving,' I say. It is a statement.

'Mandar told you,' he says.

I nod.

'See, Niharika—it happened. No matter how much I regret it, no matter how much I hate myself for not being able to maintain balance, the bike went out of control. I did not mean to smash into that divider, you know? I did not mean to end up here, at the hospital, and . . . and be the reason for Tanmay's death. I just . . . I could see it coming—the crash. And I tried to stop it, but the bike, it just . . .' Ratul says, panicking. He sounds very frustrated and it is clear to me that he has been running that incident through his head ever since it happened. He looks haunted.

'What do you mean the bike went out of control? The accident happened because of the bike?' I ask, my heart sinking a little. If it is because of Karthik's bike, he would still be partially to blame. I don't want that to happen.

'No, not the bike. I have driven bikes with equal power before, and although this one was a little rough, it was not difficult to ride. The problem was the jeep that kept tailing us.'

'Jeep? What jeep?' I did not know there was another vehicle involved in the crash.

'There was a flashy jeep following us, ever since we left the party. It kept diverting my attention, and I accelerated to get rid of them, but they just kept following me till we touched 120 km/hr . . . that was the last time I checked the speed. After that, we kept going faster . . . Tanmay asked me to slow down, but I didn't. Their intentions did not seem good. Had they caught up with us, I don't know what they would have done . . . I was scared,' Ratul says.

'Why would someone do that? Were you in a fight recently? Or Tanmay? Can it be something related to the football matches?'

'I don't know. I'm not even in the football team. I could not recognize the people in the jeep, but there was at least four or five of them. And they definitely were people one of us knew, because it was very obvious that they were doing it intentionally. They kept following us, and honking every once in a while, trying to scare us . . . and I fell for it.'

'They wanted you to crash?' I ask.

'I don't know. But they definitely did not mean well. It won't be a stretch to say that had we not crashed into the divider ourselves, they would have knocked us over.'

'Why would someone want to do that to you guys?' I murmur. Since Ratul says that he has no enemies he can think of, my mind starts thinking of reasons why someone would want to hurt Tanmay and who he might be. There could be people who might do something like this out of jealousy . . . maybe because of Tanmay's new-found and short-lived fame on the football field. But I can't think of anyone who could have done this.

But then, all this because of his success in the football field? It is hard to believe that someone would go to such lengths for football matches. This is life and death we are talking about, and even adrenaline-crazed sportspersons know that at the end of the day, it is just a game. These are not professional footballers; these are college students who play for their college teams. Can victory on the field mean so much to them? Someone's *life* . . . ?

The thought that someone wanted Tanmay dead makes me sick. But right now, there is another thing I have to take care of—*Karthik*. I need to apologize to him for all those horrible things I said to him. It is not his fault, and he should not suffer because of the things I said to him without knowing the facts. I have not seen him around recently, but I need to find him.

Chapter Twenty-seven

Slip of the Tongue

'I am not going to listen to anything. Just get up,' I say.
'But I just got into bed. It hasn't even been an hour . . .'
Pia says, checking the time on her cell phone.

'I don't care! Come with me now, and you will have a good sleep tonight. And every night after that. So, leave the bed this minute.'

'Let me sleep. Go away.'

'Don't force me to drag you out,' I say, already pulling her up. I have decided to take a stand against Pia's self-destructive regime now. She can't keep hiding in her room and drowning herself in misery, thinking about what we have lost. I know it hurts, and I feel exactly the same, but he is gone . . . *and we are still alive*. I can't let her throw away her life like this. I will not let her be like this. I have to help her get herself and her life together and this is the first step to it—getting her to go back to her daily routine, starting with gym at six-thirty in the morning.

Fifteen minutes later, we find ourselves walking towards the gym, the early January cold biting us a little. We stuff our hands deep inside our jerseys to ward off the chill, our teeth clattering. It had taken a lot of persuading and forcing to get her out of the room; pleading and begging did not work too well. She walks with a grumpy face, clearly unhappy.

'I'm telling you—this is *not* a good idea. It doesn't work like this. I am way too weak to get back to gymming all of a sudden,' Pia complains.

'And that is because you have not been eating well. Which—like it or not—is going to stop today.'

She keeps murmuring things like, 'What is wrong with you? I can take care of myself . . . stop being my mom . . .' but I do not pay her any heed. I am going to do this, with or without her cooperation.

However, once in the gym, I do not know what to do. I look around at the equipment placed against the walls and wonder what people do with them. I never really got around to working out with Pia before, so I have no idea what one does with the weirdly shaped gear all around us. It's such a shame that now when I have finally been able to drag her here, I do not know what to do next. I had expected her to start doing whatever it is she used to do here, but she just stands staring at me. I am lost, and she can see it.

'What?' I say, noticing her look at me weirdly. I walk towards the treadmill, assuming that it should be the easiest one.

'Why are you doing this?' she asks me seriously, looking at me with those big brown eyes, the eyes that have lost their spark . . .

'We pledged to do everything Tanmay would have wanted us to do, right?' I meet her eye and say softly. 'That also includes taking care of *you* and making sure that you are happy.'

She nods. I can see tears filling her eyes already.

'I am going to make sure that it happens. That's my duty now.'

~

'I am so, so sorry, Akshat. I did not mean to . . . I had every intention of coming . . .' I say over the phone. After coming

back from the hospital last evening, I had sent Akshat a last-
minute text saying that I wouldn't be able to meet him. He
must already have been waiting for me for about an hour
by then, and I felt bad about it, but after getting to know
what I got to know, I was simply not in a condition last
evening to meet him.

I had sent him a text, not mentioning the reason, but just
telling that I would not be coming. I had come back to
the college campus and tried to find Karthik, but it seemed
like no one had seen him for the last few weeks. I asked
everyone I could think of—students, teachers, the football
team, guards, the janitor and even the gardeners—but no
one knew anything about where he could be. I spent hours
roaming around the campus, but found out nothing.

In the end, I went to the chai stall Karthik had taken
me to, that time on his bike. I thought it was worth giving
it a shot. The small boy there—the one who served us our
tea the last time I was here—came running to me when he
saw me. I was a little surprised that he remembered me. I
asked him about Karthik and he told me that he came to
the stall every evening and that he was there just moments
ago—I had missed him by minutes. I heaved a sigh of relief.
I had finally found someone who had seen Karthik within
the fortnight. That meant he was okay.

But since I still did not have a contact number or address,
I decided to meet him at the chai stall in the evening today.
The boy had said that he came daily, not missing even a day.
I felt relieved that I could find him. There was nothing else
to do but wait for the evening to come. Till then, I set some
tasks for myself—a) getting myself together and being strong,
b) taking good care of Pia and c) apologizing to Akshat about
yesterday and also letting him know that as we agreed, we
are just friends and he should stop acting like my . . . *lover*
or whatever. I regret that moment when I let him kiss me in

the parking lot. I wish it had never happened; things would not have gotten so complicated.

So the first thing I do after getting back from the gym is call him up to apologize properly. I think that once that is done, I will politely ask him to stay away from me. 'What happened yesterday? All I got was a text message from you, saying you are not coming . . . Is everything okay?' Akshat says, sounding a little freaked out.

'Yes, yes. Everything's fine. I left to meet you, but I got caught up in some things before I could leave the campus. I meant to let you know immediately, but it totally slipped my mind. I am sorry you had to wait . . .'

'Relax, Niharika. It's perfectly alright. I thought you must know by now—I don't mind waiting for you. I don't mind *anything* about you . . .'

'You're too kind,' I say, mentally cringing from the cheesy lines he is using on me. It's not that I mind him being sweet to me; it's just that I want him to be more . . . *human*. And regular human beings get mad when people leave them waiting and never turn up. His niceness was nothing short of weird.

'Just for you. So, what happened?' he asks.

'Nothing. I mean—it's a long story. I am sure you do not want to get into all that. You must have better things to do.'

'Oh, come on! How can I ever be too busy for you? Tell me what's wrong. I'm all ears.'

He insists so much that I ultimately have to cave in. 'Okay, fine. I'll tell you. But I don't know much . . . it's just that—you remember that night of Tanmay's accident?'

'Yes . . . what about it?'

'I got to know last evening that Tanmay was not the one driving the bike. It was Ratul. So that means it was not Tanmay's fault. I feel so bad about blaming Karthik for everything now . . .'

'But it was still Karthik's bike. It's not like he had *no* hand in the accident!' Akshat says. I am shocked by his sudden change of tone. He has way too much hatred for Karthik, but blaming him for someone's death is really unfair. I tell him so.

'Ratul said that the bike was perfectly safe and okay to handle. The accident was *not* because of the bike. It is *not* Karthik's fault in any w—'.

'What the hell is wrong with you? Why do you always keep defending that guy?'

'BECAUSE IT IS NOT HIS FAULT. Why don't you understand? He did *nothing* to cause that accident,' I shout out, frustrated now. Akshat changes moods in a matter of seconds. One minute, he is all sweet and caring, the next, he is shouting at me like there is no one he hates more than me. They are like two different people. I hate his caustic tone.

'*Oh, really*? So you mean this other guy . . . Ratul—he banged into that divider just like that? For fun?'

'As a matter of fact—*no*. He did *not* do it for fun. He was going really fast and he lost control of the bike. And he was going fast because someone was chasing them. He got scared and panicked. And no matter how fast he went, the jeep kept following them . . . they intended to knock the bike over.'

There is a short silence from the other end, and I presume that Akshat has done his split-personality thing again. He is back to being the sweet-and-caring guy I first met. 'Jeep?' he asks slowly. 'What jeep?'

'There was a jeep full of four or five guys that was tailing Ratul and Tanmay.'

'Whose jeep was it?'

'I don't know . . .' I say, pondering over it. 'It could be guys from the college they had beaten in a match? Maybe? Or someone who didn't like him? Or Ratul?'

'Are you sure there was a jeep?'

'Yes! What do you mean—*sure*? It's not like I know everyone who owns a jeep in the entire city of Nagpur!' I joke, just to lighten the strained mood. 'In fact, I guess the only jeep I have seen since I came to Nagpur belongs to that college president friend of yours. But that does not mean that it was *he* who did it!' I remember having seen Chetan drive around in a jeep with Akshat. It was a long time ago, when Akshat had been stalking me around the college campus. It was a yellow open jeep, with flashy red and green graphics on it. It would stand out anywhere it goes, so obviously, I remember it.

There was a longer pause from Akshat's end this time, and I almost think the call has got disconnected. But then I hear his breathing. I don't know what's wrong with him. Why did he start acting so weird all of a sudden, ever since I mentioned the accident?

'What are you trying to say?' he asks, finally breaking the silence.

'What do you mean? I was just telling you how the accident happened . . .'

'Really? Then why do I feel like you are *accusing* my friends of something? Just because they have a jeep? And for what? To save Karthik? That fucking son of a whore! You're thinking too much. There was NO jeep. It's all Karthik's fault. Do you fucking get it?'

'*Akshat!* Mind your language. He did nothing to deserve this. *The accident was not his fault!*' I yell, now very angry. Things are getting way out of hand, and I have no idea why.

'Then whose fault is it? *Mine?* Are you trying to say *that*? Just because I happen to know a guy who owns a jeep?'

The angry quiver in his voice was freaking me out. It was like he was losing control.

'I never said—'

'THEN WHAT THE FUCK *DID* YOU SAY? That *I* sent them to knock Karthik over? Are you accusing *me*? Is that why you called me today? To accuse me?' Akshat shouts out.

I freeze.

Did he just say *Karthik*? I start breathing heavily, but my mind is strangely calm. It begins to process everything that has happened in the conversation. My head feels like it would implode as it dawns as on me as what might have happened. Akshat? I go over the incidents again in my head. I can't be wrong. There was no other explanation. It actually is Akshat who planned all of this. It is he who is behind that accident that killed Tanmay.

First, he freaked out as soon as I mentioned the accident. Then, he kept blaming Karthik, even when I told him that it was not Karthik's fault. He just wanted to shift the blame and change the topic. And as soon as I mentioned the jeep, he asked me if I was *sure* I did not recognize it. He was just making sure that he wasn't in any trouble. But then, when I mentioned that I remember Chetan—his friend—owning a jeep, he freaked out totally.

And when he said, 'That *I* sent them to knock Karthik over?' it became more than obvious that it really was the case. He said *Karthik*, not *Tanmay*. Now that I think of it, it makes perfect sense. Akshat had asked Chetan and his guys to knock Karthik over, and those dumb idiots had confused Karthik for Tanmay, just because it was Karthik's bike.

'Niharika?' Akshat says. He clearly does not realize what he has just said.

I hang up. I feel sick.

~

An hour passes, without me moving even an inch. I sit, frozen in my place, running it all through my head. I have always known about the hatred between the two guys—Akshat and

Karthik—but I never thought it could grow to this extent. Was the hatred, which had developed because of a stupid reason, enough to warrant someone's death? Is Akshat really capable of *killing* someone, just over a petty brawl? How could I have read a person so wrong?

Even though I do not need more evidence to confirm that it really was Akshat's plan, I decide to go one more step.

'The jeep—what did it look like?' I call Ratul and ask.

'It was night-time and I could not see much. All I could see was that it was open from the top and was yellow in colour . . .'

I was right. I really wish I was not.

Chapter Twenty-eight

The Broken-Down Workshop

*T*here is a strange stench of grease and lubricant that hangs in the air of the workshop that once used to be the boiler room of ICE. Three years ago, the boiler had exploded and the workshop had been shut down. The new lab was constructed closer to the other labs and this broken-down half-burnt old building was abandoned. Karthik had been particularly happy that day. For the past one year, he had been working on the bike he had conceptualized, and constructed—at least a few parts—on his own, but the mechanical lab was always too crowded and busy and he could not concentrate. Plus, he never really liked the questions people asked him. He preferred this new work place—discarded and hence deserted.

Karthik is sitting on the bench, a pile of cigarette butts lying nearby, and the trashed bike in front of him. It had taken him three years to build the bike he thought would be his miracle—but now it lay twisted and destroyed near him. But he took it apart bit by bit, hitting it everywhere with the heavy crowbar that lies twisted on his left. The bike is completely destroyed.

He doesn't blame it on the drinking—a habit he believes he picked up from his dad—but for what he did to Tanmay. So yes, partly, he does blame it on the drinking. Niharika was right—he is a terrible person and had he not been around, nothing would have happened. Tanmay wouldn't have started drinking, he wouldn't *have driven that bike and he would not have . . . Even though he had protested the day Niharika told him that it was his fault, now he believes it.*

Niharika—even the name brings a certain relief, a certain happiness to his heart, something he has tried and failed to understand. Ever since his father died, Karthik has been a loner—no friends, no parties and no girlfriends. He has never been in love. Busy tinkering with machines or spending his afternoons playing football with strangers he barely talked to, life had whizzed past.

He was doing fine till the time he noticed the girl in front of him in the queue of the crowded hostel mess. She was pretty, but that wasn't what caught his eye, for he had seen many pretty girls, but there was something in her eyes and her walk that intrigued him. For the next few days, he had been looking everywhere for her, and when he finally saw her—in the canteen—he felt . . . something. Something tugged at his heart and he tried to ignore it at first, but slowly and steadily, the face imprinted itself on his brain and on his thoughts.

He never had any intention of going back to the football field again—his unceremonious dropping from the team was something that was totally wrong. He had sworn he would never play again for his college. Slowly, he had started enjoying the frequent losses of his team against unworthy opponents in one-sided matches. Secretly, he had even wished the football team captain would come crawling to him and beg him to come back, to which he would obviously refuse. But it never happened.

That day, during trials, he noticed that face droop when her friend, Tanmay—the cute guy in glasses—took the field. It was almost involuntary the way Karthik stepped onto the field and played his heart out. The sheer joy on Niharika's face made Karthik the happiest he had been in the longest time. So much so, that when he had called home that night, his mother had noticed the obvious delight in his voice.

A few days later, they went out on an accidental date which he would never forget. From that day to today—when she hates him and doesn't want to see his face ever again—he keeps replaying the images of that day in his head. The muted laughter, her hand on his shoulder when they drove in the early morning wind, the eyes that looked away from him every time he gazed too hard—he remembers it all. Deep down in his heart, he knew there would be no one else who would make him feel like this new girl did, and she was all he ever thought about. It became clearer the day he saw her crying after Akshat made a move on her in the parking lot. He had felt like a part of him had died and he had then proceeded to hit the living daylights out of Akshat—to make himself feel better.

But things had only gone downhill from there. One day, he was strangely possessive and overtly protective about Niharika, and a little while later . . . he got the biggest shock of his life. It happened so quickly that he did not even have time to process it in his head. ICE's football team had won the semi-finals of the tournament and had made its way to the finals, and that, for Tanmay, was the biggest achievement of his life. He had worked hard for it and the team had done so well because of him. He had been happy beyond measure. When Tanmay came to him and asked if he could borrow his bike for a ride, Karthik could not possibly have refused, could he? He knew Tanmay would get drunk at the after-match party, but he had promised that he would not drink-drive.

When he got the news of Tanmay's accident the next morning, he had literally felt frozen for the next few minutes. The guilt he felt . . . it was crushing. No one is strong enough to have someone's death on his conscience. When he had seen Niharika, walking out of the hospital's parking lot, he had not been ready to face her at all. He had just gotten to the hospital, did not know how serious an accident it was, or how Tanmay was doing. When Niharika blamed it all on him, his brain automatically rejected the accusations. It was almost a reflex action.

But when she had left . . . it had dawned upon him. It was all his fault. He should never have influenced Tanmay the way he had.

He knew Tanmay was changing, but he had not thought that there was anything wrong with that. Secretly, he even liked the fact that Tanmay used to look up to him and was trying to be like him. It was flattering, and Karthik had never realized what it might eventually lead to. It never struck him that he was slowly pushing him to his death. He never imagined that he, Karthik, could become a . . . a murderer.

A part of him died with Tanmay. He cut himself off from the rest of the world ever since, even though it doesn't seem to lessen the pain. Two faces haunt him continuously, no matter how hard he tries to push them away from his head. Tanmay—and when tormented thoughts about him finally become less . . . Niharika. The face, her beautiful face, comes back to haunt him every time he closes his eyes.

He looks at the bike he had crashed the day he came back after the confrontation with Niharika and doesn't feel a thing. He thinks about Tanmay's innocent face looking up at him, asking for his approval. He thinks about Niharika and Akshat holding hands, and a tear escapes from the corner of his eye.

Chapter Twenty-nine

A New Beginning

When the clock strikes six, I am still lost in my thoughts. It is just too much for me to process. I still cannot believe it. I still cannot believe that Akshat is capable of taking someone's life. I am stunned and I find it hard to take it in. But it's time for me to go to the chai stall and talk to Karthik. I have no other way to find him and I don't want to miss him this time. So I get up from my bed, quickly run a comb through my hair and walk out of the room.

Things are changing, and they are not going the way I would have liked. One day, I am worried about something, and the next, I find a bigger reason to worry waiting for me. It's hard to believe that Tanmay's craze for alcohol and his change in attitude were the things I used to be worried about, just a little while ago. Now, there *is* no Tanmay, and not too long ago, I made Karthik's life hell, making him feel that he was the reason for someone's death, even though he was in no way responsible. I know it can't be undone now, but the least I can do is let him know that it was not his fault.

And I also have to make someone else's life a living hell—I can't believe Akshat could do something of this magnitude, just over a stupid brawl. These ego clashes, do they mean so much? I want to avenge what Akshat did, but I just cannot think of anything. If I tell someone, who is going to believe me? Pia, Simran and a few other people. The others would think that I have gone mad and am cooking up stories. I have no proof to justify my claim.

And I wonder if I even want to have any proof. What good is that going to do? The truth remains that the accident happened by itself. What Akshat was planning to do was exactly that—*just a plan*. And the person he was going to do it to—Karthik—was not even there. No one will buy my story, and even if they do, Akshat has a very rich and very powerful dad. If it comes down to *my* word against *his* . . .

I feel very disheartened and strangely helpless. I want to do something. I am supposed to avenge my best friend's death, aren't I? Then why am I not doing anything about it? I feel trapped, with no other way out. I don't know how to get justice for Tanmay. I don't even know whether Tanmay would have wanted me to do something like that. A part of me says that he would not, but another part of me reminds me that he is no longer here to tell me what he wants and what he doesn't.

Lost in my own disturbing thoughts, I suddenly find myself just a few feet away from the chai stall. As I contemplate hiding, in case Karthik goes away when he sees me, I see him come out from under the shed and sit on one of the plastic chairs placed outside the stall. He looks at his feet absently, not aware of his surroundings . . . and me. I *stand where I am and stare at him.*

I am seeing him after over a month, and every single feature of his face comes rushing back to my head. I had almost forgotten about that one unruly strand of hair on the right side of his forehead, which always refuses to behave. And those deep-set eyes, of a colour so dark . . . For some reason, seeing him brings with it a lot of other emotions too. Every single second of every single moment I have spent with or around him flashes through my head . . . *and I realize how terribly I have been missing him.*

I will probably never admit it to him, but ever since I first saw him, he has always been there at the back of my head. I never admit it even to myself, but I always think about him. Now, seeing him right in front of me after such a long time, I can't help but feel my heart beat furiously in my chest. I slowly walk towards him, pull a chair, place it next to his and silently sit by his side. A second later, he looks up to see me next to him. He is visibly shocked. Almost as a reflex, he gets up and starts to move away.

'Karthik! Karthik, *stop!*' I say. He stops in his tracks but does not turn around. 'Please sit down . . .?' I whisper, praying that he does not walk away.

I see him stand motionless, with his back turned towards me, for a minute, after which he turns back and takes his seat again. Looking at him, the full consequences of what Akshat has done hits me. He is not just a player, he is a monster. He is cruel and sinister and inhumane. He not only killed Tanmay, he has also caused everything that is wrong with my life right now. He did whatever he wanted to do, for his stupid revenge. What he probably does not realize, and I'm sure is not bothered about at all, is that I am the one left cleaning up the mess that my life has become because he chose to be what he is.

I look at the guy sitting next to me, his head hung low, and I feel sorry for him. Before my courage gives way, I start talking.

'Are you drunk?' I ask softly. He looks really worn out and miserable.

'No,' he replies and adds something so softly that I can barely make out the words, 'I don't drink any more.'

I nod slowly, tears filling my eyes automatically. I can see what Tanmay's death has done to him and it's hardly bearable. I ache, seeing Karthik like this. 'Where have you been?' I ask.

He shrugs.

'Tell me. I looked for you everywhere. I was so worried ... I ran out of places to look for you. I have no idea where you live and . . . I don't know what I would have done had I not come here, looking for you.'

'I didn't know you would care.'

'I do,' I say and put my hand on his arm. He looks up at me with a strange, unreadable expression on his face. All I can tell is that he is confused and a little shocked; he did not expect me to be here. I can feel the tears in my eyes and I know that I am very close to breaking down, but I hold myself together.

'You should not,' he says. 'And you should not be here. I don't deserve your caring. I don't deserve to even sit next to you . . .'

'No, Karthik. Don't say that.'

'But it's true! I messed it all up. You guys were happy on your own, before I decided to butt in and screw it all up. Nothing would have happened if it weren't for me.'

'You did nothing. It was not your fault. None of it was,' I say.

'It was! I never should have interfered. And it's not like I did not try. I did. But I just could not . . . stay away from you . . .'

'And why is that?' I ask slowly.

'I think the word they use is love,' he says. My heart skips a beat. It's hard to imagine that under the given shitty circumstances, I can still find blood rushing to my face, making me blush. I think I have always known somewhere deep inside that he loves me, but I had never had the courage to actually believe it. A part of me still cannot believe it.

'You . . . love—?'

'I guess. But it doesn't matter now. Forget I ever mentioned it. I know that you are with Akshat and you hate me anyway.'

'No, I do *not* hate you. I guess I never did. When the accident happened, I was scared and I wanted to put the blame on someone, and it seemed like you fit the bill. But I was wrong. *So wrong*,' I say, framing the words in my head to tell him what I know.

'But it *is* my fault. And you know that!'

'That's *not* what I know. And if you would just hear me out, I have something important to tell you.'

He looks at me strangely at first and then nods. I tell him everything I know, my eyes never leaving his, my grip on his arm tighter than ever.

~

'You are not going to do anything of that sort!' I shout.

'I am. I cannot let that son of a bitch live after what he did to Tanmay. It's time he paid his dues,' Karthik shouts back, his face red with anger and a vein prominent in his forehead.

'You are going to do no such thing, you hear me?' I plead, shaking him. But he gets up and starts walking towards his bike, ready to confront Akshat and do God-knows-what to him. He seems to be in some other world and doesn't even notice me running after him.

'Do you expect me to just sit here and do nothing, now that I know at least two things that give me legitimate reason to take down that bastard? He tried to kill me, and he killed Tanmay. Aren't those reasons enough?'

'You guys and your stupid power games! They are what led to this, and now you are doing it again. But it is *not* going to do any good!'

'But it will feel fucking awesome,' Karthik says. He kicks the pedal, and his bike starts up with a roar.

I stand frozen. I knew Karthik was not going to take the news lying down, but now that it is actually happening in front of me, I realize what he is going to do next. And I have to stop him.

'Karthik,' I say calmly. 'If you do anything to him, if you even so much as *move* your bike just an inch—I swear to you—I will kill myself in the most painful way I can think of. And I am *not* kidding.'

His head jerks towards me suddenly and he looks at me as if he is seeing me for the first time. A moment later, I see him walk slowly to the plastic chairs and sit down. I join him wordlessly. There is an uncomfortable silence for a bit.

'Why? Don't you want to see that asshole pay for what he did?' he asks.

'I do. But I choose to leave it up to karma to take care of him.'

'What kind of absurd logic—?'

'I know,' I cut him off. 'It's not like I haven't thought about revenge. But what's right is right. It all started with senseless brawls over senseless things, and look at where we are now. I don't want to start that cycle all over again, at any cost.'

'But this is just so unfair! Tanmay . . . he never should have been involved in all of this. I should have been the one on the bike that night. I should have died instead. It's all because of me.'

'No, it's not. Take it from me, Karthik—thinking like this doesn't help. That way I can blame myself for having become friends with Tanmay. Had that not happened, you never would have played that first trial match to help him out, and none of this would ever have started. But it just does not work like that. We cannot blame ourselves for things we never had control over . . .'

'But I just . . . it just . . .' Karthik trails away, frustrated. I can understand what he is going through; I was feeling the same desperation, the same helplessness not so long ago, but I cannot let him take any rash step either. I have already lost Tanmay—I cannot afford to lose him.

—We sit together, wordlessly, staring at the setting sun, till a zillion stars appear in the dark blue night sky. I keep holding his hand and somehow draw energy from the fact that he is with me. We don't say anything, but we are both thinking about the same thing. We are both missing Tanmay more than ever.

At long last, we get up to leave. We walk to the college campus silently. Right before I enter my hostel, I turn to him to say goodbye.

'You'll be alright?' I ask.

'I guess. I just . . . feel so helpless. I wish I could do *something* . . .'

'I can think of something,' I say.

Chapter Thirty

For Him

'Do you think we have a chance?' Pia asks. We are sitting in our college stadium, where the final football match is about to commence. Since our college is hosting the match, both Pia and I have been forced to volunteer. We're in the refreshment department. So obviously, we are ditching our duty and sitting on the stands instead, waiting eagerly for the teams to come out of the pavilion.

'I think we do,' I reply, almost involuntarily.

'You do?' she asks, looking a little surprised. She seems to have given up all hopes and I decide not to tell her about Karthik playing for our team. I'll let her see for herself. A surprise like that might cheer her up.

'Uh, I mean—the match hasn't even started yet. Anything can happen. Our team is a strong one too. So, let's not be pessimistic, right?'

'All the strength of our team was mostly because of . . . *him*. Without him now . . .'

'Relax. We can't think like that,' I say and look away. I contemplate telling her, but before I can decide, I see the opposing team making its way to the field. 'See—they are coming out.'

'AITR is a good team, I've heard. The champions for the last two years,' Pia whispers.

'I know. But our team is still . . . stronger,' I say. Pia turns her gaze away from the field to look at me. The expression on her face tells me that she thinks that I have lost my mind. I just shrug and motion towards the field, where our team is coming out of the pavilion. Fifteen players, all dressed in a deep shade of red, teamed with yellow, make their way to the field. It is a very cloudy day, and rain seems just around the corner. Against this background of dark, evil-looking clouds, the team looks very tough. We watch them, slightly in awe. The entire atmosphere is thick with excitement and nervousness; everyone seems to be whispering prayers in their heads.

I spot Karthik immediately. Even with fifteen guys dressed alike, he stands out. Just his stance is enough for me to recognize him anywhere. He walks with the team, and they huddle in the corner. The captain, Mandar, motions to everyone to come close and from what I can see, it seems like he starts his pep talk. Every player listens to him intently. Karthik, on the other hand, scans through the crowd, his brows knit together in tension, his jaws tightly clamped together.

His condition worries me. His reaction to the news about Tanmay's death, its reason and Akshat's attempt to harm him is understandable. Anyone would be furious, especially if they have a friend's death on their conscience, because of something they did not even do. But I had expected him to cool down a little by now. But by the look of things, he is still in the same condition as he was yesterday.

The only relief I can draw is from the fact that he agreed to play in the final match. Surprisingly, even Mandar did not oppose his sudden re-entry in the team. I assume the victory does mean a lot more to him than his hatred for Karthik. At least he is sane enough to realize that their stupid ego clashes and baseless rivalry is not worth losing the cup, after getting so close to claiming it.

'Is it . . . ? Is that Karthik?' Pia whispers.

'Yes, it is,' I smile.

'But . . . how?'

'Long story. Let's just concentrate on enjoying the match now.'

'We're *so* winning this,' she says, excitement showing on her face. She suddenly seems alive. We're finally a little close to getting Tanmay something he would have really wanted. No wonder she is so happy. 'With Karthik on our side, the match is definitely ours. I don't know how you did this. But . . . I just love you so much!' she shrieks and hugs me.

'Aww!' I hug her back.

Ten minutes later, after the brief initiation ceremony and a few announcements, the match starts. We knew that AITR was a good team, and we had heard that they had remained unbeaten for the entire series, but it turns out that we had still underestimated their power. We have had a simple logic—*we have Karthik on our team, we will win*. But it does not really work like that. Each and every player on team AITR seems threatening. But our team isn't too far behind either. The match is tough; it is between equals.

A nail-biting thirty minutes later, AITR's team hits their first goal. The match is suddenly lopsided. One would think that being on the winning side, the team would loosen up, but that never happens. They play as furiously as before. Maybe even more, since ICE panics and attacks with greater fervour. The only good thing I can find in the situation is that our team has not gotten defensive yet. We are still attacking; we don't have another option. But it does not seem to be working. Karthik, for the most part, seems ineffective. He runs in jogs with no real urgency. It makes me think he is not mentally ready for the match.

By the time it is half-time, AITR is leading by 1–0. At the whistle, the players make their way to the sidelines. We rush towards our team.

'What's happening—?' I ask Karthik when I reach him, but another, louder voice overpowers my question.

'YOU!' Mandar shouts, pointing at Karthik, who turns to look at him. 'What the hell do you think you are trying to do?'

'You need to relax, Mandar. It's all under control,' Karthik says.

'UNDER CONTROL? We are losing the match, can't you see? All because of you!'

'Just listen to—'

'You said you will take care of the match. We had it all planned. *You* demanded we replace our centre forward with you. Samar would have at least scored *one* goal. What do you think you are doing?' Mandar shouts furiously.

'I told you I have it under control.'

'But you can't blame me for doubting your word, can you? Because the match sure does NOT seem under control. AITR is winning!'

'Stop shouting! They just *think* that they have the lead. I can score any time I want to,' Karthik says cockily. I have to agree, his cockiness has a certain charm to itself. At least I am charmed.

'Then why don't you? What are you waiting for?'

'For them to tire themselves off.'

'What kind of stupid logic is that? *We* are getting tired too, you know?' Mandar looks very frustrated and probably a little scared too.

'*I* am not.'

'Of course not. You are not doing anything. Just standing there. How are you supposed to get tired?'

'Exactly my point. If we score now, they'll know that we are back in the match and they'll tighten their control. Then, we'll have to work harder for goals. We need them relaxed. I'll hit the goals when the time is right and we will win this match. Now, for the last time—you need to relax,' Karthik says and walks towards where Pia and I are standing.

Mandar walks away, muttering something like, 'I don't even know why I'm trusting this bastard. He might even have the match fixed . . .'

'So, how do you like the match?' Karthik asks us.

'Well, I was worried like five minutes ago!' I say. Only Karthik can be insane enough to pull a trick like that.

'You don't need to. It's all—'

'—under control. Yes, we know. We heard,' I say and smile at him. It's a nice feeling. I am smiling, Karthik is smiling and even Pia is smiling. It has happened after a long, long time.

And it changes way too quickly.

'What the hell,' Karthik mutters and Pia and I follow his line of vision. There, standing at the opposite end of the field is Akshat. Karthik starts walking towards him without wasting a breath. I rush after him and Pia follows suit.

'What's going on?' she asks. She is clearly baffled. I just keep running after Karthik.

'What are you doing with him?' Akshat asks me, when we reach him.

'What are you doing here?' I shout at him in response. He clearly does not realize that we know all about what he had done.

'YOU SON OF A BITCH!' Karthik thunders and charges towards Akshat.

'Karthik! Stop!' I shout out.

'WHAT THE FUCK!' Akshat shrieks and moves backwards in defence. He looks like a little girl, scared of the dark.

Before I can stop him, and before Akshat can make out what is happening, I find Karthik holding him up by his collar.

'Let me . . . go, you bastard,' a half-choked Akshat says.

'Not in this life,' Karthik says and lands a neat punch on Akshat's nose, loosening his hold on his collar. Akshat loses balance and falls on the ground. Karthik waits for him to get up and then launches himself at him and lands another blow, on his jaw this time.

'KARTHIK! ARE YOU OUT OF YOUR MIND?' Mandar shouts. Half of ICE's football team seems to have appeared here out of nowhere. They break up the fight and try to keep Karthik away from Akshat.

~

We are twenty minutes into the second half of the match and the scoreboard has remained stagnant. AITR is still leading, and the worst part is that Karthik is not on the field. Mandar decided it would be a risk to play Karthik immediately. One fight on the field would get him a red card for sure. The referee was taking no nonsense on the field today.

For all the time I have known Akshat, I had never realized that he would turn out to be such a coward. He was cunning and soulless enough to plan someone's murder and deceive me like this, but two punches by Karthik and he went running away out of the college campus. I knew his super-neat ways probably indicated that he was somewhat effeminate, but I had never imagined him to be such a coward. Even the thought of him fills me with loathing. And to think that once upon a time I thought I might be in love with him, and I let him kiss me . . . it makes my blood boil.

Karthik is not doing much better either. A shot at Akshat must have vented some of his anger, but he still looks very disturbed. He is sitting on one of the benches in the side lines, staring unblinkingly at nothing in particular. His face is morose and he seems to be in some other world. By now, it has started drizzling a little, and by the look of things, I feel that heavy rain is to follow.

We have just twenty minutes left in the match, when AITR scores another goal. The crowd explodes in cheers and boos in equal measure. Karthik finally looks away from whatever he was staring blankly at. The noise pulls him back to the world around him. He shoots a glance at the scoreboard and swears loudly. We are trailing by 2–0. Mandar looks at Karthik as if to ask him for help. He nods, get up and shouts something at Mandar. I feel a little relieved.

Next moment, we see a player from ICE leaving the field and Karthik replacing him.

'GO KARTHIK!' Pia stands up and shouts.

I cheer with her too, silently praying to God. Karthik stretches a bit and then stands still, as if to shake off the memory of his fight with Akshat from his head.

The team suddenly comes to life. Karthik shouts instructions to players and they seem suddenly rejuvenated. They communicate with each other through some kind of a secret sign language that only the senior players on our team seem to know. The rest of our team looks a little lost, but Karthik does not seem to care. Maybe the four senior players on our team are enough to handle what Karthik has in mind.

Even Mandar looks excited. They create a mesh–like formation on the field, baffling the opposing team. After five minutes of vigorous running around the field, they finally get to the goalpost. Mandar signals Karthik, who sends the ball flying towards the goalpost. The ball flies at top speed, until it reaches to goalkeeper, who defends it, sending the ball away.

We let out a disappointed sigh. I really thought that Karthik was going to score a goal, but it isn't all that simple, I realize.

But I am mistaken. It isn't that hard, either. A millisecond later, the ball, redirected by the goalkeeper, lands straight at the feet of our second striker. Without wasting any time, he aims it at the goalpost with full force. AITR's goalkeeper, who is still reeling from the first save, gets up hurriedly, but cannot do anything. It's a goal!

The crowd cheers and the chants of *Ratul*, who I guess is the one who hit the goal, booms across the stadium. Even though it would have made me happier had Karthik been the one hitting the goal, it is a goal nonetheless. We are back in the match. Hopes rise exponentially.

Barely ten minutes later, ICE hits another goal. This time, it's Karthik who has done it.

The cheering is ear-splitting—one of the plus points of playing in front of a home crowd. We get up from our seats and jump up and down, shouting at the top of our lungs. Even over the rain—it is pouring heavily now—we are able to make ourselves heard. While everyone else is happy just to see our team back in the game, I am happy for other reasons too. The happiness in Karthik's expression is something I would give anything for. Smeared with mud, his hair dripping water and sweat in the rain, and a happy smile on his face, he looks almost enchanting. The sheer joy in his expression . . .

I suddenly pause. Where are all these thoughts coming from? Why am I so happy to see Karthik happy? Am I . . .? Is this . . . *love*?

Before I get a chance to ponder about it, everyone sits down and Pia pulls me down onto my seat too.

'Where are you?' she shakes me and asks.

'Right here,' I say.

'You seem lost.'

'Just thinking.'

'Don't worry. He has got it. We're winning!' The smile on her face is one of relief and happiness. She has confidence in Karthik. So do I.

And sure enough, almost immediately, Karthik has the ball back at his feet. He runs with it for a while, before passing it over to the striker, who then passes it back to him. Everyone has their eyes set on Karthik. We can almost see him hitting a goal in the next second.

'KARTHIK! KARTHIK! KARTHIK!'

The chants across the stadium are deafening. The crowd gets rowdier. The rain gets heavier. This is the end of the match. One goal and it is done.

'KARTHIK! KARTHIK! KARTHIK!'

Karthik runs towards the goalpost and Ratul passes the ball towards him. I can almost see Karthik stopping the ball and directing it straight to the goalpost. But it never happens. When the ball comes to him, he lets it pass right through. The ball hits a player from the opponent side and rolls away from the field. It goes out of the boundary and the referee blows his whistle. It's an outside.

No one knows what just happened and why. It was a very easy shot. It's hard to believe Karthik missed it accidentally. He did it on purpose. It is very evident. But—*why*? I find my answer within seconds.

As he makes his way to fetch the ball, Karthik shouts out to me, 'Niharika!'

'What?' I shout back. I am sitting just three rows away from where the ball is, and I can see him coming towards me.

'Do you want us to win?' he asks.

'Yes, of course! What kind of question is that?'

'Do you *really* want us to win?'

'YES!' I shout.

'Then you'll have to do something for me.'

'What? Now?'

'Yes, *now*. Give me what I want, or else I won't go back to the game,' he smirks. He has reached the ball and bends down to pick it up in his hands.

'What is it? There are just four minutes left in the match!'

'I know. And only you can make me go back to the field and win it.'

'Karthik! What is—?' I panic. I can see the referee and the other players getting curious.

'Shh! Let's not waste time. Just—tell me you love me.'

'WHAT?'

'I know you do. You know you do. Don't you?' he cocks his head to one side and asks. He is way too smug for his own good. But I find even that endearing. Moreover, there is a certain uncertainty in his eyes. No one else could have noticed it, but I have. I have come to know him. And I have come to love him.

'I do,' I whisper. His eyes never leave mine, my eyes don't leave his. The referee blows his whistle, but we hardly notice.

'What? I can't hear you.'

'I SAID I DO!'

'Say it,' he says. Strangely, the sheer arrogance in his attitude makes me love him more.

'I love you, Karthik,' I say in a clear voice. I can feel the blood rush to my face, and my ears turn warm. The referee blows his whistle again. Mandar and Ratul shout out to Karthik, asking him what's going on. I doubt he hears any of them. He seems interested in listening only to me.

'Now—kiss me!' he says.

'Now you're pushing your luck!'

'Okay, okay!' he laughs, blows a kiss to me and turns back to the field. The referee pulls out a yellow card and waves it at Karthik. Darn. He had crossed the time limit for the outside. But it's just a yellow card; no harm done.

Karthik throws the ball to one of the players of our team and runs inside the boundary. I am still reeling from the impact of what just happened between us and feeling terribly embarrassed. People all around me, who saw it happen, are shooting me strange looks, making me blush even more. But fretting about how soon the news of my 'scene' with Karthik would travel to the entire college will have to wait. There are just two minutes left in the match. So, for now, I just worry about whether or not our team will be able to make it.

We do. Karthik hits the most spectacular goal ever. Weaving his way through the mesh of players of the opposing team, he runs determinedly towards the goalpost. His clothes are soaking with water and the rain pours down all around us, but that does not deter him. He passes the ball to Ratul, who runs with it for three seconds, before passing it back to Karthik. Without wasting any time, Karthik kicks the ball hard, right into the middle of the goalpost. The goalkeeper manages to touch it, but that does nothing more than change the direction of the ball fractionally. It deviates slightly from its path, but enters the goalpost in the next second. The crowd goes berserk; the noise around me is thunderous.

Everything blurs in front of my eyes. People leave the stands and rush to the field, towards the players. Even after about ten minutes later, I can't spot Karthik anywhere. It seems like the crowd has devoured him.

'Where is he?' I ask Pia, as we stand near our seats, holding hands.

'I don't know,' she whispers. Her voice breaks. I look at her, to find that she is crying. I hug her tightly.

'We won, Pia. Tanmay would have been so happy.'

'I know. If he is seeing this . . . he must be so . . . he wanted to bring the cup home—'

'Shh. Don't do this to yourself. We just won! Smile!' I prod her and she smiles, a little sadly at first and for real after some more prodding.

We wait for ten more minutes, watching the jubilant crowd surrounding the team, cheering, dancing and spinning around the field madly. We can't help but feel ecstatic ourselves. But . . . I still can't spot Karthik anywhere.

A finger taps my shoulder from behind. Startled, I turn around to see Karthik standing behind me, his clothes dripping water, his hair all over the place, one hand behind his back, hiding something.

'You scared me! Where were you? I could not find you anywhere!' I say.

'You were searching?' he smirks again.

'Shut up! Don't flatter yourself,' I say. I try to be a little aloof and cool, but the pinkness in my cheeks gives me away. 'I just . . .'

'You just . . .?'

'I was just looking for you because . . . Pia wanted to thank you!' I say and turn to Pia.

'What?' she looks up at me and asks. 'Oh, yes. Karthik, thank you so much for—'

'No, Pia. Please don't,' Karthik says abruptly and we all pause. There is suddenly a strange silence around us. I curse myself for dragging Pia into this just to cover up my blush.

'But I really did want to thank you. It means a lot,' Pia says.

He just nods.

'Umm . . . what are you hiding behind your back?' I ask, to change the subject.

'It's nothing,' he says. It's his turn to blush now. I have never seen him shy. So it's new, and it's also adorable.

'Show me!'

'It's just . . .' he murmurs and pulls out a red rosebud from behind his back. It looks freshly picked and has barely even opened yet. 'I plucked it just now from the college garden . . . just to . . . tell you I love you too. Next time, I promise you a dozen.'

'I don't *need* a dozen! I just need you,' I say and take the rosebud from him. On an impulse, I hug him. I shiver a little in the cold, as the water seeps into my clothes too. But he holds me firmly and I feel amazing, resting my head against his chest. I look up at him, smiling. We lock eyes, and I stand on my toes to reach his lips. I kiss him softly, before hiding my face in his chest again. 'And there's your kiss.'

He holds me tighter.

Epilogue

Eight months later

We have just gotten back to our hostel, after our annual break, following the end of the second semester exams. It has been two months since I last saw Karthik. Ever since that football match—the one in which Karthik was amazing and brought the title home for the team—we had been practically inseparable. Until the stupid break happened.

I can't even begin to tell you how hard these two months at home have been for me, away from Karthik.

I hug Pia as soon as she enters our room and she shrieks on seeing me. She throws her bags down and her caretaker, her Didi, looks at her lovingly, as she jumps up happily, hugging me. To say the least, I am relieved to see her all right. Although we all are fine on the outside, I do find myself sinking into depression, thinking about Tanmay. Sometimes, I miss him just way too much. The pain is almost physical in its intensity.

It is worse for Pia. But she has taken good care of herself. She has handled herself very bravely and tried really hard to be happy. Now, when we think of Tanmay, we think about all the good times we spent with him. All the cherished memories of that cute childish face, not the sadness of his death. We think about him all the time, and we think about him fondly.

Akshat has never shown his face again, ever since he got punched by Karthik during that football match. We let him go, leaving it to karma to take care of him. Nothing we ever did could get Tanmay back. And I did not want Karthik, Pia or myself to get into those power and revenge games. So I made Karthik swear that he won't go looking for Akshat. It has worked out fine for us.

'You can't imagine how much I missed you! I was so eager for college to start again that Mom thought I had a boyfriend here!' Pia shouts.

'My Mom thought the same. Only, in my case—she was right!' I laugh and she joins me.

'You lucky girl! So, where is he?'

A bike honks outside our hostel and my heart skips a beat. I know that sound; how can I not? We look at each other for a second and rush to the window. There, in a black Led Zeppelin tee and worn-out grey jeans, is the best sight in the world, looking up at me and smiling.

Acknowledgements

Co-authors always thank each other last in the acknowledgements page, and that, too, merely as a formality. But since we have written and re-written this book several times and ended up fighting like crazy on too many occasions, we think the first people we should thank is each other. Moreover, we deserve to be thanked for not losing our calm and killing each other.

Our families and extended families for their undeterred support, no matter how much they love or hate what we write—our parents, Nishant Malay, Rituparna Datta Ghosh, Kumar Abhinav, Prishita Singh, Tushar Deep, Vishal Kumar, Abhimanyu Singh, Shaina Singh, Shreela Singh and Pooja Singh.

For taking the trouble to read our books and lying that they like it—Maanvi Ahuja, Sachin Garg, Avantika Mohan, Alka Singh, Ashay Shukla, Abhay Mishra, Pratham Jain, Viyali Michael, Nidhi Sharma, Deepika Rathore, Naman Kapoor, Ankit Mittal, Arpit Khandelwal, Komal Rustagi and Palak Kandelwal.

We would also like to thank everyone following us at social networking sites. Thank you for all the love. We are forever indebted.

The whole team at Penguin India, for their support and encouragement. Especially Vaishali Mathur, for bearing with us over and over again, while we kept missing deadlines, setting new ones and missing them again!

Last, but not the least, we thank Guruji for his blessings.